Bullets from the hillside stitched up dirt all across the campsite. The other three prisoners lay pressed to the ground. Tim jerked his head toward the ring of keys on the ground behind them and said to Jed, "We've got to get out of here. Can you get to those keys?"

"I can try," Jed replied. "Keep me covered."

Jed hurried, turning and crawling on his belly, shots whizzing dangerously close to his back. He snatched the ring of keys and scurried back across the ground. Tim fired two shots from the marshal's pistol toward Jack Pearl, who rose up and fired down the hillside at Jed. Pearl ducked down as Tim's bullets sent chips of rock slicing into his forearm.

"I got them, Tim," Jed said, his breath pumping short and fast as he crawled back to his brother's side. He shot a glance back at the marshals in the clearing and saw that they were too busy firing to pay any attention to the prisoners. He drew into a ball on his side, unlocked the cuffs on his ankles, and let them fall. Quickly, he rolled over and did the same for Tim.

"I've only got two shots left in this pistol, Jed. . . ."

Ralph Compton

Riders of Judgment

A Ralph Compton Novel
by Ralph Cotton

A SIGNET BOOK

SIGNET
Published by New American Library, a division of
Penguin Group (USA) Inc., 375 Hudson Street,
New York, New York 10014, USA
Penguin Group (Canada), 90 Eglinton Avenue East, Suite 700, Toronto,
Ontario M4P 2Y3, Canada (a division of Pearson Penguin Canada Inc.)
Penguin Books Ltd., 80 Strand, London WC2R 0RL, England
Penguin Ireland, 25 St. Stephen's Green, Dublin 2,
Ireland (a division of Penguin Books Ltd.)
Penguin Group (Australia), 250 Camberwell Road, Camberwell, Victoria 3124,
Australia (a division of Pearson Australia Group Pty. Ltd.)
Penguin Books India Pvt. Ltd., 11 Community Centre, Panchsheel Park,
New Delhi - 110 017, India
Penguin Group (NZ), 67 Apollo Drive, Rosedale, Auckland 0632,
New Zealand (a division of Pearson New Zealand Ltd.)
Penguin Books (South Africa) (Pty.) Ltd., 24 Sturdee Avenue,
Rosebank, Johannesburg 2196, South Africa

Penguin Books Ltd., Registered Offices:
80 Strand, London WC2R 0RL, England

First published by Signet, an imprint of New American Library,
a division of Penguin Group (USA) Inc.

First Printing, January 2001
20   19   18   17   16   15   14   13

Copyright © The Estate of Ralph Compton, 2001
All rights reserved

Ⓟ REGISTERED TRADEMARK — MARCA REGISTRADA

Printed in the United States of America

PUBLISHER'S NOTE
This is a work of fiction. Names, characters, places, and incidents either are the
product of the author's imagination or are used fictitiously, and any resemblance to
actual persons, living or dead, business establishments, events, or locales is entirely
coincidental.
    The publisher does not have any control over and does not assume any
responsibility for author or third-party Web sites or their content.

Prologue

Newton, Kansas. September 7, 1871

For the past two weeks Danielle Strange had been recovering in bed in the upstairs back room of Dr. Lannahan's office. Her gunshot wounds had been healing quickly, but not quickly enough to suit her. Now that she was up and able to dress herself, she was restless and wanted to get on her way. She had spent over two years of her life hunting down her father's murderers, a gang of desperados who had left his body hanging from a tree. There had been ten outlaws in the gang that had killed Daniel Strange. Posing as a young gunman named Danny Duggin, she had used the gun-handling skills her father, the gunsmith, had taught her early in life. Danielle had tracked the killers down, one and two at a time, and had taken her vengeance upon them. Only one of those outlaws remained alive. His name was Saul Delmano, and she eagerly wanted to get back on his trail before it grew too cold to follow.

"The longer we stay here, the more time Delmano will have to prepare himself for a fight against us," Danielle said to her brothers, Tim and Jed Strange. On a chair beside her bed lay the cloth binder that

Danielle was accustomed to wearing. The binder kept her breasts flattened enough that when worn beneath her loose-fitting shirt, no one could tell she was a woman. The only reason she wasn't wearing it now was because the binder constricted her painful wounds.

Her twin brothers, Tim and Jed Strange, looked at one another, then turned back to Danielle. Tim said, "Danielle, you're still too weak to ride and fight. You've done more than most any man could have done. But you're only human. We can't traipse out of here and take a chance on that hole in your side breaking open again, or that fever settling back upon you."

"Tim's right," Jed joined in. "The way the doctor explained it to us while you were unconscious that first week here, is that you'll be walking on new legs for a while. He said it could take half the coming winter getting all your strength back."

"I can't spend half the winter here, if that's what you're getting at," said Danielle. She nodded toward the supper her brothers had brought her on a wooden tray. The plate and bowl on the tray sat empty on the nightstand beside the small featherbed. "I've got an appetite again, and I'm starting to get around pretty good, all things considered." She patted the mended bullet hole in the side of her clean boiled shirt. "By morning I ought to be able to ride."

"By morning?" Tim Strange shook his head. "That's pushing things too hard, Danielle."

Danielle turned a firm gaze toward him. "Quit calling me Danielle. I'm Danny Duggin until this thing is over."

"Sorry," said Tim, "I just wasn't thinking there for a second."

"All right, but be more careful," she replied. She offered him a slight smile to show she wasn't angry, and said, still patting a hand on her side, "I'm still pretty sore in my ribs, but it'll go away soon."

"Yes, it will," Tim Strange said, "and when it does, we'll talk about leaving here and getting on Saul Delmano's trail. But not a minute before. Besides, the doctor still needs to give me and Jed a clean bill of health."

Danielle took a breath and tried to regain her patience. In her attempt to convince her brothers that she was ready and able to ride, she'd almost forgotten that they, too, had suffered wounds at the hands of the outlaw gang they had fought and left dead on the ground before coming here to Newton. "I'm sorry, Tim," Danielle said, looking from one of her brothers to the next. "How are you two doing?"

The twins nodded in unison. "We're doing all right, Danielle," said Tim. "We're mostly healed up pretty good." He nodded at Jed. "Just so you won't think we're not keeping busy, listen to what Jed found out at the saloon."

Danielle looked at Jed expectantly. "Well, what is it?"

A grin spread across Jed's face. "You remember Bob Dennard, the bounty hunter you had trouble with back in Fort Smith?"

"I remember him," said Danielle. "He wanted us to ride with him and find Saul Delmano."

"That's right," Jed said. "Well, I've talked to him some, and he knows a lot about Saul Delmano. He said Delmano's family operates a large cattle business that stretches all the way across the border into Mexico. He said Saul Delmano's father, Lewis Delmano, is not much more than an outlaw himself, except that he's made lots of powerful political connections over the years. Dennard says if Saul Delmano is holed up with his crew along the border, he's going to be awfully hard to get to."

"Sounds like Bob Dennard is still trying awfully hard to throw in with us," Danielle said. "I appreciate him giving you the information, but we've still got no room for him riding with us. Does he still think I'm Danny Duggin?"

"Yep, he does," said Jed, "and so does everybody else except the doctor. We've done good keeping your secret. I told Dennard that Tim and I are your younger brothers, that we're here as family helping you out. He seems to believe it. He wants to ride with us awfully bad. Said if he's not riding with us, he'll be going after Saul Delmano alone. If he does, let's hope he doesn't cause us trouble getting to Delmano."

Danielle Strange thought things over for a moment, pacing slowly back and forth across the small room, one hand held to her tender side. Tim and Jed Strange stood quietly watching her.

Across the street, other eyes were watching her, too. Atop the mercantile store, an outlaw named Clyde Branson stood with his rifle lying across the edge of the roof. He watched Danielle each time she stalked past the dusty window. Thinking Danielle was the deadly young gunman, Danny Duggin, Branson whispered to himself, "Come on, Duggin, let's get this over with."

Danielle was pacing slowly, and that was to Branson's advantage. He knew he would only get one shot, so he'd better make it count. He wet his thumb against the tip of his tongue, then ran it across his rifle sight. There was two thousand dollars riding on this shot. He couldn't afford to miss.

Clyde Branson counted off the seconds it took Danielle to walk past the window in the light of the lantern, then turn and come back. For a moment there she must have stopped, out of sight, probably talking to someone. Branson had eased down and waited. When nearly a full minute had expired, he saw her move past the window again, and he tightened his hand on the rifle stock. He would let her make a couple of more passes, then he would take her down. It would take a few days for word of Danny Duggin's death to make its way to the Delmanos. But that was all right with Branson. He would already be waiting at the Delmano spread by then. All he'd have to do was pick up his money and head over into Mexico.

Inside the room, Danielle stopped pacing again and said to her brothers, "How are the horses doing? I haven't seen Sundown since the day we got here." Sundown was the chestnut mare her father had ridden the day his killers had come upon him. The big mare had managed to find her way back to the Stranges' small ranch, and Danielle had been riding the animal ever since.

"Sundown's fine," said Jed Strange. "All three of our horses are fine. To tell the truth, they needed the rest. We've pushed them pretty hard all summer."

"Well," Danielle said, turning and starting to pace again, "they've had all the rest they'll be getting for a while—"

Her words stopped short when she stepped in front of the dusty window and the sound of the rifle exploded across the street. The shot sprayed shattered glass across the room, the bullet barely missing Danielle's head.

"Look out!" Jed shouted as he and Tim sprang forward to grab Danielle. But she had already dived past the window and onto the floor.

"I'm not hit!" she said, crawling back hurriedly across the floor toward her brothers. A trickle of blood ran down her cheek from where a small piece of flying glass had nicked her. "Give me my guns!"

"Stay down!" Jed shouted as Tim reached over, grabbed one of Danielle's pistols from its holster slung over a chair back, and pitched it over to her.

Danielle caught the pistol and, rising into a crouch beside the window, peeped around the edge of the frame into the darkness outside. Another shot exploded, this one ripping a long sliver of wood from the windowsill. Danielle ducked back, but not before seeing the rifle's muzzle flash. "Quick! It's coming from the mercantile roof!" Danielle shouted to her brothers.

The twins wasted no time. They were out the door and running down the wooden stairs as Danielle poked the barrel of her Colt through the broken window and fired three shots toward where she'd seen the rifle flash.

In seconds Tim and Jed had raced across the dark empty street. Cutting through an alley as they saw Danielle's pistol firing from the broken window, they turned and ran through mud and broken whiskey bottles to the rear of the mercantile store. A few feet back from the rear wall, Tim stopped and brought his brother to a halt beside him. He nodded at the ladder reaching up to the roof and said, "We've got him. There's only one way down unless he makes a jump for it." Twenty feet back in the darkness, partially hidden by stacks of firewood, a horse stood waiting, its reins hitched to a cedar post.

"I'll get his horse just to make sure," said Jed in a lowered voice.

"Yeah, good idea," Tim agreed. "Do it while Danielle keeps him pinned down up there."

Pistol shots barked from the window where Danielle stood, taking aim at the roofline. Tim ventured forward, Colt in hand, and kicked the ladder away from the wall. Meanwhile, Jed slipped across the muddy path to the waiting horse, calming it with a raised hand. He unhitched its reins and led it farther back into the darkness, noting the animal's fancy silver-trimmed bridle and reins. "Whoever he is, he rides in style," Jed whispered to himself, running a hand along the hand-tooled California saddle with its Mexican silver inlay.

At the rear of the mercantile, the shooting had stopped as Danielle reloaded her Colt. "You up there!" Tim called up to the roof. "You best come down with your hands raised. We've got you surrounded."

There was no answer from the roof, but behind Tim came the sound of running boots, and he almost turned and fired before he recognized the red-bearded face of the bounty hunter, Bob Dennard, coming closer. "Don't shoot, it's me!" Dennard called out.

"You better hug this wall, Dennard," Tim called out, gesturing toward the roof with his pistol barrel.

"If he's alive up there, he might start shooting down here any second."

Bob Dennard flattened back against the wall beside Tim Strange, glancing up along the roofline, drawing his pistol from his tied-down holster. "I heard the shooting and came running. What happened?"

"Whoever's up there took a shot at Dan—" He caught himself, about to say Danielle. "Somebody shot at Danny through the window!"

"I should have figured as much," said Bob Dennard, peering upward, scanning the roofline as he spoke. "I tried telling you, these are big people you're wanting to lock horns with."

"I believe you, Dennard," said Tim Strange, "but Danny says he wants nobody else riding with us— no offense." As he spoke, Tim's eyes searched along the edge of the roof, sweeping darkness in case the rifleman tried to jump down and make a run for it.

"No offense taken," said Dennard.

"Hey up there!" Tim called out again. "Either give it up and come down with your hands raised, or I'm coming up after you. Make up your mind!"

This time a weak voice called out from atop the roof, "I can't come down ... I'm hit bad."

"Then throw down some hardware, pronto!" Tim responded. He looked over through the pitch of the night and saw that Jed had taken the horse to a spot where if anybody jumped down from the roof on the far end of the building, he would spot it immediately.

"Here ... comes my rifle," the halting voice said. After a second, a rifle fell to the soft ground a few feet out from the building.

"Now your pistol," Tim Strange demanded.

"I . . . can't get it drawn. I'm hit . . . bad, and laying on it."

Tim gave Bob Dennard a questioning look.

Bob Dennard shrugged.

"I wouldn't take his word for it," Jed warned.

"I'm not going to," said Tim. He called up to the roof, "We're coming up. If I don't see both your hands empty when I step onto the roof, you're worm bait. Is that clear enough?"

Danielle came limping from the alley, a Colt in one hand, her free hand pressed to her side. She'd thrown on a riding duster and closed the front to conceal her woman's figure. "He's not lying about one thing," she said, stepping up to her brother and Bob Dennard. "He is hit. I don't know how bad, but I shot him when he raised up with his rifle."

As Danielle spoke, her eyes met Bob Dennard's. "I reckon you remember me," Dennard said, looking a bit sheepish.

"Yes," Danielle replied none too friendly. "You're the one who mistook me for an outlaw and tried to ambush me outside of Fort Smith."

"I sure don't want any hard feelings between us, Danny Duggin," Bob Dennard said, taking a quick glance at the cocked Colt in Danielle's hand. "I made a mistake and I admit it. Lucky you didn't shoot me for my ignorance. I've been telling your brothers that I want to—"

"Not now," said Danielle, cutting him off. She turned her gaze to Tim. "Help me raise the ladder. I'm going up there."

"No," said Tim, taking her forearm and preventing her from walking over to the ladder on the ground. "You've got no business climbing a ladder, the shape you're in." He raised a hand and waved Jed in from the darkness. "Jed and I will go up there."

Danielle started to protest, but thinking about it, she knew Tim was right. She let out a breath. "All right, I'll stay here," she said. "You and Jed be careful."

"I'm going, too," said Bob Dennard, "in case you two need some help."

Tim gave him a firm look. "You can go up there, Dennard, but don't think you need to watch over me and my brother Jed."

Bob Dennard looked embarrassed. "I should have said that a different way. I'm only interested in seeing who that is. Call it my nosy nature."

Danielle stood back and watched with her Colt ready in her hand as Jed joined Tim and Bob Dennard. Tim and Jed raised the ladder and set it in place while Bob Dennard kept an eye on the roofline.

Tim was the first to carefully climb the ladder, his Colt poised and ready. Jed climbed close behind him, then Bob Dennard followed, seeing Tim step over onto the tin roof.

Tim stepped across the roof as quietly as possible. Seeing the man lying in a heap against the front façade of the building, his hands empty and slightly raised, Tim called out, "Don't try any tricks, ambusher, or I'll kill where you lay."

"It's no . . . trick," the man said, lying over on his right side, his holster beneath him. "I'm . . . done for, sure enough."

"Serves you right, mister," Tim said, stepping

closer, hearing Jed move in and beside him. "You tried to kill, but ended up getting killed yourself."

"I don't . . . need no sermons," said Branson.

"And you're getting none either," Jed Strange cut in. "Who are you anyway? Why'd you bushwhack our brother?"

"Name's Pete . . . Bristol. I was going to—"

"He's a damn liar," Bob Dennard interrupted. "He's a hired assassin named Clyde Branson. I've seen him a dozen times over the years. Most likely he's working for the Delmanos. Ain't that right, Branson?"

Clyde Branson raised his face weakly and said, "Is . . . that you, Dennard?"

"Yes, it's me. Tell these men who you're working for, Branson, before you make your trip to hell, you back-shooting snake."

Branson coughed, struggling to catch his breath. "Don't . . . act . . . so innocent, Dennard. You've done the . . . same thing before."

"Who is it, Branson?" Dennard insisted, ignoring Branson's remark. "It's the Delmanos, isn't it? They're paying you to kill Danny Duggin."

"What's . . . the difference," gasped Branson. "It never got done."

"How much?" Dennard asked, stepping in closer, looking down at the wounded man.

"Two . . . thousand dollars," Branson said, his voice faltering more and more. "But not . . . just for me. It's open to all takers. Saul Delmano wants . . . Duggin dead . . . real bad. You might even be tempted—"

"How many men know about this two-thousand-dollar reward?" Dennard hissed, cutting him off.

Even as his breath weakened, Branson murmured, "Hell . . . every gunman from here . . . to El Paso. Now tell . . . these boys how you make . . . your living."

"That's enough of your mouth!" Bob Dennard cocked his pistol and aimed it at Branson's head.

"No! Don't shoot him!" Tim started to reach over and stop him, but even before he could grab Bob Dennard's gun hand, Dennard let the pistol down with a sigh and nodded at Clyde Branson.

"Never mind, this mangy cur is dead," said Dennard, straightening up and lowering his Colt into his holster.

Tim and Jed Strange both looked at the dead, hollow eyes of Clyde Branson, then back at Bob Dennard. "We don't hold with what you were about to do, Dennard," said Tim.

Dennard shrugged. "Well, as you can see, it never got that far."

The three of them turned at the sound of Danielle's footsteps on the tin roof behind them. "Is he . . . ?"

"Yes, he's dead," said Jed Strange. "Bob here knew him. His name is Clyde Branson—a killer for hire. He said Saul Delmano has a two-thousand-dollar reward on your head."

"Yeah," said Danielle, "heard most of it while I was back there on the ladder."

"What are you doing up here, Danny?" Tim asked. "You were supposed to stay down there and take it easy."

"Don't worry, I took it as easy as I could," Danielle said. As she spoke to Tim, she turned a cold gaze to Bob Dennard. "You were pretty quick to want to kill a dying man, Dennard. What's wrong, was he saying things you didn't want known?"

"Now look, Duggin," said Dennard, "I don't deny what I am. I make my living hunting down men for money. If it's wrong, why do you think the law allows it? Because the law knows it can't keep up with all the riffraff out here, that's why."

"I don't care how you go about making your living, Dennard," said Danielle, "but I saw what you were about to do." She looked away from Dennard to Tim and Jed, getting their approval from the look in their eyes. "My brothers and I won't be having you ride with us, will we, Tim, Jed?"

The twins only shook their heads, lowering their pistols into their holsters. Danielle stepped past Clyde Branson's body, over to the front edge of the roof, where she looked down at the gathering crowd on the dirt street below. "Somebody go get the town sheriff," she called down to the uplifted faces. "Tell him there's a man shot."

The people on the street looked back and forth at one another, then a young man turned and raced away toward the sheriff's office where a light now glowed through the window.

"You're making a mistake not riding with me, Duggin," said Dennard, as Danielle turned back around. "Ask your brothers here. Branson said the price on your head is open to all takers. Do you realize how many cold-blooded killers there are between here and the border? You'll never make it past Dodge City."

"I already know there's a lot of cold-blooded killers out here," replied Danielle. "But at least none of them will be riding beside me." She turned to her brothers.

"Come on, Tim, Jed—we've got to make some plans and get out of here."

As the three turned to walk away across the tin roof, Bob Dennard called out, "All right then, play it your way, Duggin. But I'm going after the reward on Saul Delmano and anybody with him, with or without you!"

"It's a free country," Danielle called back over her shoulder.

"Damn right it is!" Bob Dennard called out. "We get out there in the thick of things, I'm warning all three of you . . . stay out of my way!"

At the threat in Dennard's words, Tim Strange started to turn from the ladder and issue some warnings of his own. But Danielle grabbed his arm, stopping him.

"Let it go, Tim," she said. "Dennard just showed you what kind of man he is. Let him rave and threaten and curse all he wants to. We've got work to do."

Chapter 1

September 8, 1871

Danielle recounted the events of the past months in her mind, most of the memories bringing a bitter taste to her mouth. Before Daniel Strange's death at the hands of his killers, he had been known as the best gunsmith in or around St. Joseph, Missouri. He and his wife, Margaret, had raised all three of their children to be decent, God-fearing, law-abiding, and equally as important, to be respectful of others regardless of that person's station in life. Along with these indisputable values, the Stranges had taught their children to be independent to a fault, for life along the western frontier was not a kind place for the meek, the helpless, or the reluctant of spirit. While the Strange children were honest and soft-spoken, they had a presence beyond their years and knew how to handle themselves in most any situation.

Along with all the other things a frontier child must learn, Daniel Strange had taught his daughter and sons at an early age the skill, safety, and responsibility of handling and carrying a firearm. By the time his children were able to read and write, they could handle a Colt as well as any grown man and, of the three, while Daniel didn't make it a habit of saying so to Tim and Jed, young Danielle was by far the best. And the fastest. At thirteen, Danielle Strange could strike sulphur matches at a distance of thirty feet with the customized Colt her father had designed to fit her hand.

Tim and Jed Strange had taken up their father's trade at gunsmithing and had mastered it at an early age—so had Danielle. When it came to repairing or even designing and building a firearm, the Strange children were equal in every regard. Yet, when it came to pulling the trigger, while the Strange twins were both excellent marksmen in their own right, it was daughter Danielle who had what her father always referred to as the *gift*. Whether firing from the hip or from horseback, Danielle Strange's talent was undeniably the best in the family.

Had it not been for the tragic death of Daniel Strange nearly two years earlier, Danielle might well have spent the rest of her life in St. Joseph, Missouri. She may have married and raised a family, or have taken courses at the women's college in St. Louis and spent her life teaching school. But these things were not to be, not for now anyway. Fate had dealt her a different hand, and all she could do was play the few cards left to her. She thought of this now, in the dark hours of night as she sat cleaning and checking her brace of Colt pistols.

Her father, Daniel Strange, had left home on Sundown, the big chestnut mare, and had gone off on a cattle-buying trip, his trail snaking across Indian Territory. Days later, the chestnut mare had returned by herself, lathered and weary from the road. The following day, a note from U.S. Federal Marshal Buck Jordan had arrived along with Daniel Strange's wallet at the sheriff's office in St. Joseph. From that day to this, Danielle Strange had ridden the vengeance trail, seeking out her father's killers one at a time. What had begun as a list of ten names—the names she'd extracted from one of the killers before he'd died—was now down to one. Saul Delmano.

Danielle whispered the name to herself in the darkened room. The only light was the halo of the lantern by which she'd cleaned and checked her Colts. She looked around at Tim and Jed, the two of them having fallen asleep in her room, Tim leaning back in a wooden chair against the wall, Jed curled down on the floor, wrapped in a blanket he'd taken from the closet. Danielle smiled to herself, feeling closer to her brothers than she ever had.

It had been Tim and Jed who had come and found her in Indian Territory, where she'd taken up with some of her father's killers in order to draw all of them into a trap. Tim and Jed had broken the news to her about their mother's death, and she had suffered her loss alone, with no time for proper grief. "Sorry, Mom," Danielle whispered now in the darkness, thinking about it. Feeling herself give in to deep sadness, Danielle shook the melancholy off before it got the best of her. She stood up from the side of the bed and dressed herself quietly, winding the cloth binder methodically around her torso, as she had done so many mornings before on this trail of blood. Then she clenched her teeth against the pain in her side, pitched the pistol belt around her waist, buckled it, and tied the rawhide strip around her leg, securing the oiled holster in place.

Finishing, she walked over to her sleeping brothers, looked at each of them in turn, and said, "Rise and shine, we've got a long day ahead."

In a moment the twins were up on their feet, picking up their hats and adjusting them down on their foreheads. Having slept no more than a hour or two, and in their clothes and gunbelts at that, Tim and Jed rubbed their hands on their faces, forcing themselves awake, and soon the three of them left the room and descended the wooden stairs. On the front porch of the doctor's office, Danielle took an envelope from inside her shirt and slipped it under the door. She looked back at Tim and Jed, who stood watching her questioningly. "I wouldn't think of leaving without paying the doctor his due," she said.

They turned and walked abreast to the livery barn at the far end of the street. Before dawn, Danielle, Tim, and Jed Strange were in the saddle and riding single file along the dirt street out of town. There was no more to say about whether or not Danielle was fit to ride. They had talked it out last night until both Tim and Jed saw there was no use in arguing any further on the subject. Danielle had made up her mind to go, and nothing was going to change it.

As the three of them rode past a darkened alley, they did not see the five men standing back in the far shadows watching them ride by. One of the men, a gunman named Loot Harkens, started to raise his pistol from his holster, but beside him a deep, gruff voice whispered, "Don't be a fool, Loot. Want to end up like Clyde Branson? Let them go for now. Once they get out there in the wilds, there won't be nothing to keep us from killing them."

"Yeah, Loot," the voice of Hank Phipps whispered, "Tarksel's right. They're not going to get very far. I've got news for Mr. Danny Duggin, and his two look-alike brothers . . . there ain't none of the three going to live to see their next birthday."

"I like your attitude, Phipps," said Al Tarksel. "See if you can get Loot here to settle down, before I have to backhand him into the next county." Al Tarksel was a big man, weighing over two hundred and fifty pounds, all of it hard muscle and bone. He spread a flat smile at the other men in the darkness. "Boys, I know that since Axel Eldridge got himself killed last month, there ain't been nobody to really take charge of this gang." He let his eyes cut from one to the other as he spoke. "But just to keep things well organized, I've decided that from here on, I'm taking over." His smile faded as he added, "Any objections?"

The four men looked at one another, then turned back to Al Tarksel as he said in his deep voice, "If there is, let's get it settled here and now." He called each of them by name, looking them square in the face. "Loot, any problem with me taking over?"

Loot Harkens shook his head, saying, "No. Far as I'm concerned, you're the boss."

"Hank?" Tarksel asked.

"Fine by me," Hank Phipps replied, sounding a bit nervous.

"Hector?" Al Tarksel stared coldly at Hector Sabio.

After a pause, Hector shrugged, looking sullen. "*Sí*, you are in charge. But I say to you the same thing I say to Axel back when I join." He thumbed himself on the chest. "I am a free man. I come and go as I choose. If I decide to quit and return to Méjico, I do so without asking anyone's permission."

"I can't run this bunch if everybody does as they damn well please, Hector," said Al Tarksel. "Are you sure that's your final say on it?"

"*Sí*, I say nothing more," said Hector in a firm tone.

"All right then." Al Tarksel reached out a big hand, clamped it around Hector's throat, and lifted him nearly off the ground. Hector's boot toes scrapped back and forth in the dirt as if running in place. His eyes bulged, both hands clamping around Tarksel's thick wrist. Al Tarksel only stood smiling, flat and cold. Hector reached down with his right hand and tried to snatch his pistol from his holster. But as he raised the gun, Al Tarksel slapped it away and kept squeezing.

"God almighty!" said Jack Pearl. "Let him go, Al, you're killing him!"

But Al Tarksel didn't let go until Hector Sabio hung limp as a wet towel. Then he dropped Hector to the ground and looked at Jack Pearl. "What about you, Pearl? Any objections to me taking over as boss?"

"Hell no. What do I care?" Jack Pearl looked down at the Mexican. "You didn't have to kill ole Hector, though. He was a damn good man. He was just running his jaw some. He wouldn't have quit us and gone back to Mexico. Hell, he's wanted in every province down there! They've been wanting to cleave his head off for years."

"Then I just saved everybody a lot of trouble," said Al Tarksel. "Now, are we all through here?" He stared at Jack Pearl as the others nodded in agreement.

"I told you, I've got no problem with who's in charge," said Jack Pearl. "I just want my part of that two thousand dollars when we kill this Danny Duggin."

"Don't worry, Jack," said Al Tarksel, "anybody who rides with me, I'll see to it they get what's coming to them."

Jack Pearl only stared at Tarksel, realizing what Tarksel had just said could be taken a couple of different ways. But Jack Pearl didn't need to have it spelled out for him. He knew that two thousand dollars was worth more to one man than it was to five. For the time being, Jack Pearl thought, the best thing for him to do was keep a close watch on his back and keep his mouth shut.

"Are we ready to ride?" Tarksel asked, still staring at Jack Pearl.

"Yep." Jack Pearl smiled. "I'm just waiting on you to make the first move, boss."

"Then let's get going." Al Tarksel stepped over Hector Sabio's body and walked toward the horses that were hitched back at the far end of the alley. In minutes the five men were mounted and riding along the dirt street as the first rays of sunlight seeped upward on the eastern horizon.

The young U.S. federal marshal's name was Charles Fox McCord, but most of the other marshals called him C. F. for short. The outlaws along the Cherokee Strip had taken to calling him The Fox. It was a name they used with a great deal of respect, if not with much affection. During the brief two and half years that C. F. McCord had been riding for the federal district court out of Fort Smith, Arkansas, his reputation as a lawman had become almost legendary. When folks who had only heard of C. F. McCord met him for the first time, they had a hard time believing that this thin, clean-jawed young man could be the same marshal who had brought in some of the most hardened killers in Indian Territory.

But C. F. McCord had learned to take it all in stride. Whatever work he had done in his short life, he had always tried to do his best at it. Law work was no different, he thought, riding his lineback dun at a walk along the center of Newton's main street. Mid-morning sunlight fell glaring and harsh on the passing wagons, buggies, and foot traffic.

At the hitch rail out front of the sheriff's office, McCord stepped down from his saddle, stretched his back, hitched his sweat-streaked dun, and stepped up onto the boardwalk. As he swung the creaking door open and stepped inside the small dusty sheriff's office, Sheriff Bart Lynch looked up from the stack of papers and wanted posters atop his desk. The sheriff's expression was stiff at first, but when he saw who'd just walked in his expression changed. A slight smile even came to his lips as he spoke.

"Come in, Marshal McCord," Sheriff Lynch said. "To what do I owe this honor?" He rose from his chair and gestured a hand toward the empty chair in front of his desk.

"I'm here to see a man by the name of Danny Duggin," said McCord, "the young fellow who got shot out front of the saloon here a while back."

"Yep, I know him," said Lynch. "What can I tell you about him?"

"For starters," said McCord, "does he happen to ride a chestnut?"

"Yes, I believe his mount is a big chestnut mare come to think of it. Why? Lots of people ride a similar mount, I reckon."

"Yeah, just curious," said McCord. "Word has it he's been laid up in the room atop the doctor's office."

"Yep, that's right," said Sheriff Lynch, "he has been. But he ain't now. I went by to see him earlier to talk some about a shooting he was involved in last night. But he's gone. Him and his brothers, too. The liveryman said they left before daylight, headed toward Dodge City."

"Gone?" McCord gave the sheriff a look of surprise. "After being involved in another shooting here?"

"That's right. He was innocent of any wrongdoing. A paid assassin by the name of Clyde Branson tried to ambush him through a window. Danny Duggin shot him from across the street . . . in the dark mind you." Sheriff Lynch cocked a bushy eyebrow. "I mention that fact in case you and Duggin have anything to settle between yas. It appears this young Danny Duggin has nine lives, like a cat, and can see through the night just like one, too."

"Nope," said the young marshal, "there's nothing that needs settling between him and me." McCord shook his head, pulled the empty chair back and slumped down in it, dropping his dusty hat on his lap. "The judge sent me out to clear up some things for the record."

"Yeah? What's that?" Sheriff Lynch asked. "Can't

the judge keep busy enough in Indian Territory? Now
he's gonna start telling us how to run Kansas?" Lynch
grinned, but C. F. McCord heard him loud and clear.
No local sheriff wanted federal marshals interfering
with how they ran their towns.

"You know how Judge Parker is, Sheriff. He can't
stand not knowing what's going on—says he loves a
good riddle." McCord smiled. "This Danny Duggin
sort of popped up out of nowhere this past summer.
He was in the territory when Parker sent in a posse
to clean up a gang of outlaws. The next day or so
Duggin gets in a shoot-out here with some of the same
bunch who were fleeing the posse. You have to admit,
it makes you wonder who this boy is and what he's
out to do. The judge takes a dim view of vigilantism."

"Vigilantism . . ." Sheriff Lynch considered it, then
said, "Well, I ran a check on him the best I could after
the first shooting here. Nobody was holding wanted
papers on him that I could find. I'm not big on vigilantism myself. But no innocent bystanders were
harmed. The only gripe I've got about the ones he
shot is that the town had to foot the bill for their
coffins. If I'd had time, I'd liked to have given him a
list of a few others that needed killing, since the federal law can't seem to keep the riffraff from converg-
ing on my town."

C. F. McCord chuckled, then said, "I might *person-
ally* agree with you, Sheriff, except Judge Parker is a
curious man. He called me in all the way from the
strip, just to find out more about this man Duggin.
I've been scratching around all the way from St.
Joseph, Missouri, finding out what I can about him
and his brothers."

"Anything interesting?" Lynch asked.

McCord shrugged. "Nothing much out of the ordinary. These so-called brothers of his are Tim and Jed *Strange*, the best I can figure. I found no family with twins in it by the name of Duggin. The only twins in the area around those boys ages are the Stranges.

"Maybe they're stepbrothers then," Lynch offered.

"That's what I wondered at first," said McCord, "but then I checked around town, couldn't find a soul who ever even heard of a Danny Duggin being from there, let alone of him being any kin to the Strange brothers."

"Hmmm," said Lynch, looking puzzled.

McCord continued. "I did hear about a young man named Daniel Strange who killed some gunmen last summer over in Texas. Rumor has it they killed his father, and he went on a vengeance trail after them. But then, he supposedly got himself killed in a knife fight last winter." McCord gave Lynch a knowing look. "Now, this summer, here comes Danny Duggin, doing the same thing, and he just happens to be traveling with the Strange twins, Tim and Jed."

"So, you think Duggin is really this Daniel Strange, the one who was supposed to have gotten killed?" Lynch rubbed his chin. "I can see where you might think that." He thought about it for another second, then asked, "What about Tim and Jed Strange's family? Were you able to talk to anybody kin to them?"

"Here's the real trump card," said McCord, leaning a bit closer to the edge of the desk. "Tim and Jed Strange's folks are both dead. The mother only died last spring . . . but the father, whose name just happens to also be Daniel Strange, mind you, was killed over a year ago down in the Territory. Now, do you see why Parker considers this quite a riddle? What do *you* make of it?"

"It's confusing all right," said Sheriff Lynch, still rubbing his chin. "And these boys, Tim and Jed, have no brother named Daniel?"

"Nope," said C. F. McCord in a flat tone, carefully phrasing his words, "they have no other *brothers* at all." He watched Sheriff Lynch's eyes as Lynch tried sorting it out to some reasonable conclusion.

"Well, they *do* have a brother somewhere, or a cousin, somebody that nobody knew about, and he was going by the name Daniel Strange till he got knifed. He lived through the knifing, then took on another name. That name is Danny Duggin."

"You think that's it?" McCord asked, a faint smile on his face.

"It has to be," said Lynch. "There has to be a brother, a cousin, or something."

"What if this Tim and Jed managed to find themselves a hired gunman?" McCord asked, just to introduce the possibility. "Maybe he was just going by their father's name to rattle the killers?"

"Naw, that ain't the way Missouri boys do things. They settle their own trouble."

"Yeah, that's the way I figured it, too," said McCord. He stood up, raised his hat, and dropped it on his head. "But whatever the case, Parker wants to know, so I'm on Duggin's trail until I can find something out. Do you suppose the doctor is in this time of day?"

"Our doctor's in at all times of day or night," said

Sheriff Lynch. He started to rise up from his chair, saying, "Hold up. I'll get my hat and go with you."

"No, you've been plenty of help already, Sheriff. I'll talk to him alone."

"He might be more helpful if I'm there," said Lynch.

"Or," said McCord, "he might be more helpful if you're not."

"Suit yourself then," said Sheriff Lynch, dropping back into his chair. "I've got plenty to do here anyway. Somebody damn near choked a Mex to death last night and left him for dead in an alley."

"Where is he?" McCord asked, seeming interested.

"He's back there in a cell. Tried to leave him at the doctor's to recuperate, but all the danged fool could do was try to break away and run off. I figured he'd be better off here for a few days, leastwise till he can talk and tell us what happened to him."

"Care if I take a look at him?" McCord asked.

"Help yourself," said Lynch. "He's a handful though. Something sure has got him awfully upset."

McCord and Sheriff Lynch walked back along a row of cells to the last one. Lynch kicked his boot against the bars until Hector Sabio rose up from beneath a blanket on a sagging cot, looking at them through puffy, bloodshot eyes.

"What's his name?" McCord asked.

"Beats me," said Lynch. "Like I told you, he can't say a word. Lordy, look at his throat!"

McCord winced and whistled low under his breath. "Did somebody hang him?"

"No . . . those aren't rope burns," said Lynch. "If there were any claw marks I'd swear he got snatched up by a grizzly bear."

McCord nodded, then turned to Hector Sabio. *"Habla lngles?"*

Hector groaned, trying to nod, and cupped a hand to his swollen throat.

"Good," said McCord, "you understand English. Then listen to me. The man who did this to you . . . was he about this tall?" McCord held a hand above his head. Hector only looked up, giving no acknowledgement.

"Was he a big man, named Al Tarksel, used to ride with the Axel Eldridge Gang?" McCord saw that the man was not going to tell him anything, but he watched Hector's dark eyes as he spoke, seeing if they revealed anything.

"See, he's a knothead," said Sheriff Lynch. "I can't say that I blame him though. If somebody done me that way, I wouldn't want nobody going after them but me and a smoking shotgun."

"Is he charged with anything, Sheriff?" McCord asked, staring through the bars at Hector.

"No, he's not. I was hoping he'd tell us something before I let him go. But it doesn't look like he's going to. The poor devil can't eat . . . nothing but soup and broth, that is. Can't hardly manage even that."

"Let me take him off your hands, Sheriff," said McCord.

"Suits me, if it's all right with him," said Sheriff Lynch. "I can't hold him here much longer."

McCord looked back at Hector, seeing that he had been listening close to everything they were saying, a look of distrust shadowing his dark eyes. "You heard him," said McCord. "You want to ride south with me, see if we can round up the man who did this to you, maybe let you and him settle things between you?"

Hector's expression changed. He stood the rest of the way up and walked over to the bars, his eyes turning to black fire as he leaned close with a hand cupped to his throat. He motioned Marshal McCord closer until McCord held his ear between the bars. Then with all his effort Hector struggled until he managed to whisper in a strained rasp, *"Sí, por favor!"*

"What did he say?" Sheriff Lynch said, leaning in closer.

McCord smiled. "He said 'yes, please!' Seems he's real interested in running into whoever did this to him."

"Well, I'll just go get the key and be right back," said Lynch.

"No," said McCord. "Just wait until I get back from the doctor's." He turned to Hector Sabio. "Is that all right with you, mister?"

Hector nodded, with murder smoldering in his eyes.

C. F. McCord left the sheriff's office and walked the length of the boardwalk until he came to the doctor's office. Inside, McCord took off his hat and stepped over to a divan, where he waited until a woman and a young boy wearing a sling around his right arm came out of the next room. After the doctor had walked the woman and boy to the door and closed it behind them, he turned to McCord and, seeing the badge on McCord's chest, said, "Now then, Marshal, what seems to be your problem?"

McCord smiled, standing up, gesturing the doctor toward the other room. "I seem to have an identification problem, Doctor. I sure hope you can give me something for it."

In the other room, McCord declined taking a seat when the doctor offered it to him. Instead, McCord stood restless, and waited until the doctor seated himself. "Now then, Marshal"—Dr. Lannahan smiled cordially—"since identification has never been a serious ailment, what *really* is the problem?"

C. F. McCord stepped in close and leaned down in front of the doctor. "I'm not going to beat around the bush, Doctor," McCord said. "Tell me what you know about this patient of yours, Danny Duggin."

Dr. Lannahan was taken aback. He tried to collect himself as he spoke. "Well—he—that is, Mr. Duggin, was severely wounded in a gunfight. He left here against my advice. He has no business being on horseback. He'll likely kill himself if he's not careful. Other than that, I'm not really at liberty to discuss any particulars with you."

"Then don't," said McCord. "But you said his wounds were severe. Then tell me this—did you have to perform surgery and take any bullets out of him?"

"Well, yes, in fact, I did," the doctor said reluctantly.

"So you took his shirt off of him, maybe even his trousers?"

"I don't see why you're asking me this, Marshal. Of course I had to remove the patient's shirt ... trousers, too—"

"All right," said McCord, cutting him off. "Now tell me an honest yes or no to this next question, then I'll be on my way."

Dr. Lannahan stared at McCord, feeling pressed

and nervous, as if already knowing what that question would be.

"Is Danny Duggin a woman?" McCord asked bluntly.

Dr. Lannahan shifted his eyes away from McCord and tried to look unruffled by the marshal's abrupt manner. "Now, see here Marshal," Lannahan said, "has Mr. Duggin broken the law? Because unless this question has some relevance to—"

"No, I don't think he has broken any laws," said McCord, again cutting the doctor off. "But unless I can stop him, he might very well end up dead. Now let me ask you again."

"You might as well not ask," said the doctor. "When I give my word to a patient, Marshal, I keep it."

McCord relented and took a step back; the doctor's eyes had given away any secret he'd promised to keep. "I respect you for that, Doctor," McCord said. "When I give my word I'm the same way, nobody can make me break it. So you've got my word right now, that whatever you tell me about Danny Duggin, I'll never repeat. Fair enough?"

The doctor stared at him. "No, I'm not going to discuss this with you. If Danny Duggin is indeed a woman, you'll have to hear it from someone else ... I gave my word."

Marshal C. F. McCord smiled. "Thank you, Doctor. That's all I wanted to know. The secret's safe with me." He put his hat on and walked out the door. Outside, C. F. McCord walked along the boardwalk until he reached the hitch rail where his dun stood with its muzzle raised, sniffing toward him. McCord stepped down into the street and ran his hand along the dun's neck.

"Don't worry," McCord said, "we're not going anywhere till we get fed and rested." He turned his gaze southwest toward the trail leading out to Dodge City. "I know where they're headed," he said to himself and the horse. "We'll catch up to them quick enough." He paused as if thinking of something. "I hope you're as tough as you think you are, *Miss* Danny Duggin, he said quietly to the distant sky. "We've never met . . . but from what I'm hearing, I like you already."

Chapter 2

Shortly after noon, Marshal C. F. McCord walked into the undertaker's parlor, and back to a small room in the rear where the undertaker's assistant, Martin Cobb, had just poured a fresh bucket of ice into the pine coffin that lay flat between two sawhorses. Cold water dripped steadily from the bottom of the pine coffin onto a cushion of wet sawdust. Martin Cobb set the ice bucket on the floor, keeping a small chunk of ice in his hand. He looked up at Marshal C. F. McCord as he wiped the ice across his sweaty forehead. "It's about time you got here, Marshal," said Cobb, perplexed. "Sheriff Lynch said you'd be here over two hours ago. We've been keeping his man iced down so's you can recognize him."

"I appreciate it," said McCord.

"Well, I hope so," said Cobb. "Do you realize what a premium ice is at, having it shipped by rail all the way from St. Louis?"

McCord didn't answer, instead only looking down at the naked body of Clyde Branson and the gaping bullet hole in his chest. Clyde Branson lay naked save for the wet towel thrown over his privates. Flustered, Cobb answered himself, saying, "Well, it's very *very* expensive, I can tell you that!"

"I bet it is," McCord murmured, looking at the parchmentlike face of the corpse. His eyes went to the pale, folded hands on Branson's belly and saw that the man's trigger finger was missing.

"Well?" said Cobb, while McCord studied the dead face with the drops of cold water on its cheeks and brow. "What do you say, Marshal? Is that Clyde Branson or not?"

"If I said it wasn't Branson, would whoever bought the trigger finger get their money back?" McCord asked.

Cobb's face reddened in embarrassment. "I don't make the rules here, I'm only an assistant. Is it him, though? Is it Clyde Branson? Sheriff Lynch said he'd never seen him in person, but that you had."

"It's Branson all right," said McCord. "If you need me to sign something, give it here."

"I'll just be a moment!" Cobb's voice grew excited at the good news. He scurried from the room, wiping his hands dry on his mortician's apron. Alone with the corpse, McCord cocked his head sideways and studied the bullet hole dead center of Branson's chest.

"Good shooting, Danny Duggin," McCord whispered to himself. Yet, knowing the circumstances, with the gunfight having taken place in the dark, and Duggin having shot from a window, McCord couldn't help but think that luck had played its role in this shot.

"Here we are, Marshal!" said Cobb, returning with an affidavit and an ink pen and dipping bottle. "Just sign right here on the bottom and we put this matter to rest."

"Tell me something, undertaker," said McCord as he dipped the pen and scrawled his name across the bottom line. "Who's claiming this body?" He nodded at the shipping tag tied to Clyde Branson's big toe.

"Well, now that we have a signed identification, our Mr. Branson here will be packed in ice, hauled to the railhead, and shipped to Chicago on the first available train!" He reached out and patted Branson's stiff foot as he spoke. "My boss, Mr. Tull, has had an open arrangement with a traveling show, for them to purchase an unclaimed body of any outlaw of notoriety. Mr. Branson here came along at just the right time!"

McCord looked down at the cold, wet body, and shook his head, saying, "Sorry, Clyde. Hope you enjoy the show."

In his excitement, Cobb continued to babble. "Thank heavens it wasn't one those awful deals where they only want the bones, after the deceased has been boiled and stripped and—"

"I get the idea," said McCord, interrupting him. McCord turned to leave but found himself staring into the red-bearded face of the bounty hunter, Bob Dennard.

"It's a terrible end, ain't it, Marshal McCord?" said Dennard, nodding at Branson's body. "But one that befits the life he lived, nevertheless."

"You slipped in here awfully quiet, mister," said McCord. "Do I know you?"

"No, you do not, sir," said Dennard, hooking a thumb in his vest as he turned facing McCord. "That is, we've never met. But I've certainly heard a lot about you. Down on the Cherokee Strip the outlaws all call you The Fox, I believe?"

"So I've heard," said McCord. "Now that's me . . . who are you?"

"Dennard, sir . . . Bob Dennard, at your service." Dennard beamed as he spoke. "I saw you in Fort Smith a few months back whilst I was delivering the bodies of a couple of cattle rustlers."

"A bounty hunter, huh?" McCord said flatly. "Now I recognize the name. You used to be a preacher of some kind or other."

"Yes, it's true I was at one time a minister of the Gospel," said Dennard. "But now I am a private lawman, or, as you so distastefully put it, a *bounty hunter.*"

McCord turned to Cobb and said, "We're all through here, right?"

"Yes indeed, Marshal." Cobb nodded, wiggling the signed affidavit in his hand.

"Wait, Marshal McCord," Bob Dennard called out as McCord turned to leave. "I have a proposition for you . . . don't you want to hear it?"

"Whatever it is, Dennard, I've heard it before," said McCord without turning around.

Dennard spoke hurriedly. "McCord, I know who you after—you're after the Delmanos, and you've been after them for a long time! I can help you. Danny Duggin and his brothers are after them too. I know Duggin, I know all about him!"

C. F. McCord stopped with his hand on the doorknob and turned it slowly: "What do you know about Danny Duggin?"

"First things first," said Dennard, seeing if he could

get the upper hand on the conversation. "You are looking for the Delmanos, aren't you?"

McCord only gave him a flat stare, not wanting to
let his expression give anything away about who he
was after, or why. "You said you know about Danny
Duggin," McCord said. "Now what exactly do you
know?"

"Well, I know he's on the vengeance trail, looking
for the Delmanos," Dennard said, not knowing much
else to say. "I know if I'm riding with you, we'll catch
up to him and his brothers . . . I know where they're
headed!"

"So do I. They're headed for Dodge," said McCord.

"No, I mean after Dodge, I know where they're
headed and what they're gonna do once they get
there," Dennard responded.

McCord stared even harder at him. "Is there anything else you know about Danny Duggin? Anything
that I might find *real* interesting?"

Dennard squirmed in place, searching for something. Finally he had to shrug in submission. "I just
know you're gonna need my help, McCord."

"You don't know nothing, Dennard." McCord
started to turn back to the door, satisfied that Dennard had no idea about Danny Duggin's secret.

"I know that two guns are always better than one!"
Dennard called out in a last attempt.

"That's a good thing for you to remember, Dennard," McCord said, looking back over his shoulder.
"Because if I catch you out there fanning my trail,
that *one* little gun you're carrying won't do nothing
more than get you killed."

When C. F. McCord had left, Bob Dennard turned

to Martin Cobb with his fists clenched at his sides. "Damn his hide! Damn them all! We'll see who comes out on top of this thing! We'll see!"

Martin Cobb eased back a step from Dennard in his rage and said in a guarded tone, "I hope this doesn't change anything as far as our agreement?"

Dennard calmed himself, picked up a chunk of ice from inside Clyde Branson's coffin, and ran it across his forehead. "No, this doesn't change our agreement. Where is it?"

"Twenty dollars first," said Cobb, his wet hand outstretched toward Dennard.

Bob Dennard grumbled under his breath as he took out a wallet from his inside coat pocket. He riffled through his money until he snatched out twenty dollars and flung it down on Clyde Branson's icy leg. "There's you damn money, where's the finger?"

"I'll get it," said Cobb, "it's in a jar, in ice, just like you wanted it."

"Hurry up then," Dennard barked, "I haven't got all day. I've got to get it shipped to Cleveland, Ohio, before it turns rank!" As Cobb hurried to a wooden cupboard and swung its door open, Dennard looked down at Clyde Branson and said under his breath, "Damned outlaws. It's getting to where they're worth more in parts than they are whole."

Leaving the undertaker's parlor, C. F. McCord walked to the livery stable and bought Clyde Branson's horse, complete with its California saddle and fancy bridle. Once he'd looked the horse over—a solid little roan barb gelding with a white blaze on its forehead—he saddled it, tacked it out, and led it to the hitch rail outside the sheriff's office. Inside the sheriff's office door,

McCord looked at Sheriff Lynch and Hector Sabio, who both sat sipping hot coffee at Lynch's desk, Hector having a hard time getting the coffee down.

"Are you ready to ride, mister?" McCord asked Hector, still not knowing his name.

"For crying out loud, C.F.!" said Sheriff Lynch. "Let the man get something in his belly first."

But Hector rose up and set his cup on the desk, raising a hand toward Sheriff Lynch, letting him know it was all right.

"See? He's eager." McCord smiled. "Ready to get under way." He looked at Hector. "Aren't you, mister?"

Hector cupped his hand to his bruised, swollen throat, "*Sí*." He gasped, with much agony and effort.

At the hitch rail, Hector was surprised to see Clyde Branson's horse standing beside C. F. McCord's. "It's yours for now," said McCord. "Ole Clyde never rode nothing but the best. I'll say that for him."

Hector looked around nervously, as if to make sure it was all right. Then he unhitched the roan's fancy reins and swung up into the saddle. Beside him, C. F. McCord swung atop his dun and together they turned the horses to the street. On the boardwalk, Bob Dennard appeared and called out, "This beats every damn thing I ever saw, McCord! That man is nothing but a heathen outlaw! He rode with the Eldridge Gang!"

Marshal C. F. McCord stopped his horse and swung it around, facing Bob Dennard. "You watch your language, bounty hunter." McCord seethed. "This man is riding with me. I might even deputize him before it's over." He looked at Hector Sabio. "You're not an outlaw, are you, mister?"

Hector Sabio shook his head slowly, cupping a hand to his sore throat.

"There, you see, Dennard? This man is not an outlaw. He just said so. He's an innocent victim who wants to see justice done."

Hector Sabio gave McCord a strange look, his hand still cupped to his throat as he nodded slowly in agreement.

"You damn fool," Bob Dennard cursed under his breath, seeing the two men turn their horses and heel them out along the rutted dirt street. "I hope he kills you in your sleep."

At the edge of town, McCord slowed his dun to a walk and reached over and caught the roan barb by its bridle, bringing it over near him. "Just so we don't get off on the wrong foot, mister," he said to Hector, "I think I best tell you now. We're going after Al Tarksel and what's left of the Eldridge Gang, because they're going to lead us to the Delmanos. What you do with Al is your business. But make no mistake, if you cross me in any way, shape, or form, I'm bound to kill you graveyard dead, *comprende?*"

"*Comprende*," Hector managed to croak.

The Dodge City Trail. September 9, 1871

Owing to the pain in Danielle's wounded side, the ride to Dodge City was taking longer than it should have. The first day they had ridden across the flatland and made a camp in a dry wash surrounded by waist-high prairie grass. The autumn grass stood brittle in its shoots and served as a good guard against anybody approaching the camp unannounced. Jed boiled a small pot of coffee and turned some jerked beef above the low flame to work some of the stiffness out of it. Once the coffee was ready and the jerked beef hung from the ends of their knife blades, Danielle and the twins sat around the fire, having their supper.

Seeing the pained expression on Danielle's face, Tim asked his sister, "Are you doing all right? You look pale and feverish."

"I'll do," said Danielle, forcing down a bite of warm jerky. "I knew I'd be stiff and sore the first day or two."

Tim and Jed looked at one another, then back at their sister. "I brought along a bottle of whiskey if you need it for the pain," Jed offered.

"Maybe just a short sip," said Danielle. "But I'll use some to clean this wound and change the dressing, soon as I rest some and get my strength back."

"We could always lay up a day or two once we get to Dodge," said Tim. "We don't want to travel hellbent-for-leather you know."

"I know, Tim," said Danielle, "but you can feel in the air that winter's coming early. I want to settle all accounts with Saul Delmano aforehand. Once he's dead, I'll take all the time I need to heal up properly."

"If we had to," said Tim, "Jed and I could finish this thing out. We'd come back for you afterwards, you know that."

"I know," said Danielle, sipping her coffee, "but it's something I've got to do—I made a promise at Pa's grave marker. I started with ten names on my list and crossed them off one at a time. I'll stop when I crossed off the last name, not before."

A silence passed as the night wind rustled through the wild grass. Then Jed spoke in a lowered voice as he gazed into the low flames. "Sometimes I wonder if there ever will be an end to it. Seems like the more of these kind of men you kill, the more spring up in their place. We thought we only had Saul Delmano left to deal with. Now it turns out he's got his pa and whoever works for him on his side, not to mention that hired killer, Branson. Are you sure you're going to be able to let it all stop when Delmano's dead?"

"It'll stop," Danielle said with conviction. "I haven't developed a taste for killing if that's what you're asking, Jed."

"I needed to ask," Jed said softly, still staring down into the flames.

"And now you have," said Danielle.

After their meal, Tim and Jed brought her the whiskey along with the fresh bandages she'd brought in her saddlebags. As Danielle dabbed the whiskey on a wad of gauze and carefully touched it to the wound in her side, Jed and Tim led the horses a few feet from the camp and picketed them to graze. "I'm awfully worried about her," Tim said, the two of them stopping on their way back to the campfire.

"Both of us, brother," Jed replied. "I believe she'd keep on going on this even if she knew it would kill her."

"Yeah, and I'm afraid it just might," said Tim. "We'll be in Dodge tomorrow evening. If she's not looking any better, we've got to find a way to make her stay there till she's well."

"She won't take kindly to it," Jed warned.

"I know," said Tim, "but it's something we'll have to do, if we don't want to end up burying her."

"We'll see," Jed whispered, as the two of them walked into the camp as Danielle looked up at them from tending her wound.

September 10, 1871

Tim and Jed noticed the way their sister had begun to slump to one side in her saddle, her hand pressed her side. But when Tim sidled his horse close to Danielle's chestnut mare, she looked up at him from beneath her hat brim through fevered eyes and waved him away. "I just need to catch my breath is all," she said. "I'm feeling lots better." Beads of sweat stood on her cheeks. Her face looked pasty and pale.

Tim let his horse fall back beside Jed with a worried look on his face. "That does it," he said to Jed, keeping his voice low so Danielle wouldn't hear him. "We'll be at the Arkansas River this afternoon. As soon as she's rested some, we're pushing on into Dodge tonight and getting her some help, whether she likes it or not."

"I agree," Jed replied, nudging his horse forward. Behind him, Tim had started to do the same, but then he stopped short when he caught a glimpse of a hat moving through the tall grass fifty yards to his right.

Jed, hearing Tim's horse jerk to a halt, looked back at his brother, saying, "What's wrong, Tim?"

Tim Strange kicked his horse forward a step, speaking under his breath. "Don't look over there, but we've got somebody watching us."

"What should we do?" Jed resisted the urge to look all around the flat grassland.

"Get up there and tell Danielle," Tim whispered. "We don't want to get caught by surprise out here. I'll lag back some, keep anybody from riding in on you two."

"But what about you, Tim?" Jed asked.

"Just do it, Jed," Tim hissed. "I'll be all right. You get past that low rise," he added, nodding toward a short upward roll in the land ahead of them. "Both of you get moving as fast as you can to the river. There's plenty of cover there. Don't worry about me, I'll find you."

Fifty yards to the right, Jack Pearl watched Jed bolt forward as Tim stayed back and drew his rifle from his saddle boot. "Well, they're on to us," Pearl said, scooting back down the side of a low natural cutbank. He looked at Al Tarksel. "It can get real bloody out here with sparse cover. Since you're in charge now, what do you want to do?"

"Damn it!" Tarksel cursed under his breath. He shot a harsh gaze at Loot Harkens, saying, "You had to raise your ugly head up and see what was going on, didn't you?"

"I only did it for a split second," said Loot, feeling the hard eyes of the other men on him, making him nervous. "We could go ahead and rush them."

"For two cents I'd make you go rush them by yourself, you slab-sided fool!" Al Tarksel growled, trying to keep his deep voice from carrying across the flatland. "Pearl's right . . . this is bloody land for a gun battle. The whole idea of shooting somebody for money is to not get shot yourself—Clyde Branson wishes he was here to agree with that notion."

"We could take this one," Jack Pearl said, jerking his head in Tim Strange's direction. "It'd be one less to deal with."

"That would be real smart, Pearl," Tarksel said in sarcastic tone. "We'll shoot the one that's not worth shooting, then let the one worth two thousand dollars hear it and get away. Are you sure you're smart enough to carry a loaded firearm?"

Jack Pearl bristled, but remained silent.

Hank Phipps rose high in his saddle, looked across the tops of swaying grass, then dropped back down. "They'll probably take cover and spend the night along the Arkansas. We can close them up and hit them first thing in the morning . . . what do you say?"

Al Tarksel sat atop his horse, brooding for a moment. Then he nodded, saying, "Yeah, that's our best shot." He looked around at each man in turn, then added, "The next son of a bitch who messes up, I'm going to grab by his head and his ankles and snap him across my knee for kindling."

Meanwhile, Tim Strange took his time, carefully moving forward, keeping a good distance back from Jed and Danielle, and swinging his horse slightly to his right, keeping an eye along the grassy horizon.

Once out of sight across the roll of the grasslands, Jed and Danielle pushed their horses up into a fast pace. Jed stayed a few feet behind Danielle, seeing the difficulty she had keeping to her saddle. By the time they reached the low banks of the Arkansas River, Danielle was hunched down low, fighting the pain.

Jumping down from his saddle when they reined their horses to a halt, Jed reached forward just in time to catch his sister as she swayed and toppled out of her saddle. "Easy, easy!" Jed said to her, cradling her in his arms and lowering her to the ground on his lap. He pulled her hat off and ran his hand across her forehead. "Lord, you're burning up with fever!"

"No," Danielle said, nearly delirious, her voice trembling in a chill, "I'm freezing . . . freezing cold. Where's Tim?"

"He'll be here, just lay still. I'll get a blanket and some water."

"Don't leave him here!" Danielle cried, her voice strained and weak.

"Oh, Lord," Jed whispered, looking down at the fresh bloodstain seeping through her bandages and through her shirt. "Don't worry, we won't leave Tim behind."

But as Danielle spoke, Jed could see she wasn't even talking about Tim "Ma? Pa . . . ?" Danielle's eyes rolled back and forth aimlessly across the sky. "Where are they, Jed . . . ?"

"Oh, Danielle, Danielle, please!" Jed cried out, holding her shivering body against him. "Don't you dare slip away on me, you hear?"

"I—I won't," she whispered, her voice sounding more distant.

Jed hurried to the horses, racing back with a canteen and a blanket. He wrapped her in the blanket and poured tepid water over her face, swabbing it with the tail of his shirt. He splashed water across her burning lips, then into her mouth, much of it gushing back up as she swallowed. Then he waited, holding her against him, clutching her as chills racked her body.

When Tim rode in, he found the two of them there in the long evening shadows. Leaping down from his horse, his rifle in hand, he slid down beside Jed and looked at Danielle's sweaty face. "How is she?" he asked.

"Better, I think, for now," Jed replied, sounding spent and worried. "But if we don't get her to Dodge, I'm afraid she ain't going to make it."

"You're right," said Tim. "Be ready to ride as soon as I water the horses." He hurried to the river's edge, loosened the horses' cinches, and let them draw water while he stood among them, wishing he could hurry them, but knowing he couldn't. Once the horses had their fill, Tim hurriedly drew their cinches and led them over beside Jed and Danielle. "Let's ride," he said.

"What about them, back there?" Jed jerked his head in the direction of their back trail.

"They know I saw them," said Tim. "They stayed back. I figure they'll hit us tonight or first thing in the morning. We've got to get out of here."

"I'm with you, brother," said Jed, rising to his feet with his sister in his arms. "I'll carry her on my lap. You lead Sundown."

Dodge City, Kansas. September 11, 1871

It was deep into the night when the three Stranges rode into Dodge City. Lights along Front Street formed pale circles on the ground and along the edge of the boardwalks. The sound of cattle lowing resounded from the holding pens, their musky smell looming heavily in the darkness. The sound of a twangy piano danced upon the nearly empty street where a few late-night drinkers, cigars glowing in one of their hands and a whiskey bottle or a beer mug hanging from their other, staggered from one saloon to the next.

Tim and Jed reined up out front of a doctor's office, recognizing the painted wooden sign hanging above the door. A dim light glowed in the window. Beyond the light, a silhouette moved toward the door. "Thank God, he's in," Tim said, stepping down from his saddle and letting Jed hand Danielle down into this arms.

The light in the window turned dark, then the door creaked open and a man stepped out onto the boardwalk, pulling his coat on. He looked around at the faces of Tim and Jed Strange as he began to lock the front door. "My goodness, gentlemen," he said, looking from the twins to Danielle. "What have we here?"

"It's our brother! He's fevered up real bad, Doctor," said Tim. "He got shot three weeks back up in Newton. I reckon he tried to get up too soon."

"I see," the doctor said, putting his key back in the lock and swinging the door open. "Watch your step back through there until I light the lamp. I was just on my way home. Luckily I stayed late to do some paperwork."

By the time the doctor had lit the lamp and turned it up, Tim had already stepped across the dark parlor and into the adjoining room. Jed followed and, taking out a match, found another lamp and lit it as well. In the glow of light, Tim saw the gurney standing in the middle of the floor and laid Danielle down upon it. "Fellows, I'm Dr. McFee," the doctor said, already out of his coat and rolling up his sleeves. "Since this happened in Newton, I assume it was Dr. Lannahan who treated your brother?"

"Yes it was," said Tim. "Dr. Lannahan tried every way in the world to keep him from leaving. But our brother, Danny, is pretty headstrong sometimes."

"I see," said Dr. McFee, stepping in close and leaning down near Danielle's face. "Well, from the looks of him, he won't be putting up much of an argument about leaving this time." He turned to Tim and Jed and looked them up and down. "There's nothing you two can do here for now. Why don't you go get yourselves something to eat and drink—looks like you could both use it. I'll take over now."

"Doctor," Tim said, hesitantly, "there's something maybe I ought to tell you about our brother . . . it's sort of a secret."

"Unless it pertains to his health, you can tell me later. This young man needs treatment quickly."

The twins nodded, Jed saying, "Thank you, Doctor, we'll be waiting right outside."

Tim and Jed weren't about to leave Danielle unprotected, knowing the men on their trail were probably not far behind. Tim stood back in the shadow of the boardwalk overhang with his rifle in his arms and kept watch on the street while Jed led the horses around the side of the building, out of sight in the darkness. Then he hurried off to an open saloon halfway up the long boardwalk. When Jed came back, he carried a bar towel with a half-dozen boiled eggs and sour pickles wrapped in it. In his other hand he carried a small tin bucket of foamy beer and two empty mugs. "Is everything all right?" he asked, laying the food down on a wooden chair sitting against the front of the building.

"So far, so good," said Tim, scanning the dark street. He then looked down at the eggs and pickles as Jed unfolded the bar towel. "I haven't seen anything that looked so bad, and smelled so good in my life," Tim said, reaching down, picking up a boiled egg and popping it whole into his mouth.

"I know," said Jed, filling the beer mugs, "it's all I could rustle up this time of night. The bartender said he wants this towel back. I ran into the sheriff and he asked what was going on up here—reckon he saw the horses. I told him what had happened, about our brother Danny getting shot a while back."

"What did he have to say?" Tim asked, chewing on the boiled egg as he spoke.

Jed sucked back a mouthful of beer foam, then spoke. "He said he'll drop by in a few minutes just to see how things are going."

"Yeah," said Tim, "he probably thinks we're up to something we shouldn't be up to."

"Well, that's his job," said Jed. "It might be good, him being here for a while, in case we need him."

"Maybe," said Tim, taking the beer-filled mug Jed

handed up to him. "But it's also a sheriff's job to ask, and we don't need to be answering a lot of questions."

"Why?" Jed asked. "We've got nothing to hide from the law."

Tim didn't answer. His eyes had gone to the single line of horsemen riding their horses in at a walk on the far end of Front Street.

Jed saw them, too, and he set his beer mug down and stood up slowly, wiping his left hand across his mouth. His right hand went down to the Colt on his hip and rested there. "Do you think that's them?" Jed whispered.

"I don't know," Tim replied. "There's nothing we can do but wait and see." His thumb reached across the rifle hammer and pulled it back quietly. "Ease inside, Jed," he added in a whisper. "See how much longer that doctor's going to be."

At the hitch rail out front of the dirty and less frequented Aces High Saloon, Al Tarksel swung his big frame down from the saddle, the horse beneath him blowing out a long breath and straightening its back. He looked around at the others, who stepped down as well. "Check around, boys, they're here somewhere. I know they are."

"Yeah," Jack Pearl grumbled half aloud, "you knew they were on the riverbank, too."

"What's that, Jack? Speak up," said Tarksel, "I didn't hear you."

"Nothing," said Jack Pearl. "I just want to get this job done and go on to something else."

"Well, so do we, Jack," Al Tarksel said, stepping past Loot Harkens and shoving him aside to get closer to Jack Pearl. "So, do like I said and start looking for them."

"And where will you be?" Jack Pearl asked, tired and irritated from the long, hard ride.

Al Tarksel motioned with his hand toward the darkened front of the Aces High Saloon. "I'll be right inside . . . any objections?"

"No," said Jack Pearl, "except the place is closed." He looked closer at the faded sign hanging by one rusty chain, the other chain broken and dangling from the overhead ceiling. "It looks like it's out of business." A sheet of corrugated tin stood covering a large broken window. In the closed doorway, a thin gray cat lay coiled in a ball, asleep.

Al Tarksel stepped closer to Jack Pearl, saying, "I happen to know the owner, Jack. He'll open up for me. Any other questions?"

Jack Pearl stepped back, looking at the dilapidated saloon, shaking his head. "Come on, Pearl," said Loot Harkens, "we'll check along the other side of the street. Hank and Al can take care of this side. Does that sound all right to you, boss?" he asked Al Tarksel.

"Yeah," said Tarksel, "if you find them, don't do nothing till you come and get me." He stepped up onto the rickety boardwalk and kicked the cat away with a sweep of his boot. The cat let out a shriek and shot off into the darkness. Jack Pearl and Loot Harkens walked across the street toward the row of all-night saloons and gaming houses.

"Pearl is right about this place," said Al Tarksel, looking through the dusty window at the dark, cluttered insides of the Aces High Saloon. "How does Bernie Odell make a living in a place like this?"

Al Tarksel knocked on the door, then shook it, then rapped again, louder this time. "Open up, Odell, it's me, Al!" he shouted. He shook the door again, stepped back, and lunged against it with his shoulder, crashing it open as Bernie Odell came walking through the bar, hooking his galluses up onto his shoulders. Odell jumped back in surprise as the door barely missed hitting his face. Al Tarksel came charging through and stopped, seeing Bernie Odell in the darkness.

"I was coming!" Odell said, looking at the splinters on the floor and the busted wooden door latch. "Damn it, Al, you've ruint my door!"

"It couldn't be helped, Bernie," said Al Tarksel, chuckling as he brushed splinters off his shoulder. "We're passing through, on the trail of an ole boy Saul Delmano wants dead. I knew you would want us to stop by and say howdy." He looked around in the darkness, smelling the musty air full of stale whiskey and cigar smoke. "So this is your Aces High Saloon . . . well well, ain't she something?"

"It was when I first bought it," said Bernie Odell, walking around behind the bar and striking a match to a lantern. "But I've fallen on hard times the past couple of months. I haven't been able to compete with the big saloons here. To tell you the truth I've done more drinking than my customers."

"Well, I reckon a couple of friends can still get a bottle of rye and a beer here, can't they?" asked Tarksel, as he and Hank Phipps stepped over to the bar.

"Yep, but just barely," said Bernie Odell, fishing a

hand along beneath the bar until he came up with a half bottle of rye whiskey and sat it on the bar. "I've been thinking about closing this place, long enough to go out on the trail and make myself some operating capital."

"Have you sure enough?" Al Tarksel grinned. "In that case you're lucky we came along when we did. I could use a good man like yourself, to replace a sore-headed Mexican I left laying dead back in Newton."

"Yeah?" said Bernie Odell, getting interested, rubbing his hands together. "What kind of money is Delmano paying?"

Al Tarksel pulled the cork from the bottle with his teeth and blew it away. "Two thousand dollars," he said. "Your end of it will come to four hundred dollars, for just a quick piece of work."

Bernie Odell leaned forward, saying, "For four hundred dollars, I'll help you shoot a whole string of people. Tell me more."

While Al Tarksel, Hank Phipps, and Bernie Odell talked at the bar of the Aces High Saloon, Jack Pearl and Loot Harkens made their way along the other side of the dark street, stopping first at the livery barn, where a sleeping hostler rose up from a bale of hay and met them, looking at them through bleary, bloodshot eyes.

"Has three men come by here in the past few hours?" Jack Pearl asked, looking past the old hostler and along the row of stables for any sign of Tim, Jed, and Daniel Duggin's horses.

"Nope, business had been slow here since before

noon. You needing to leave your horses here for tending?" the old hostler asked.

"Not right now," Jack Pearl replied. "We'll let you know." He and Loot Harkens turned and left. They made their way along the nearly deserted street, looking at horses lined up at the hitch rails out front of saloons, looking closely at the faces of cowboys as they staggered by. "I wonder if our new boss, Al, ever stopped to consider that those three might have kept on riding?" said Jack Pearl, his voice sounding a bit sarcastic.

"We followed their tracks right to the main trail leading here," said Loot Harkens.

"Yeah, and once on that heavily traveled trail they could have cut off anywhere. We'd never have seen it," said Pearl.

Inside the saloon where Jed had purchased the beer and food, Jack Pearl and Loot Harkens walked up to the bar, where three cowboys stood leaning with their faces lowered over their whiskey glasses. When the bartender came forward to them, he asked, "What can I get you?"

"Two whiskeys," said Jack Pearl. Then he said as the bartender set two glasses up and filled them, "We're looking for three young men who might have come by here earlier, one of them is limping from a gunshot wound. Have you seen anybody like that?"

"Nope, I haven't. All's I've seen here today are these same ugly faces." The bartender pushed the two shot glasses forward and considered it while Pearl and Harkens tossed back their drinks and set the glasses back on the bar. "A young fellow came in here a while ago though, bought some eggs and pickles, said he was taken 'em to the doctor's office for his brothers. Do you suppose that might be them?"

Jack Pearl grinned, running his hand across his mouth. "I'd bet on it," he said, pushing his empty glass forward. "Give us one more quick one, ole buddy."

"Hadn't we better hurry over and tell Al?" said Loot Harkens.

"You heard the bartender," said Jack Pearl, "they're at the doctor's office. We've got time to wet our whistles first. That's what our new boss is doing right about now."

Inside the doctor's office, Tim and Jed hurried, picking up the gurney with Danielle on it and heading toward the rear of the building. "Watch your step, boys," the doctor cautioned them, moving ahead of them to open the back door.

"Are you sure you can trust the woman you were talking about, Dr. McFee?" Tim asked, almost stumbling in the dark.

"Sarah Sims is as steady as a rock, boys. She'll tend to young Danny and never tell a soul he's there."

Dr. McFee moved quickly. As soon as the gurney passed though the door, he closed the door and locked it. Then, as Tim and Jed stood anxiously waiting with their sister on the gurney between them, the doctor ran around the corner of the building, unhitched their horses, and returned, leading them behind him. "This way, boys," he said.

Tim and Jed rushed along behind the doctor and the horses until they reached a small white cottage sitting back on a quiet side street.

Dr. McFee hitched the horses to a white picket fence, swung the gate open, and held it as the twins passed through. Then he hurried ahead of them again up onto the small porch, where a dim light glowed in the window. He knocked softly and kept his voice lowered, "Miss Sarah, it's Dr. McFee. Please hurry!"

"Dr. McFee?" The door opened an inch, then swung open all the way as Tim and Jed slipped in quickly with the gurney. "My goodness, Doctor, what's going on?" said the spinster, Sarah Sims, stepping back and reaching for the lamp in the window.

"Don't turn the light up, Sarah," said the doctor. "These boys need some help. I'll explain it all later. I thought you might be willing to look after a patient of mine for a while."

Sarah Sims hesitated, but only for a second. "Why, of course, Doctor," she said, picking up the lamp from the small table at the window. "Just follow me."

Inside the Aces High Saloon, Loot Harkens stood back by the broken door and said to Al Tarksel, "We found them, boss. They're down the street at the doctor's office."

"Where's Jack Pearl?" Tarksel asked, setting his glass down, then turning from the bar with Hank Phipps and walking to the door.

"Pearl is headed there now. Said to meet him," Loot Harkens replied.

"He said to meet him?" Al Tarksel bristled. "I told you both to come get me before you did anything."

"I know, boss," said Harkens, "don't blame me. I'm right here, ain't I?"

Behind them, Bernie Odell hurriedly shoved the cork back into the rye bottle and snatched a gunbelt from beneath the bar. "Wait for me," he said, strapping on the gunbelt as he walked across the dirty floor.

"Who's this?" asked Loot Harkens.

"This is Bernie Odell, a friend of mine," said Al Tarksel, lifting his pistol from his tied-down holster and checking it as he spoke. "Bernie's going to be riding with us."

"For a share of the reward?" Harkens asked, looking Bernie Odell up and down. "But, boss, that's going to mean less money in all our pockets."

"You're not a bookkeeper, Loot," said Al Tarksel, "so let me handle how the reward gets split up." He tapped the pistol barrel against Loot Harkens's chest as he spoke. "Any objections?"

Harkens shrugged and turned to the door with a begrudging look on his face.

"Al, if my being here is one too many," said Bernie Odell, "I can always shoot one of these peckerwoods."

"See?" Al Tarksel grinned, headed out the door. "That's what I always liked about Bernie here. He'll work with you any way he can."

Dr. McFee had barely made it through the back door of his office when he heard the footsteps on the boardwalk out front. He quickly snatched up the bloodstained cloth and the old dressing gauze that he'd left lying on a table beside the gurney while he'd cleaned Danielle's wound. When he heard loud knocking on the front door, he called out, "Just a minute," then he threw the telltale items in a trash basket and went through the dark front parlor as the loud knocking resounded once again. "Hold your horses!" he said, ruffling his hand through his hair and loosening his necktie.

"Open it, or I'll kick it down," Jack Pearl demanded, rattling the doorknob.

Dr. McFee opened the door, giving the appearance of a man who'd been asleep. "What on earth is going on?" he asked, looking right into the bore of Jack Pearl's pistol. In the street beyond, Dr. McFee saw the other four men arriving, Al Tarksel's head and shoulders towering above his companions.

Jack Pearl shoved the doctor back and stepped inside the office as the other four men hastened their steps to join him. "Where are they, sawbones?" Jack Pearl asked in a threatening tone. "Try lying to me and see what you get." He cocked the pistol loudly.

"Who in the world are you talking about, sir?" McFee asked indignantly, buying as much time as he could for Tim and Jed Strange, who'd left town only moments before the doctor had returned to his office.

"You know damned well who I'm talking about." Pearl sneered. He stepped sideways to the lamp in the window and raised the wick, bringing a circle of light into the dark parlor. Before he could say anything more, Al Tarksel and the others came through the door. Tarksel shoved Jack Pearl aside.

"I told you to come get me first, Jack!" Tarksel growled. He turned to the doctor. "Where are they, Doc?"

Dr. McFee looked back and forth at the faces of the men, holding out as long as he could. "I have no idea what you're talking—"

"We'll see!" said Tarksel, cutting the doctor off, shoving him backward to the other room. The men followed, advancing on McFee until he stood with his back against the wall, his hands up as if to protect his face.

"Please, gentlemen, I was sound asleep," McFee pleaded. "I don't know who you're looking for!"

"Yeah, take a look at this, Al," said Jack Pearl to Tarksel. Pearl reached down and picked up the blood-stained gauze from the trash can, then dropped it and wiped his fingers on his dirty trousers. "Let me pistol whip it out of him." Pearl hissed, stepping forward, his hand on his pistol butt.

"Easy now, young man," said the voice of Sheriff Harrington, stepping into the room, a shotgun pointed at the four men, both hammers cocked. "Dr. McFee is the only doctor we've got. If you hurt him, who's gonna dig all this buckshot out of your bellies?"

Thinking quickly, Al Tarksel said, "Sheriff, we're not breaking any law here. I'm looking for a gunman named Danny Duggin. I'm a bounty hunter, you see."

"You've broken two laws that I can name," said Sheriff Harrington. "First of all, you barged in here against the doctor's will. Second of all, you've made me cock this shotgun." He stared coldly at Al Tarksel.

"All right, Sheriff," said Tarksel, giving a nasty smile. "We'll play this your way. You've got two loads of buckshot. But two loads ain't going to get you out of here alive."

"I know that," said Harrington, "that's why I asked Harvey here to join me." He took a step to one side of the door, and a short man moved into the room with another double-barrel cocked and pointed at them. "Harvey, no matter what happens, you make sure this big sucker gets both barrels, all right?"

"Sure enough, Sheriff," Harvey said in a tense, quiet tone.

A nerve twitched in Al Tarksel's jaw. A sheen of sweat glistened on his brow. "You know what, Sheriff, I can't help think this is all just some sort of misunderstanding. We meant the doctor no harm. Hell, I always liked doctors, always thought they did a lot of good. If I had it to do over again I might even—"

"Shut up, mister," said Harrington. He looked at Dr. McFee, saying, "Doc, where are those three young men who were here earlier?"

Dr. McFee let out a breath, hoping Tim and Jed were well on their way by now. "All right, I did treat a patient here a while ago for an infected gunshot wound. But they moved on. They headed southwest out of town."

"See, Sheriff, a gunshot wound," said Al Tarksel. "That's the gunman we're after. We really are bounty hunters. We're just doing what the law abides."

"So am I," said Sheriff Harrington, jiggling the shotgun in his hands. "I'd jail the lot of yas, but then I'd have to feed you and have the whole jail fumigated." He slid a glance over at Bernie Odell, who stood beside Loot Harkens with his face ducked a bit in an effort to go unnoticed. "What about you, Odell? Are you a bounty hunter now, after poisoning half the town with your rattail rye?"

"Rattail rye?" said Hank Phipps, swallowing back a sudden bitter taste in his mouth.

"Weren't nothing wrong with my whiskey," said Bernie Odell, "but yes sir, I'm bounty hunting now—this town never appreciated my drinking establishment."

Sheriff Harrington turned his gaze back to Al Tarksel. "It's worth letting you go just to get this two-bit grifter out of town. Doc, you bringing any charges against this bunch?"

Dr. McFee looked the men over. Seeing how bad things could get all of a sudden, two shotguns and five pistols all firing at once in a small room, he said, "No, Sheriff, I just want them out of here."

"You heard the doctor," said Harrington, motioning with his shotgun barrel, "get your ragged asses out of here, and don't come back. Harvey, keep these buzzards covered till their knees are in the wind."

"Sure enough, Sheriff," said Harvey, his finger tight across the triggers.

Filing out the door, Bernie Odell grumbled toward Sheriff Harrington, "I can't leave this town quick enough to suit me. I hope everybody who ever drank at my place dies with the bleeding runs."

"I'll tell them you said so," said the sheriff.

Once the men had left town, and Sheriff Harrington and Harvey had lowered their shotguns across their forearms, the sheriff stepped up onto the boardwalk where Dr. McFee stood. "Now what went on here, Doc? Why was you protecting those three boys?"

"They just looked like hardworking farm boys to me, Sheriff. I felt like they needed protecting." McFee shook his head. "This was a most peculiar situation."

"Yeah, how's that?" the sheriff asked.

Dr. McFee seemed to consider something for a second, then said, "Well, it doesn't matter. The main thing is that there was no bloodshed here tonight, right, Sheriff?"

"Yes, that's the main thing, Doc. Come morning I'll be leaving town for a couple weeks, to give testimony in a murder trail in Abilene. I don't like leaving here with bad dust hanging in the air. Is there something you ain't telling me, Doc?" Sheriff Harrington asked, lifting a bushy eyebrow.

"Why no, Sheriff, not at all." The doctor smiled.

Chapter 3

Three miles out of town where the trail swung south-
ward into a stretch of rocky brushland, Tim drew up
his horse and looked back through the moonlight toward Dodge City. Jed reined down beside him and
brought Danielle's chestnut mare to a halt between
them. "I hate leaving Danielle unguarded back there,
Jed," Tim said. "It's too risky."

"It's the best we could do for now, Tim," Jed replied.
He reached over and adjusted the heavy sack of feed
across the chestnut mare's saddle, placed there so its
tracks would look like it was carrying a rider. "We'll
let them follow us around out here, then the first
chance we get, we'll shake them off of our trail and
head back for her. The best thing for Danielle is a few
more days' rest to get rid of that fever and infection."

"She's going to throw a fit," said Tim, inching his
horse forward into the brush.

"Yep, but at least she'll be alive to throw it," Jed
replied. While the twins headed off into the brush, a
mile past the outskirts of Dodge City, Bernie Odell sidled his horse close to Al Tarksel and motioned him
away from the other three men.

Al Tarksel let Jack Pearl, Hank Phipps, and Loot
Harkens drift past them. Then Tarksel checked his

horse down and said in a lowered tone, "Yeah, Bernie, what is it?"

Bernie nodded at the backs of the three men riding on ahead of them. "How close are you and these boys?" he asked, in the same low voice of secrecy.

Al Tarksel just looked at him for a moment, then replied, "I'm two thousand dollars close to them, why?"

Bernie Odell nodded at the three fresh sets of hoofprints they'd been following. "I didn't want to say it in front of the others, but what we're doing here is fool's play, Al."

"Oh, really?" said Tarksel, his tone turning cold, offended. "And now you're going to start right off, telling me how to run things?"

"Hell, no, but I've been living in Dodge, I know more about the doctor than you do."

"What are you getting at?" Al Tarksel asked.

"Listen to me, Al . . . suppose I told you we could split that reward two ways between us and not have to ride all over creation to do it? Would you be opposed to it?"

"I'm listening," said Tarksel, "but you better tell it quick, before these boys look around and wonder what we're talking about back here."

Again Bernie Odell nodded at the prints on the ground. "There's only two men we're following, Al. One horse ain't carrying no rider."

"It looks to me like it is, Bernie," said Tarksel.

"I know it looks like it, but it ain't," Bernie replied. "These boys are being real cagey. Did you notice anything out of the ordinary back at the doctor's office?"

"No. What?" Tarksel asked, getting a little put out.

"There was no gurney there." Bernie smiled. "Ever seen a doctor who doesn't keep a gurney set up for emergencies?"

Tarksel didn't answer.

Bernie Odell continued. "No you've haven't, and neither have I. It's a known fact that Dr. McFee always keeps one set up. I saw it there one night when one of my customers got to upheaving and couldn't stop."

"What was wrong with him?" asked Tarksel.

"Something he et or drank I reckon, but that's not important. The thing is those two boys moved Danny Duggin on that gurney. They took him somewhere and laid him up back in Dodge. Alls we're doing out here is chasing wind."

Realization lit up Al Tarksel's eyes. "I'll be damned. Now I get you. These two are only leading us away from Duggin."

"Exactly," said Bernie Odell. "I didn't have to tell you this, Al. I could've stayed back there and collected that reward from the Delmanos myself. I'm doing it because you and I have known one another a long time. Now the question is, are me and you going to split that two thousand between us and let these three peckerwoods whistle for their supper?"

Before Al Tarksel could answer, Harkens, Phipps, and Pearl turned in their saddles and looked back at Tarksel and Odell in the moonlight. "What's the holdup?" Pearl called back to them.

"Nothing," All Tarksel called back to them, kicking his horse forward. "Me and Bernie here were talking. It makes no sense, all of us bunched up together. We might need to split up."

"What for?" asked Jack Pearl. "Hell, we can see they're all three riding together!"

"Yeah, they were when they made these tracks," said Tarksel, "but that means they haven't rode apart since then. I'm thinking we need to spread out some as we go forward here." He gestured a hand at the dark land in front of them. "You three stay on their tracks here, and me and Bernie will ride over to the right a mile or so. We'll all meet inside of Texas, if we haven't caught up to Danny Duggin first."

The three men looked at one another, baffled.

"I don't like it," said Jack Pearl.

"I don't recall asking if you like it or not, Jack," said Tarksel. "I'm the boss, and that's what we're going to do!"

"I understand," said Jack Pearl, "but why are you two going over there and us three are staying here? Why not you, your friend Bernie, and me over there, and Hank and Loot over here?"

Al Tarksel jerked his horse close to Jack and drew back his big hand. "I'm tired of your mouth, Pearl!" He moved to backhand Jack Pearl out of his saddle as Pearl shied back with his forearm raised for protection. But Bernie Odell jumped his horse forward, stopping Tarksel.

"Hold it, Al," Bernie Odell said, "this ain't worth arguing over. Let this knothead ride with us. We're wasting time here."

"Who are you calling a knothead?" asked Jack Pearl.

Bernie Odell raised his hands chest-high in a show of peace, saying to Jack Pearl and the others, "Look, boys, I know I'm a stranger to you all, except for Al here. Al knows I rode with the Axel Eldridge Gang long before any of you came along. All I'm wanting to do is see us get that money, four hundred each. If nobody wants me here, that's too bad. But as long as I am here, I'm going to do my part. If Al Tarksel's in charge then, by God, I'm going to do what he says without any back talk. I don't know how this looks to any of you, but I'd be damned ashamed to face the Delmanos and admit that five of us couldn't run down one wounded gunslinger and a couple of his buddies and smoke all three of them out without raising a sweat."

"Listen to him, boys, he's got a point," said Al Tarksel.

Bernie Odell continued, saying, "Four hundred dollars apiece ain't the biggest chunk of money in the world, but it's damn good pocket change. Now, I'm sorry as hell that ole Axel Eldridge got his brains blown all over his shirt. If you can't do something this simple without him along, how are you ever going to rob another bank, or railcar, or payroll?" He looked at each of them in turn, watching them lower their eyes in shame. "Now Axel Eldridge did a good job leading this gang, robbing, killing, pillaging, and I say God bless him for it. But he's gone and ain't coming back. The question is, can you men pull together, act like you've got some sense, and go on with the fine work he started?"

A silence set in, then Jack Pearl said in a humble voice to Al Tarksel, "Al, I'm sorry . . . you just tell me how you want to do this, and that's what I'll do."

"That's more like it," Bernie Odell said, looking

down and nodding his head. "I know that's what Axel would want to hear."

In a few moments, as the three men rode forward following the three sets of horse's hooves, Al Tarksel and Bernie Odell cut off to the right, seeing Jack Pearl and Loot Harkens look back at him in the moonlight. "As soon as we get out of sight," said Bernie Odell, "we'll circle, find this Danny Duggin, and make a quick piece of work out of him." He chuckled, adding, "The only thing those boys needed was a little rallying speech, Al. I'm surprised you hadn't already given them one. You know, sometimes a good talking to goes a long ways."

"I figure choking Hector Sabio might make them straighten up and follow my lead," said Al Tarksel. "I've never had a way with words like you do, Bernie. To tell the truth, that might be why I came and got you."

"Then that was a smart move on your part," Bernie Odell said in a smug voice.

Al Tarksel gave him a solemn look and asked, "You're not thinking about taking this gang over, are you, Bernie, because I'll not stand for it, I'm warning you."

"What gang?" Bernie Odell laughed, heeling his horse forward. "I just need some money, fast. We can't help it if we followed this Danny Duggin back to Dodge while they're out there looking for the other two, can we? We'll tell them that's how it happened. They can't expect a share of the money if they had no hand in the work. As far as I'm concerned, after it's over, if you want to ride with these boys again, that's your business. I'll go somewhere else and start me a gang of my own, if I take a notion."

"What about that shotgun-toting sheriff?" asked Tarksel. "He ain't going to stand still for us snooping around town looking for Danny Duggin."

"Don't worry about Sheriff Harrington," said Bernie Odell. "I happen to know he ain't going to be in town for the next couple of weeks. As far as Harvey Bain, or any of Harrington's half-wit deputies, they'll back off without the sheriff around. Besides, there's a couple of cousins named Clem and Otis Gooden in Dodge that'll help us out. We'll let them do most of the work." He grinned.

"For part of the reward?" Tarksel asked.

"Hell no," said Bernie Odell, his grin disappearing. "These boys will do it just because I asked them to. They both owe me bar bills. We won't tell them why we're killing Danny Duggin, we'll just say it's personal business of yours. We might give them twenty or thirty dollars apiece when it's over."

"Sounds good to me," said Tarksel, "but just out of curiosity, what would you have done if Jack Pearl had of rode over with us instead of with Hank and Loot?"

Bernie Odell grinned and ran a finger across his throat. "What do you think I would've done, for half of two thousand dollars?"

Al Tarksel laughed and said, "That's what I figured you'd have done. You're still the same ole Bernie—nothing's changed a bit, that I can see."

"That's right," said Bernie Odell. "Now that I'm back in the saddle and getting the smell of other people's whiskey off my shirt, I'm fixin' to make up for some lost time."

Tim and Jed Strange had ridden farther south than they'd intended to, but with the gunmen close on their trail they wanted to be sure they'd completely lost them before turning back to Dodge City. After two more hours of riding, the twins stopped at the crest of a higher land swell and looked back through the clear gray moonlight. "What do you think?" Jed asked, leading the chestnut mare by its reins.

"I think it's safe for us to circle around now," Tim replied. He looked ahead of them at a wide stand of cottonwood and juniper. In the moonlight, the black outlines of the trees swayed on a night wind. "Let's drop the bag of feed in there, then stay in the trees for a half mile or so to our left, then head back."

"That's fine by me," Jed said, booting his horse forward.

A few yards inside the cover of the trees, Jed dropped the heavy bag of feed from the mare's back. They turned east, staying deep inside the trees, hoping to leave very little tracks for the gunmen to follow. When they'd gone a half mile or more and started to turn back toward Dodge City, Tim stopped his horse and raised a hand to have Jed do the same. After a second of sitting in silence, Tim looked back at his brother, saying in a whisper, "Did you hear that?"

Jed quietly stepped his horse up beside Tim, leading the chestnut mare. "I might have heard something, but I don't know what it was," he whispered in reply, his hand poised on the butt of his Colt.

"It sounded like a wheel creaking," Tim whispered.

They sat in silence, listening until the faint sound came again. They looked at one another, then inched their horses forward to a sapling. They stepped down from their saddles without making a sound and, hitching the horses, they moved forward on foot. The sound came again, this time more clearly, followed by a horse blowing out a deep breath in the darkness.

Looking past the trunk of a cottonwood, Tim made out the dark form of a horse and the outline of a tall wagon behind it. "I don't know what it's doing here, but I don't like it," Tim whispered. He backed away a step. "We best get out of here, I think that's the posse that rode through the territory and chased everybody out."

"That's good thinking," a voice said, breaking the deathlike quietness. "Now get your hands in the air before we open fire. In the second that Tim and Jed stood stunned in surprise, the sound of rifles cocking filled the close space around them. Tim and Jed hesitated, their hands ready to snatch their pistols from their holsters. But the voice said, "Don't even think about it. There's five armed U.S. federal marshals surrounding you. You're both under arrest."

The twins slowly raised their hands chest-high, but stayed poised to make a grab for their Colts. "If you're lawmen, we better see some badges," said Tim.

A lantern flared in the small clearing, then grew into a corona of light. The man held the lantern out from himself at arm's length to his side, not making himself a target for them. The voice chuckled, saying, "You damned outlaws are all alike. The first thing you do is start trying to call the shots."

"We're not outlaws," said Jed Strange, "and we still haven't seen any badges."

"Then look around real easy-like," said the voice, "you'll see more badges than you ever wanted to."

Taking a cautious look around, Tim and Jed saw the lantern light glint on badges and rifle barrels. Tim let out a breath of relief as the two of them raised their hands a few more inches. "All right, you really are lawmen," Tim said. "But you've no reason to arrest us. We're not wanted for anything."

"Maybe, maybe not," said the man holding the lantern. He stepped closer, the riflemen doing the same, closing the already small circle. "I'm U.S. Marshal Christian Dane," he continued, "and we heard every word you said a moment ago." Hands reached in and lifted the twins' Colts from their holsters, then they stepped back, the barrels of cocked rifles leveled on them less then three feet away. Marshal Dane looked at the twins with a flat smile, his tired eyes going up and down them. "And you were right . . . we *are* the posse that swept through Indian Territory a while back."

"Chris, I found their horses," said another voice. An older deputy stepped into the light behind Marshal Dane, leading all three horses.

"Good work, Seals," said Marshal Dane over his shoulder. "Take them over and hitch them to the back of the jail wagon. "We're headed back to Fort Smith at the crack of dawn." He looked back at Tim and Jed, saying, "We're plumb tuckered out rounding all you boys up. If we had missed you two tonight, you'd have gotten away free and clear for a while longer."

"Marshal Dane," said Tim, "listen to me, please.

We were in the territory when your posse hit there . . . but we're not outlaws. I'm Tim Strange, this is my brother, Jed. If you want some real outlaws, there's some on our trail right now, about an hour or two behind us. If you arrest us, you're arresting innocent men."

"You might find this hard to believe, Tim Strange, if that really is your name," said Dane, "but in my whole career, all I've ever arrested is *innocent* men."

The other lawmen stifled their laughter. Two of them stepped in behind Tim and Jed, drew their arms down roughly behind their backs, and handcuffed them. When Tim stiffened and started to resist, the man behind him said, "Take it easy, young man. We'll remove these cuffs once you're in the wagon."

"You men are making a big mistake!" Jed hissed, struggling as two pairs of hands turned him and Tim around and shoved them toward the wagon in the larger clearing ahead.

"Settle down," Marshal Dane demanded behind him. "If you boys aren't wanted, we'll soon find out. If we've made a mistake, you'll have our sincerest apologies."

"But you don't understand, Marshal!" Jed insisted. "We've got to get back to Dodge City before—!"

"Shut up, Jed," Tim hissed under his breath. "You heard the marshal. We're innocent . . . we've got nothing to worry about."

One of the deputies swung open the door to the jail wagon and helped Tim and Jed take a step upward inside. When the door slammed shut and a deputy locked it, Marshal Dane said, "You two back up against the bars, we'll take the cuffs off . . . and

we'll leave them off so long as you can behave yourselves."

On the floor in the darkness an old man looked
up, his face almost entirely covered by a gray tangle
of beard. He chuckled and said to the twins, "Good
to get some company for a change. Ole Cooley and
Sipes here are too cross to converse with." He
stretched his leg out and nudged his boot against one
of the two figures lying against the wall of the wagon
wrapped in blankets.

One of the figures growled, "Keep your boot to
yourself, Alley Cat, or I'll rip your leg off."

"See what I mean?" the old man snickered. "They're
both salty as hell." He raised up slightly, looking the
twins over. Seeing to his surprise that they were twins,
his eyes widened a bit. "Say now, you boys are look-
alikes, ain't yas?"

Neither of the twins answered. Instead they slid
down to the floor of the wagon and watched one of
the deputies hitch their three horses to the rear of the
wagon. Marshal Dane stepped close to the wagon,
asking Alley Cat Catlin, "Do you recognize these two,
Alley?"

"Yep, I sure do," said Catlin, "they was there all
right. Do I get some extra beans for breakfast for iden-
tifying them?"

"Sure, why not," said Marshal Dane. He turned
and said to one of the deputies as he walked away,
"Paris, you get up in the seat for a while, give Dooley a rest. We're going to push on tonight while we've
got good moonlight. Once you get back on the trail,
it'll be easy going."

Tim turned to Alley Cat Catlin as the men prepared

to get under way. "You're a liar, mister. You didn't see us in Indian Territory."

Alley Cat Catlin shrugged and laughed. "What's the difference? Hell, I weren't there myself! But these boys feed good. If you stand the heat, this wagon ain't a bad way to travel."

"Shut up, Alley," a muffled voice growled from within one of the blankets. "You keep running your jaw, I'm going to twist your head around backwards."

"That's Lon Cooley," said Alley Cat, lowering his voice. "Him and Lawrence Sipes weren't in the territory either, but the marshals come upon them leading a string of stolen Indian horses three days ago."

"Keep it up, Alley Cat," Lon Cooley warned, "see if I don't kill you."

"We've got to get out of here, Jed," Tim whispered to his brother as the wagon made a short lurch forward and began to roll. "What's going to become of Danielle if we don't get back there to her?"

"I know," Jed whispered in reply. "I started to tell the marshal everything a while ago. It's a good thing you cut me off. They wouldn't understand, would they?"

"No, they wouldn't," said Tim. He looked around in the darkness at the passing black outlines of trees and brush swaying in the night wind. "It's up to us to get back there and look after her. Lord help her if those gunmen figure out where she's at."

Chapter 4

Without pushing their horses too hard, Marshal C. F. McCord and Hector Sabio reached the banks of the Arkansas River at the end of a two-day ride from Newton, Kansas. Along the way they'd picked up the tracks of four riders. One of the horses left the distinct print of a Double Diamond brand horseshoe, which Hector said belonged to the big lineback dun Al Tarksel had been riding. Hector's voice began coming around by the end of the first day on the trail, with the help of honey-laced whiskey and a hot poultice of cayenne oil wrapped around his throat. Although his voice was still raspy and strained, and he still cupped his hand near his throat, once Hector started talking, C. F. McCord had no problem finding out anything he wanted to know about the Axel Eldridge Gang and the bounty the Delmanos had placed on Danny Duggin's head.

"This Danny Duggin is one bad hombre, *sí*?" Hector said as they rode along the trail, seeing where the three sets of hooves ran along the trail. A few yards to the left and off the path, four other sets followed. "Why else would Saul Delmano and his family pay so much to have someone else do their killing for them? I think they are afraid of him."

"It would appear so," said Marshal C. F. McCord. McCord wasn't about to tell Hector that he suspected Danny Duggin was really a woman. That was one piece of information the marshal wasn't about to reveal to anyone. "My main concern is finding the Delmanos and putting them out of business. It just happens that Danny Duggin's interests and mine are the same in that regard."

"So you mean what you say, McCord," Hector asked, "about letting me settle with Al Tarksel on my own?"

"Yes, I meant it, Hector. So long as it's on the other side of the border, it's out of my jurisdiction."

"You *Americano* lawmen," Hector said, a crafty smile forming on his lips as he tapped a finger to his forehead. "I have never understood how this jurisdiction works. When I meet this Tarksel on a street in Méjico and shoot him like the pig that he is, you will not interfere because it has nothing to do with your American law. Yet, you go into Méjico to hunt these Delmanos, and when you find them you will feel justified in shooting them, *sí?*"

C. F. McCord grinned, saying, "You promised to lead me to the Delmanos' place in Mexico. As soon as we cross the border, this badge comes off my chest and goes into my vest pocket, Hector. The Delmanos have taken advantage of the border too long. I don't think the *federales* or the U.S. federal law will either one shed any tears over the Delmanos."

Hector nodded. "Nor will the world be worse off when I kill this dog Tarksel and spit in his dead face."

Hector's expression turned to stone just thinking about it.

McCord gazed off along the riverbank to where the three sets of horses' hooves bunched up. Stepping his horse over amid the tracks, he looked down at scrapings in the dirt where boot prints and knee prints sank deep, picturing in his mind how one person had laid in the dirt, perhaps being cradled in the arms of another. Surrounding the area were the four other sets of hoofprints, one of them bearing the Double Diamond marking.

"Looks like Danny Duggin's wound wasn't as healed as he might've thought it was," McCord said. His eyes followed the tracks down into the water. "They left here, one of them leading a horse and two of them riding double, Hector. Now what do you make of that?"

"I do not know." Hector shrugged. "But perhaps it is time you give me a pistol in case we run into trouble across the river?"

"Don't push things, Hector," McCord replied. "We're still a long way from Mexico."

"This is so," said Hector in his raspy voice, "but you had the sheriff in Newton check and see that I was telling you the truth. I am not a wanted man, nor am I a dangerous man. I think for my protection you should give me a pistol now."

"Soon, Hector," said McCord, nudging his horse down the bank to the edge of the water. "First let's see how things shape up in Dodge City."

"Why do you hunt so hard for the Delmanos?" Hector asked, gigging his horse along behind him. "Is there not enough desperados to keep you busy?"

McCord looked along the rippling water, then out across the sky as if recounting an event in his mind. Then, letting out a long breath, he said, "Right after the war, there was a young sailor who came all the way from the port of New Orleans to El Paso to ask for a young lady's hand in marriage. He'd saved himself six hundred dollars before leaving the navy. The night before he was to travel out to talk to the young lady's father, he got into a poker game in town and won himself another three hundred dollars before he quit. But one of the men he'd won the money from was Saul Delmano. The next morning someone found the young sailor's body in a rubbish heap, with his throat cut and his pockets empty. Dogs were licking at his blood."

"This is a terrible thing that happened," Hector said, shaking his head slowly. "I have done many things that I am not proud of, but never have I stooped to such a low thing as this." He paused as if thinking about it, then added, "Well . . . I did once stick a man for grabbing the behind of a woman I was dancing with. But I only stick him a couple of times, just to make him apologize. But I never would do such a thing as this."

McCord sat staring out across the river, his expression slack and unchanged, yet his hand clenching his reins tightly.

After another moment of silence, Hector said, "And this man's killer was Saul Delmano?"

"Yep," said McCord.

"But how do you know he did it?" Hector asked.

"It wasn't hard to find out. Saul Delmano bragged about it, after he left Texas of course," said McCord.

"This young sailor?" Hector asked, his raspy voice lowered. "You knew him, *si?*"

"Yes, I knew him," said McCord. "He was my kid brother."

"Oh, I see," said Hector. "So there is bad blood between you and Saul Delmano, the same as it is between him and this Danny Duggin."

"The very same," McCord said in a firm tone, nudging his horse into the rippling water.

Dodge City, Kansas. September 14, 1871

C. F. McCord and Hector Sabio swung wide of the main trail leading into Front Street and circled around onto a narrow path leading into Dodge through an assortment of shacks, small houses, and tents. At a small private stable behind the cattle pins, McCord swung down from his saddle and handed a young boy the reins to his horse. "Grain them short, then wait two hours and grain them again," McCord instructed as Hector stepped down and also gave the boy his reins. McCord handed the boy a dollar, saying, "Don't let me come back here in a hour and find they haven't been rubbed down real good."

"Right away, Marshal," the boy said, snatching the dollar from McCord's gloved hand.

"Now then, Hector, let's take it one alley at time, see who we come up with on the streets," said McCord.

"So, this is how you do things," said Hector, falling in beside the marshal, keeping up with him across the rutted ground. "You do not ride boldly down the middle of the street the way some lawmen do."

"I always found that to be a foolish practice," McCord said, "especially if you want to look things over and find out what's going on first. I prefer to go unnoticed until I'm ready to make a move."

"I see," said Hector. "No wonder all those outlaws on the strip call you The Fox, eh?"

C. F. McCord just looked at him.

Hector added quickly, "Or so I have heard. I myself have never ridden with those cattle rustlers and stagecoach robbers along the strip."

"What exactly have you done that rates you an outlaw, Hector?" McCord asked, turning his gaze straight ahead with a trace of a wry smile. "Are you telling me that all those times you rode with Axel Eldridge you never committed any crimes?"

Hector didn't answer as they walked on through rubble and broken bottles, past garbage barrels and stray dogs that crept along the backs of the row of buildings facing Front Street. "Where do we start looking for this Danny Duggin and his brothers, if they are still here?" Hector asked as they entered a littered alley.

"Knowing he's wounded, seeing how they started riding double at the river crossing," said McCord, "my best hunch would be to start at the doctor's office. From there I'll go to the sheriff's office, let him know what I'm doing here."

"*Sí*, that would be wise," said Hector, "and let the sheriff know that I am with you, so he will know I am on the side of the law, eh?"

Stopping at the front corner of the alley and looking out along the busy street, C. F. McCord said over his shoulder, "But I'm going to see the doctor and the sheriff alone, Hector. I want you to start here and work your way one alley at a time, looking for Al Tarksel or any of the others. I've got a feeling they'll be doing the same thing we're doing, looking for Danny Duggin."

"Then you must give me a gun!" cried Hector, cupping his hand to this throat. "If I see Tarksel, I will shoot him many times and be done with it!"

"That's exactly what I *don't* want you to do, Hector," said McCord. "You're leading me to the Delmanos, remember?"

"*Sí*, I gave you my word that I will take you to the Delmanos, and I will keep it. But how can I lay eyes on Al Tarksel and not blow his brains out? What kind of man would I be to not do so, after he does this to me?"

McCord turned to Hector with a cold gaze. "You're not going to disappoint me, are you?"

Hector relented, grudgingly, rubbing his boot back and forth in the dirt as he looked down. "No, I will work the alleys as you say. But you must hurry, because if I see this pig Tarksel, I don't know if I can keep myself from killing him with my bare hands!"

"Do the best you can, Hector," said McCord, taking his badge from his chest and slipping it down into his vest pocket, "I'm counting on you." He moved forward, up onto the boardwalk, blending into the passing crowd with his hat brim low on his forehead.

McCord took his time, working his way along the boardwalk until a few yards ahead he saw people milling about in front of the doctor's office. Among the group a small, restless boy stood with a sling around his arm, a woman beside him jerking his other arm to make him settle down. Across the street from the doctor's office, two rough-looking men wearing low-slung gunbelts stood lounging against a striped barber pole, one of them picking his teeth with a matchstick. Upon seeing the men, McCord stopped for a second and pretended to look into a shop window. After a moment, he slipped sideways a couple of steps and cut back through an alley to the back of the doctor's office.

Before knocking on the rear door, McCord tried turning the knob to see if it was locked. Before he could let go of the knob, a tense voice called out from inside, "Go away! The office is closed! I'm armed, I'm warning you!"

McCord stepped to one side of the door, took his badge from his vest, and pinned it on. "Doctor, this is U.S. Federal Marshal C. F. McCord speaking. I'm here to help you."

After a short pause, the door opened an inch and Dr. McFee eyed McCord up and down. McCord saw the small pistol in the doctor's hand. "A marshal, huh?" said the doctor, letting out a sigh of relief. "Thank God you're here." He swung the door open, then shot a glance both ways along the alley before closing and locking it. "My office is being watched by some gunmen! I haven't even been able to slip away and go for help. The sheriff's out of town, but he has a couple of deputies. Yet from the looks of things, I'm afraid I'll only get the deputies killed!"

"I understand," said McCord. "I saw two men across the street. Do you recognize them?"

"Yes, they're the Goodens," said the doctor, wiping a hand across his forehead, "a couple of hardcases who've been hanging around town for the past three or four months. I don't know why Sheriff Harrington has allowed it."

"Settle down, Doctor," said McCord in a calming voice. "If they've broken no law, your sheriff can't do much about them being here." He looked the doctor up and down. "What do they want from you?" McCord had a pretty good idea already.

"There are two others involved," said Dr. McFee. "A fellow named Al Tarksel, and a local thug named Bernie Odell who owns a saloon here. I treated a young man here the other night for a gunshot wound. This Al Tarksel wants the young man dead. He thinks they can pressure me into telling them where the young man's staying. Bernie Odell met me out front yesterday evening. Said if I didn't tell them what they wanted to know, they'd be back this afternoon. Said I'd tell them one way or the other."

"I see," said McCord, "but you *won't* tell them because you've given your word, right?"

"In a nutshell, yes." The doctor slipped the small pistol into his pocket as he continued. "What kind of doctor would I be to turn these wolves loose on a wounded man?"

"Not much of one, I suppose." McCord considered things, then said, "Doctor, which is the most important to you, keeping your word, or saving this Danny Duggin's life?"

The doctor looked surprised. "How do you know his name?"

"Because I'm looking for him, too."

"To kill him? Is he wanted by the law?"

"No, he's not wanted for breaking the law. I've got a feeling he's been on a vengeance rampage. I want to bring it to an end before some innocent people get hurt—one of them being him. Are you going to help me?"

The doctor eyed McCord closely, suspicious of the marshal's intentions. Then he said, "There's something about this young man that I don't think anybody knows. Can you tell me what that is?"

"I could," said McCord, "but I'm not going to. If there comes a time when Danny Duggin wants to reveal his secret, it'll be up to him. Until that time, I don't care *who* he is, or *what* he is. I'm only here to do some good, whether Danny Duggin wants me to or not."

The doctor wrestled with it in his mind. McCord watched, not offering another word. Finally coming to a decision, McFee let out a breath and said, "All right, Marshal. It looks like I'm going to have to play this your way."

When McCord left the doctor's office, he walked along the long alley behind the building, looking around the corner of each smaller alley in turn until he spotted Hector watching the horse and foot traffic on Front Street. He approached Hector quietly from the rear, seeing him reach down and pull a wooden slate from an abandoned packing crate. McCord realized what was about to happen and, hurrying forward, he grabbed Hector by the back of his collar and yanked him back just as Hector had started to bolt out of the alley.

"You gave me your word, Hector!" McCord said, turning the Mexican around and pinning him to a clapboard wall. He jerked the wooden slat from Hector's hand and pitched it away.

"I know, Marshal! But there is that pig!" He gestured a hand toward the other side of Front Street where Al Tarksel stood in the doorway of the Aces High Saloon with a bottle of whiskey hanging from his hand. "I am sorry, but when I see him, I lose all control, I want to kill him so badly!" Hector said in a voice still strained and raspy.

McCord held him against the wall with one hand and stood watching Al Tarksel for a moment. "You're going to have to pull yourself together, Hector," he demanded. "I've got some things set up for us. If you do like I ask, you might get a chance at Al Tarksel right here in Dodge, tonight. But I won't let you mess things up, *comprende?*" He stared into Hector's eyes, letting him see the warning there.

"*Sí, comprendo,*" said Hector with resolve, easing down and calming himself. "Tell me what you want me to do."

McCord loosened his grip on Hector's shirt and patted his shoulder, saying, "That's more like it. I spoke to the doctor. He told me where Danny Duggin is staying. This evening he's also going to tell Tarksel. There's three men in this with Tarksel. When they come to kill Danny Duggin, we'll be waiting for them. If you bring down Tarksel, it'll be in self-defense, but only if you still take me to the Delmanos. Do we understand one another?"

"Ahhh, I see!" Hector grinned. "This is how you work, eh, The Fox? You do not step out and call these men into the street like some big *pistolero*. Instead you use your head, eh?" Hector tapped a finger against his temple and winked. "I think I like this way you do things."

"Boot hill is plumb full of big *pistoleros*," said McCord. "I don't plan on being one of them. I want you to go to the stables and keep out of sight until I come and get you."

"Oh? And where will you be?" Hector asked.

"I'll be going to see Danny Duggin, make sure he doesn't shoot at us by mistake. Then I'm going to keep an eye on the doctor until the time comes. I don't want this riffraff getting carried away and hurting him."

"You are sure they will come tonight and try to kill this Danny Duggin?"

"Yes, I'm sure," said McCord. "If these men know Duggin, they know they've got to get him while he's still recuperating, otherwise they won't stand a chance." McCord looked across the street and saw Al Tarksel turn and step back inside the Aces High Saloon. "They're probably talking it over right now."

"I think it is time you gave me a pistol, eh, Fox?"

"Not yet, Hector," said McCord. "But don't worry, tonight when the time comes, I'll see to it you're armed."

Chapter 5

Inside the small wood-framed house surrounded by its picket fence, Sarah Sims stood in the bedroom door, tying the strings of a fresh clean apron around her waist. She looked over at the sleeping form on the bed and cleared her throat, not too loudly, but just loud enough to cause Danielle to open her eyes. "Oh dear, I hope I didn't wake you, Mr. Duggin," she said.

"No," Danielle replied drowsily, "I was only dozing." She raised up on one elbow and started to swing her feet down to the floor.

"No no," said Sarah Sims, "you lie still now." She moved forward as if prepared to press Danielle back down onto the feather mattress. "I'm going over to the restaurant to help prepare the evening meal. I wanted to know if there was anything you needed while I was out."

"No, ma'am, not that I can think of." Danielle laid over on her side, and Sarah Sims pulled the thin white sheet back over her, tucking her in like a child. "I haven't been this well cared for since I was a little—" Danielle caught herself on the verge of saying, "little girl." But then she stopped herself and added quickly, "a little *boy*."

Sarah Sims glanced away with a knowing look in

her eyes, saying, "Well, it doesn't hurt to be cared for now and then. I'm glad to see you're feeling better."

"I'm feeling just fine," Danielle said, patting her bandaged side. "The swelling is down, my fever has broken. I don't how to thank you and the doctor."

"But see?" Sarah Sims smiled. "You just did." She pressed her palm to Danielle's forehead, then said with relief, "Yes, your fever is all but gone." She glanced at the empty bowl on the tray beside the bed. "I'm glad to say you're appetite is much improved too. For two days you didn't eat a thing."

Danielle relaxed, easing her head back onto the pillow. "Two days? I can barely even remember coming here." She looked up at Sarah Sims and was reminded of her mother, and of home, and of countless memories of her family. Then her eyes went around the room, to the chair back where her clean washed trousers hung beneath her pistol belt. Her boots sat on the floor beside the chair. "I need to get up and on my way," she said.

"Nonsense," Sarah Sims said firmly, a look of motherly authority on her face. "You need to spend at least another day or two in bed. Gunshot infections may appear to be gone, but as you saw before, they have a way of springing back up on you."

"I—I know," said Danielle, "but I have to get going and find my brothers."

"Dr. McFee explained all that to you, young man," said Sarah Sims. "They told him they would be back for you, and I'm certain they will."

Danielle decided not to pursue it. There was no way of explaining to this gentle woman what a harsh destiny life had forced upon her and her brothers.

"Yes, ma'am, you're right, another day or two would be wise, I suppose. But I have to say, the treatment you and the doctor have been giving me has worked. My mind is cleared more than it has been since all of this happened. I feel stronger, too."

Before Sarah Sims could reply, a voice behind her in the doorway said, "That's good to hear, Danny Duggin, because you and I have a lot to talk about."

Danielle's first reaction was to bolt upright, ready to flee, but seeing the badge on the young marshal's chest caused her to hesitate for a second. In that second, C. F. McCord stepped in between her and the chair and looked down at her. "There's nothing to get excited about, Danny. I'm U.S. Federal Marshal C. F. McCord." A trace of a smile flickered. "I'm one of the good guys."

"But . . ." Sarah Sims was lost for words.

McCord turned to her, seeing the look of apprehension on her face. "Don't worry, ma'am, the doctor knows I'm here. He told me you worked evenings at Delmonico's restaurant. I started to wait until after you left for work, but I decided it best to come on in now, make sure you understand what's going on." He swept his battered Stetson from atop his head and continued. "I'll be spending the evening here with Danny. Some men are coming to kill him. I intend to see to it they don't."

As the marshal spoke to Sarah Sims, Danielle lay watching him, his calm manner, the way he seemed to keep an eye on everything around him, yet looking Sarah Sims squarely and gently in the eyes as he'd spoken to her. Sarah seemed flustered, confused, and frightened, her fingertips pressed to her lips as she spoke.

"Then perhaps I shouldn't leave," said Sarah. "I have an old ten-gauge shotgun behind the pantry . . . some shells, somewhere."

"No, ma'am, " said McCord, "but much obliged anyway. What I'd really like for you to do is to go on about your business, the same as you do every day." Danielle noted how the young marshal's voice remained calm and soft as he spoke to Sarah Sims, as if it were only the two of them in the room, as if he might have just as easily been talking about the weather. "Don't you worry about Danny and me. We'll both be just fine." His gaze cut back to Danielle. "Won't we, Danny?"

It took a conscious effort for Danielle to look into his slate-gray eyes and speak at the same time. "It's fine, Sarah," she said at length, not taking her eyes from McCord's. "The marshal's right. If someone is coming here to kill me, we best make them think today's the same as any other."

Sarah Sims calmed down, looked back and forth between the two of them, then said as she turned toward the door, "Then I'll just take down my grandmother's mirror from the wall before I leave. I wouldn't want to see it broken."

"We'll do our best not to leave a mess here, ma'am," McCord said to Sarah Sims without taking his eyes from Danielle's.

No sooner had Sarah Sims left the house than C. F. McCord picked up Danielle's gunbelt from the chair back, slipped one of her Colts from its holster, and said to her as he turned the pistol back and forth in his hand, inspecting it, "This is some set of pistols you have here . . . shaved barrels, raised hammers . . . looks like the grips were custom-fit for a smaller hand than usual. I bet if I spun a cylinder these babies would tick as quietly as a Swiss clock." McCord raised his eyes to Danielle beneath his lowered brow. "Bet your pa must've done all this custom work, back in St. Joe?"

Danielle didn't answer, but she could see he'd done his job well, checking her out, probably her brothers, too. No lawman had done such a thorough job before that she knew of. McCord shoved the big Colt back down into the holster and hung the belt back on the chair. "You know something, Danny," he said, taking a deep breath and letting it out patiently, "if I've learned anything at all about you, I figure you've got a derringer or some such small pistol under that sheet somewhere, figuring if I'm not who I say I am, or if I'm here for any reason than to help you, all you've got to do is pull the trigger and be up and on your way. Am I right?"

Danielle only stared at him, her hand steady and poised beneath the sheet, her palm dry, her strength and senses sharp. She held a poker face, not revealing a thing. Yet the young marshal shook his head and smiled, saying, "Yep, that's what I thought." In no hurry, he stepped over to one side of the partly opened window, turning his back to Danielle. Pulling back a lace curtain with one fingertip, he peered out and toward the front yard. "If you think you need that pistol cocked and pointed, it's okay with me, so long as you don't sneeze and set it off accidentally. I've found out enough about you to know I can trust you. Do you think you'll learn enough about me in the next couple of hours to say the same?"

Beneath the sheet, Danielle let the hammer down and let the small pistol she indeed had hidden lay against the side of her thigh. "I've broken no law, Marshall," she said.

"I know it," McCord replied, turning back from the window and walking over to the side of the bed. "Like I said, I've done some thinking and some checking. If I was to pull out a few names of outlaws reported dead or missing over the past year, I bet those names would match up well with where you've been."

"Any killing I've done has been in self-defense," Danielle offered.

"Well, we won't get into that," said McCord. "It'd be your word against the word of outlaws . . . since they're dead, it'd be hard for them to dispute you."

"What's your stake in this, Marshal?" Danielle asked. "If you were already after these men who are coming to kill me, why didn't you take them down when you got here? Why all the cat and mouse games?"

"It's the way I work," said McCord. "I hate shooting up a town, taking a chance on getting some innocent folks killed. Back here, we're out of the way. If there's going to be shooting, this is the best place for it, don't you think?"

"What I think, Marshal," Danielle said, "is that you're beating around the bush."

"Well, maybe, a little," McCord admitted, "but I reckon it's because I don't know yet how to act around you, Danny Duggin. I know all about your secret, and maybe I just didn't know how to approach the subject."

Danielle felt her chest tighten. "Marshal, you don't know nothing about me."

McCord raised a hand slightly, to try and calm her. "Now, don't get upset . . . I've only done my job. The fact is, it doesn't matter at all to me how a person wants to present themselves. But call me curious," he said as he shrugged. "I can't help wondering why."

Danielle lay in silence for a moment, deciding how far to trust this man. Finally she said, grudgingly, "It's a man's world, Marshal. I had a job to do and I figured this was the best way to get it done. You've got your way of doing things . . . I've got mine." She raised her brow in question. "Is there any need to talk about it further?"

"No, none at all," said McCord. "I only wanted to clear the air before we get down to business tonight." He gestured a hand toward her gunbelt. "Are you able to ride after we finish up with these men?"

"Yes, I can. Why?" Danielle asked.

"Because with a bounty on your head, there'll be more gunmen coming to collect it. I figure the best thing for you to do is to head south of the border and cut this trouble off at the source."

"You mean ride with you when I go looking for Saul Delmano? Sorry, Marshal, when I get to Delmano, I want it to be just the two of us, face-to-face. Don't concern yourself about me, Marshal, I can take care of myself. I want to see myself in Saul Delmano's eyes when they close for the last time."

C. F. McCord looked at Danielle as if running something through his mind. "We'll see," he said. "Let's take it one step at a time. A lot can happen between here and the border ... maybe I'll grow on you by then." He sat down in the chair, took his pistol from its holster, checked it, and let it lay across his lap. "We might as well get comfortable. This could be a long evening."

As a slivered moon touched the horizon, McCord left Sarah Sims's house long enough to go to the stable where Hector Sabio was waiting. "What has taken you so long?" Hector asked, reaching out and snatching the rifle McCord held out to him. "I started to go over to the saloon and beat that pig Tarksel to death with a rake handle." He raised a finger for emphasis. "It is only because I gave you my word that I have not already done so."

"And I'm proud of you for that, Hector," said McCord. "I told Danny Duggin that you'll be behind Tarksel and the others, making sure they don't escape."

"What? Behind them? But I want to be in front of Tarksel! I want to call out his name and watch my bullets nail him to the ground!" Hector's raspy voice grew louder as he spoke.

"Take it easy, Hector," said McCord. "If he comes into your sights, he's all yours. But keep in mind I've got a job to do here. Work with me."

"*Sí*, I will do as you say," said Hector, a bit crestfallen.

"Good man," said McCord. "I'm going past the doctor's to see what's going on, then I'll get back to the house and take cover outside somewhere. Be careful you don't have me in your sights once this gets under way.

Leaving the stable, McCord kept to the shadows and crept up across the alley from the rear door to the doctor's office. He saw that the door was ajar and, without approaching any closer, he caught a glimpse of the two men he'd seen earlier standing outside of the barbershop. "You better not be lying to me, sawbones," warned a voice. "Come on, boys, let's go."

McCord hurried away before the door opened all the way. He had disappeared up the alley by the time Al Tarksel, Bernie Odell, and the Gooden cousins walked out into the clear night. Al Tarksel pulled a leather glove from his right hand and opened and closed his fist a few times, loosening up. "Boys, we're going to wait here a few minutes, let it get good and dark, make sure this doctor don't try to go warn him. Then we'll go open this Danny Duggin up with some .45 slugs and see what he had for supper."

Clem Gooden looked at his cousin, Otis, then turned and asked Al Tarksel, "So, you've taken over the Axel Eldridge Gang?"

"Yeah, what of it?" Tarksel replied gruffly. He reached over, took a bag of chopped tobacco from Bernie Odell's shirt pocket, and began rolling himself a smoke.

"Nothing," said Clem Gooden, "except Otis and me are looking for somebody to throw in with full time. Pickings are a little slim around here. We figured if we did a good job for you killing this Duggin fellow, maybe we'd be able to ride on with you?"

Al Tarksel ran the cigarette in and out of his mouth, licking it, then looked them both up and down, saying, "We'll see how it goes. Bernie here vouched for both of you or you wouldn't be here. It takes some top-notch men to ride with me. I've got big plans for the Axel Eldridge Gang. What do you say, Bernie? Do these boys have what it takes?" He struck a match and lit the cigarette.

"We're fixin' to find out, ain't we?" Bernie Odell grinned, the palm of his right hand rubbing back and forth on the butt of his holstered pistol.

Darkness covered the town like a black shroud by the time Al Tarksel finished smoking his cigarette, dropping it to the ground and crushing it beneath his boot heel. Without a word he started walking in the direction of the picket-fenced house where the light of a dimmed lamp glowed in the front window. Bernie Odell and the Gooden cousins followed, spreading out and halting as Tarksel did at a distance of thirty yards. "Get ready, boys," Bernie Odell said. "Both of you circle around, hit the house from the rear. Al and me will take the front. Right Al?"

"Right," said Tarksel, lifting his pistol from its holster and letting it hang down his side. "Bernie, you get over at the other front corner. Anybody inside will never know what hit them." Tarksel stood only a few feet from the side door of the stable where Hector Sabio had taken cover behind a large pile of used straw. Hearing Al Tarksel's voice, Hector felt his hands tighten on the rifle stock. He watched and listened as the other three figures moved away into the darkness. Then he cursed silently to himself and raised the rifle butt to his shoulder.

His thumb across the rifle hammer ready to cock it back and let it fall, Hector stared at his target for a full ten seconds, thinking how good it would be to feel the kick of the rifle butt against his shoulder and watch Tarksel sink to the ground. Yet there was something incomplete, almost unsatisfying in the deed. He wanted Al Tarksel to know who was going to kill him. This wouldn't do at all, he thought, lowering the rifle the second that Al Tarksel began walking slowly toward the house.

Hector turned the rifle around, gripping the barrel in both hands, hefting it like a club. Yes, this was more like it. He made a couple of short practice swings and moved forward, falling into Tarksel's footsteps, stalking him closely.

From his position behind a short bush in the corner of the picket fence, C. F. McCord sat hunched down in his riding duster, his Colt already cocked as he watched the dark shadow of Bernie Odell approach the right front corner of the house. The other two men had passed the front yard and were headed for the rear. Just as McCord started to stand up and aim his Colt toward the unsuspecting Odell, the sound of a loud thump and a deep grunt came from the direction of Al Tarksel, followed by Hector's hoarse voice. "It is I, *Hector*, back from the dead, you *pig!* Now *you* die!"

In the split second of distraction, C. F. McCord caught only a glimpse of Bernie Odell drop down out of sight. The next thing McCord saw of Bernie Odell was him running along the picket fence in a crouch. McCord's shots followed him, pieces of fencing flying into the air with each explosion of McCord's Colt.

At the rear of the house, fire from Danielle's blazing Colts flashed in the night. As McCord raced along the front yard, he heard the loud thumping sound of Hector's rifle stock, followed by the cries of pain from Al Tarksel. Now Bernie Odell had found cover behind a pile of firewood. Two shots whistled past McCord's head. But rather than duck for cover himself, McCord ran straight toward the muzzle flash of Odell's shots, firing back repeatedly until he caught sight of Odell breaking from cover and making a run for it. McCord halted, raised his Colt out at arm's length, took aim on the fleeing dark figure, and watched it fall as his pistol bucked violently in his hand.

Without hesitation, McCord ran to the back corner of the house, then sprang out with his pistol ready, fanning it back and forth, looking for a target. But he stopped and lowered his pistol as he heard the sound of six spent pistol shells fall to the wooden porch, and saw Danielle standing in a drift of smoke, reloading. "I got two," she said, her voice tight and flat, "where's the others?"

"I got one out front," said McCord, stepping forward, looking down at the body near Danielle's feet. A bullet hole above Clem Gooden's right eye oozed blood into a widening puddle on the wooden porch. "It sounds like Hector's got the fourth one taken care of."

Danielle clicked her Colt shut with the snap of her wrist and stepped down off the porch to where the body of Otis Gooden lay facedown in the dirt. "It didn't go quite as smooth as you wanted, did it, Marshal?"

McCord felt a twinge of embarrassment. "Hector got a little carried away," he said, looking down at the body on the ground. "I meant to be here before these two doubled up on you. But apparently you had it under control."

"Like I told you earlier, I can take care of myself. I've been doing it for a long time now."

McCord heard the defiant self-confidence in her voice, but he also heard a weariness, perhaps even a loneliness there. "I know you can, Danny," he offered gently, "but now and then all of us need somebody we can—"

His words stopped short at a rustling sound from the side of the house. Both he and Danielle swung their pistols toward it at the same time.

"Don't shoot!" Hector Sabio shouted. "It is me!" His hands went up, the stub of the broken rifle butt trembling above his head. Danielle and McCord lowered their pistols as one. McCord stepped forward, took the rifle from Hector, and looked at it, shaking his head.

"Well, you've ruint a good rifle, Hector," McCord said, seeing that even the barrel was slightly bent. He tossed the rifle to the ground. "Do you mind telling us why you didn't do the way you were supposed to?"

Hector squirmed in place, saying, "The rifle jammed, I think."

"The rifle didn't jam, Hector," McCord said, sounding clearly put out with him.

Hector shrugged. "It might have, I think. But what does it matter? We have killed them all, *sí?*" He clenched his fists as he spoke and held them close to his throat. "I killed that pig who did this to me!"

Danielle just watched.

"Did you make sure he was dead, Hector?" McCord asked.

"Of course he is dead," said Hector. He patted the pistol in his waist belt. "I even take back the pistol he took from me."

McCord shot Danielle a glance. "We better go check."

Chapter 6

Danielle, C. F. McCord, and Hector Sabio walked to the spot where Hector had left Al Tarksel lying bloody on the ground. Hector stood back with a gasp, seeing that Al Tarksel was not only still alive, but from the markings on the ground had managed to drag himself through the side door of the stable. "This can not be!" Hector said.

"Wait here," McCord said over his shoulder, running forward with his pistol drawn. Hurriedly but with caution, McCord made his way through the length of the barn and out the opened front door. At the far end of the street, the sound of hoofbeats pounded away in the night. McCord didn't even raise his pistol, for already people were rushing from the saloons toward the sound of earlier gunshots. McCord slumped and lowered his Colt into his holster as the townsfolk slowed to halt before him.

"It's all over, folks," he said, raising his voice to them. "This was law work ... everybody go on with what you were doing." But the townsfolk wouldn't hear of it. They slipped past McCord and through the barn, curiously looking all around.

McCord made his way through the gathering crowd, finally spotting Danielle and Hector. McCord hurried and caught up to them just as they stopped and looked down at Bernie Odell's body on the ground. "At least you managed to hit something," Danielle said, dropping her Colt back into her holster.

"I usually do," McCord replied, catching the touch of sarcasm in her voice.

"*Sí*, it is true," said Hector, in McCord's defense. "If you have ever heard of The Fox, you would know that he is—"

"The Fox?" Danielle snapped her eyes to McCord, cutting Hector off. "Is that who you are?"

McCord looked a bit embarrassed, saying, "That's what some of the outlaws along the strip call me. My name is Charles Fox McCord. I mostly go by C. F. I thought I told you that."

"No, you didn't tell me." Danielle looked him up and down as if having just seen him for the first time. "I've heard of you, C. F.," said Danielle. "There was a story about you in the *Carver's Illustrated* a few months back, about how you had cleaned up the strip single-handed!"

"Well, don't make a lot of it, Danny," said McCord. "Somebody cleans up the strip ever year or two." He smiled. "It just gets dirty again."

"*Mi amigo bueno* is being too modest now," said Hector, butting in on McCord's behalf. McCord noted with a wry smile how all of a sudden he had become Hector's *good friend*. Before McCord could say anything, Hector continued in his hoarse voice. "It is true he has sent many outlaws fleeing for their lives! Now, the two us go face a gang of outlaws below the border!"

Danielle looked at Hector closely, then asked Mc-

Cord, "Who is this, and what's he talking about, going to Mexico with you?"

"This is Hector," said McCord, "the man I told you I had waiting back at the stables. I ran into him after Tarksel almost choked him to death. He used to ride with Tarksel and some others, and he knows where the Delmanos' place is below the border."

Danielle narrowed her gaze at Hector, saying, "So, you were after the reward the Delmanos are paying for me?"

"No, no!" Hector said, lying quickly. "I was riding with Al Tarksel because I needed to make some money. When he said there was a price on your head, I told him I wanted nothing to do with it!"

"I bet you did," said Danielle coldly. She turned back to C. F. McCord and said, "I'll ride with you, Marshal, but only because it'll be quicker finding the Delmanos' spread. Then I'll be on my own. But before I do anything, I've got know what's happened to my brothers. The doctor said they were coming back. I figure they've run into trouble or else they would have been back here by now."

"Good enough for me," said McCord. "We'll look for them on our way."

Sarah Sims ran forward out of the milling crowd, and coming up to Danielle, she looked at the body on the ground and gasped. Then she turned to Danielle, saying, "Merciful heaven! Danny, are you all right?"

"Yes, ma'am, I'm fine," said Danielle, clasping Sarah's shaking hands. "I'm sorry for this happening at your home, but we'll get everything in order before we leave. I'm afraid part of your picket fence will have to be replaced."

"Oh, I'm not concerned with picket fences," said Sarah, tossing the matter aside. "The main thing is that neither of you are hurt." Her glance went to McCord. "Marshal, are you all right?"

"Yes, ma'am," said McCord, stepping in between Sarah Sims and the body on the ground, to block her view of it.

"And so am I," Hector said, without being asked.

Sarah Sims only gave Hector a curious glance.

"He's with us," said Danielle.

"Oh, then I'm glad you're all right too, Mr. . . . ?"

"Allow me to introduce myself," said Hector, trying to soften his rough voice, "I am Hector Sabio . . . I work with The Fox. He gestured a nod toward McCord.

"The Fox?" Sarah Sims looked puzzled.

"It's a long story, ma'am," McCord said. He looked at Danielle and added, "If we're going to be looking for your brothers on the way, we best get a move on."

"Then let's get to it," said Danielle. "We'll see if we come across this Al Tarksel on our way." She shot Hector a cold glance, saying to him, "Maybe you better stay in front of me, mister, until we get to know one another a little better."

Hearing Danielle, and seeing the look on Hector's face when Danielle shoved him ahead of her, McCord smiled to himself as the three of them walked back toward Sarah Sims's house. "I think we're going to like working together, Danny Duggin," he said.

"With a bounty on my head, every two-bit gunman on the trail will be out to make himself some money," Danielle said. "I hope you know what you're getting yourself into, Marshal."

"If I had any doubts, I wouldn't be here, Danny." McCord smiled without facing her. "From now on why don't you just call me C. F.?"

"All right, C. F.," Danielle said, liking the way the young marshal tried to hide his smile from her. She even smiled herself, feeling better, her wound not bothering her any longer as she walked along in the pale moonlight at McCord's side.

Outside the Dodge City limits, Al Tarksel rode hard, not slowing the horse down until the town lights grew small and dim behind him. In the gunfire and confusion he'd headed east out of Dodge, going the wrong way. But that didn't matter. Once he put some distance between himself and the shooting, he could swing wide, circle past the town, and ride south. The main thing was that he was still alive. He'd grabbed the horse from the first stall he'd dragged himself into, luckily finding one that was already saddled and ready for the road. It was only when he'd stopped the horse and sat, feeling himself over carefully to assess the damage Hector had done to him with the rifle, that Tarksel looked down at the fancy reins and saddle and realized the horse he was riding was none other than Clyde Branson's roan barb.

"Jesus!" Al Tarksel said through swollen lips, leaning down, looking the horse over in surprise. What were the odds on this? he thought. But he didn't have time to wonder about it. He continued checking himself over, wiping blood from the gashes and lumps on his head, neck, back, chest, and shoulders. Hector had given him a terrible beating, catching him off guard. For a second when he'd heard Hector's voice and saw his face, twisted in rage in the darkness, it stunned Tarksel so badly he hadn't been able to think, let alone defend himself.

The whole thing had happened so fast and his senses had been so dulled from the rifle clubbing him over and over, looking back on it now, most of it was still a blur. Tarksel blinked his swollen eyes and took a few deep breaths, trying to get a better grip on what had really happened. In his foggy state of mind, it appeared that he'd just been beaten half to death by one dead man and was now fleeing on another dead man's horse. "Jes-*us!*" he said again, this time feeling an eerie chill run the length of his spine.

His hands shook as he lifted the canteen from the saddle horn by its strap, uncapped it, and poured out a palmful of tepid water. He dashed water on his battered face and rubbed it around gently, tasting blood as some of it seeped through his split lips. In a moment he reached down and felt the horse's mane, as if to make sure the animal was alive, and not some ghostly creature. He turned up a mouthful of water, then sat for another full minute, slumping in the saddle, trying to make sense of it all.

"Damn you, Hector," he said finally, capping the canteen as the realization set in and the events of this night became more real to him. He touched his wet palm to the pistol at his hip, glad that he'd at least managed to scrape it up off the ground before dragging himself to the stables. He shot a nervous glimpse back over his shoulder along the dark trail. Then he batted his boots to the horse's sides and brought it up into a quick trot, still headed east for the time being, his pain causing him to bow forward unsteadily in the saddle.

Before Tarksel had gone two miles, he caught sight of a dark figure on horseback rise up in the moonlight ten yards ahead of him. Before he could even get his pistol up from his holster, he saw the flash of a pistol and braced himself as the roan reared and whinnied, the dirt from the shot hitting the ground too close to the horse's hooves. As the roan touched back down and twisted sideways beneath him, Tarksel struggled with the reins, trying to right both himself and the horse, his right hand still wrapped around the holstered pistol.

"Raise it and die," said a gruff voice. The dark figure had stopped his horse and turned it crosswise in the trail. Tarksel weighed his chances quickly, then raised his right hand chest-high as his left hand wrestled the reins and settled the roan.

"Mister, I don't know who you are, but if it's money you're after, you're lost out of luck," said Tarksel.

"Pipe down," said Bob Dennard, stepping his horse forward. "This is no robbery. I just don't like to be come upon at a gallup this time of a night. What's your big hurry, mister?" But as Dennard drew closer and sidled his horse three feet from Al Tarksel, he squinted and recognized the big man even through the blood on Tarksel's battered face. "Well, my my, look who we have here," Dennard said under his breath, hardly believing his eyes.

"Bob Dennard?" Tarksel asked, almost as stunned as he'd been at the sight of Hector Sabio. But recognizing Dennard, Tarksel had already begun wondering how to get himself into a better position. Now that the roan wasn't working against him, Al Tarksel knew he would have to make a grab for his pistol.

"Don't even think about it," said Dennard, as if reading his mind. Dennard kept him covered with the cocked pistol as he reached out and snatched Tarksel's Colt from his holster. He winced, looking closely at the knots and cuts on the big man's face. "From the looks of you I'd say you've had one hell of a day."

Al Tarksel allowed himself a deep breath, and he exhaled slowly. "I'm not wanted for anything, Dennard. All you're doing is committing murder if you let that hammer fall."

"So?" Dennard chuckled, his eyes agleam, his red bristly beard lending him a look of pure evil.

"You used to be a preacher, Dennard," Tarksel said, his voice nearly pleading. "Doesn't that mean anything?"

"It don't to me if it don't to you," Dennard said, his voice going low and menacing. "All those years I preached . . . gave sinners like you a chance to atone themselves, and none of you ever did. I just call this getting back the time I wasted on you heathens."

As Al Tarksel spoke, he gave the appearance of resting his right forearm across his lap, getting into position for a good swing. But again, Bob Dennard was a step ahead of him. "If you try backhanding me, Tarksel," Dennard said, "you might get it half done. But then I'll spend the rest of the night shooting chunks off of you a little bit at a time. You won't weigh fifty pounds by the time I let you die."

Tarksel eased down, looked away into the darkness for a moment, then said, "You know what, Dennard?"

"What?" Dennard grinned.

"I think if you was really going to kill me, you already would have," said Tarksel.

"You're not as stupid as you look, Tarksel." Dennard backed his horse a step, looked the roan barb up and down, noting the fancy saddle and reins, then said to Tarksel, "I'm going to ask you a question that I might already know the answer to . . . so whether I kill you or not depends entirely on the next words coming out of your mouth." He wagged his pistol barrel at the roan. "How'd you end up on Clyde Branson's horse?"

Al Tarksel stared at him with a bewildered expression, shaking his big swollen head back and forth slowly. "To tell you the God's honest truth, Dennard . . . I don't have any idea in the world how it came about. The last I saw of Clyde Branson he was deader than a gob of chicken fat. I took this horse because it was the first one I could grab after Hector Sabio beat me into the ground with a rifle. If my life depends on explaining this horse to you, you might as well drop that hammer."

"Hector Sabio, eh?" Dennard jerked his pistol barrel upward, and saw Tarksel breathe a sigh of relief. "See, Tarksel? This is one time the truth has set your free. I saw Hector leave Newton on that horse."

"You did?" Tarksel gave him a strange look, partly amazed that Hector really was alive, and partly relieved that what had happened in Dodge was not the work of some unearthly demon.

"That's right," said Dennard. "I heard about somebody almost choking a Mexican to death. Then, when

I saw Hector leave Newton with The Fox, I put two and two together."

"Hector is riding with The Fox? That's who it was with him back in town?" Tarksel still looked baffled.

"Yep," said Dennard. "Ain't you glad you didn't lie to me just now?"

Tarksel sat speechless, raising his free hand and rubbing his forehead.

"What happened in Dodge?" asked Dennard.

"Oh, Lord, you don't even want to know," Tarksel said, his jumbled thoughts trying to piece everything together. "I don't suppose you have a bottle of whiskey, do you, somewhere under your Bible maybe?"

"I might have," said Dennard. "Step down off the horse easy-like and let's see if the two of us can't do some business together."

Al Tarksel hesitated. "What kind of business?"

Dennard said, "I'm interested in the two thousand dollars on Danny Duggin's head, Tarksel, same as you are."

Tarksel stared at him for a second. "Is this a trick? I never heard of you taking an interest in collecting for anything but dead outlaws."

"Well, I tried to throw in with Danny Duggin and his brothers, but they wouldn't hear of it. I tried to ride with The Fox, but he wouldn't go for it either." Dennard shrugged. "A man has to make his living some way."

Tarksel's cracked and swollen lips spread into a painful-looking grin. He swung down slowly from the saddle and stood with a forearm pressed to his aching ribs. "Hell, Dennard, it sounds to me like you was after the two thousand all along."

"It doesn't matter now what I was after," said Dennard, without answering one way or the other. "It's what I'm after now that counts." He reached over and took the reins to the roan barb and pulled the horse around behind him. "Start walking, Tarksel," said Dennard.

"Walk?" Tarksel looked up at him, pain etching his bruised and lumpy face. "Dennard, I was doing all I could to stay in the saddle. I'm beat to a pulp here."

"Hush now," said Dennard, "a big ole boy like you? It would take three Hector Sabios to do any serious damage."

"I might have some broken ribs," Tarksel offered, almost pleading.

"You'll have worse than that if you try my patience. Now get going. Walking is the best thing for them broken ribs. It'll keep you from stiffening up."

Tarksel turned reluctantly and staggered forward along the trail, heading back in the direction of Dodge City. Bob Dennard nudged his horse along at a walk behind him. "What happened to the men you were riding with?" Dennard asked.

Tarksel thought about it quickly. Somewhere out there was Pearl, Harkens, and the others. It might work to Tarksel's advantage if Dennard didn't know about them. "What men, Dennard? I was riding alone," Tarksel said over his shoulder.

A shot rang out. The dirt kicked up by the bullet hitting the ground an inch from Tarksel's boot caused him to jump sideways, the movement causing pain to shred throughout his sore body. "Lord, Dennard! Give a man a chance to explain!" Tarksel shrieked.

"Do you think I'm just making conversation here?" yelled Bob Dennard. "I won't tolerate any lying!"

"All right! What I meant was, I've been riding alone ever since my men got separated out there while we were tracking Danny Duggin! Me and a buddy of mine couldn't find them, so we circled back to Dodge. That's when we got ambushed!"

Bob Dennard fell silent for a second, considering it. Then he said, "So, what it sounds like is you and your buddy decided to cut the others out of the reward. The two of yas must've had an idea that Danny Duggin was somewhere in Dodge?"

"No, it was *nothing* like that, Dennard," said Tarksel. As soon as he spoke, he heard Bob Dennard cock his pistol behind him, and he said quickly, "Wait, Dennard, let me finish! What I mean is, it wasn't *exactly* like that! But it was close. We figured since the others weren't around, if we ran into Danny Duggin, we'd go ahead and kill him ourselves! That's the way I meant it!"

"Well, I reckon that's about as straight an answer as I'll get out of you," said Dennard. The pistol uncocked and Tarksel let go of a tense breath. But then Tarksel braced up again as Dennard said, "Stop at the first tree or tall stand of grass you come to."

"You're not going to kill me are you, Dennard? I thought you said you wouldn't—"

"Shut up, Tarksel," said Dennard. "We're going to stop and talk a while, figure out what move to make. I'm not going to kill you. We're partners now."

"We are?" Tarksel stopped short, Dennard's horse bumping into him before it stopped too. "You mean, fifty-fifty, on the Danny Duggin bounty?"

"That's right," said Dennard, "unless you rather I leave you lay out here and feed the buzzards."

"But how about collecting the money, Dennard?" Tarksel asked, already figuring out how to use Dennard, then cut him out of the reward. "If you showed up at the Delmanos', they'd kill you before you could say howdy, then they'd kill me for bringing you there."

"Then I expect I'll have trust you, Al," said Dennard, getting on a first-name basis now. "Once we kill Duggin, you'll have to collect the money and bring it back to me. You'll do that won't you, *partner?*"

"Why sure I'll do that," said Tarksel as he started walking forward again. "But I want you to promise me one thing."

"Yeah, what's that?" Dennard asked, already knowing that Tarksel had no intention of sharing the reward with him.

"If we run into Hector Sabio . . . let *me* have him."

"You've got my word on it, Al," Dennard agreed, nudging his horse forward.

Chapter 7

Marshal Christian Dane sat close to the low campfire, sipping coffee from a tin cup. The other marshals had pitched their saddles and blankets in a wide circle surrounding the jail wagon. In planned rotation, each man would stand a two-hour watch throughout the night, then awaken the next man to his right to take his place. When Lowell Metcalf—the newest marshal of the group—had finished walking a wide, quiet circle around the camp, he came back to the fire and looked at Marshal Dane, saying, "What's the matter, Chris, can't you sleep?"

Dane looked up at him from beneath his hat brim and shook his head. "There's something about taking those look-alikes into custody that don't sit right with me."

"I know what you mean," said Metcalf. "Dooley and Ryan says the same thing. But Seals says they're right out here where all the outlaw action has been going on, so they must've be involved. Besides, Alley Cat identified them from being with that bunch we routed."

"Seals might be right," said Dane, "but as far Alley

Cat Catlin goes, he would identify his own mother as an outlaw if it benefited him some way."

Dane looked out across the darkness, then said, "Go get yourself some sleep, Metcalf. I'll stand the rest of this watch for you."

From a thousand yards away, Hank Phipps, Loot Harkens, and Jack Pearl had been tracking the jail wagon ever since the hoofprints of Jed and Tim Strange's horses had led them to the spot where the posse had taken the pair into custody. Now, deep in the night, Harkens and Phipps lay listening quietly to the sound of bending brush as Jack Pearl worked his way back to them in a low crouch. "What'd you find out?" Harkens asked in a hushed tone.

Jack Pearl took a few breaths before answering. "Boys, I'll tell you, getting close to that jail rig gives me the jitters."

Phipps and Harkens looked at one another in the moonlight. "Damn your jitters," said Phipps, "what did you find out? Is Danny Duggin in there?"

"Yep, he's there," said Pearl.

"You saw him?" asked Harkens.

"No, not exactly," said Pearl, still catching his breath.

Harkens and Phipps looked at one another again. "What do you mean, not exactly?" said Phipps. "Either you saw him or you didn't!"

"I didn't see Duggin," said Jack Pearl, "but I saw the other two's faces plain as day when a deputy took a lantern over near the bars. There was others in the wagon, wrapped in blankets. I figure one of them has to be Duggin."

"We've got no way of knowing that," said Phipps.

"I wish we could have gotten a closer look during the daylight. It could be that Duggin got away."

"We saw all three of their horses, Hank!" said Jack Pearl, getting a little testy. "If he got away, he did it on foot. If he was on foot, where's his boot prints? We've covered every inch of ground! I'm telling you, unless he flew away like a bird, he's got to be in that wagon!"

"All right then," Phipps said, giving in. He rubbed his jaw. "I just wish Al was here. He's supposed to be running this gang, not us."

"Hank," said Jack Pearl in a flat, impatient tone, "we *are* the gang and we *are* running it. If we can't figure things out for ourselves, what are we doing out here?" He looked back and forth between Phipps and Harkens, then said, "I don't know why you can't get it through your heads that Tarksel and his pal, Bernie Odell, has run out on us."

"Maybe so, maybe not," said Hank Phipps. "But if we're the ones who kill Danny Duggin, we still get the money. I don't know about you boys, but I *need* that money bad. Winter ain't far off, and I don't have a dollar put away. I don't have to tell you how hard it's been making a living since ole Axel got himself killed."

"Yeah, good ole Axel," said Loot Harkens in a reverent tone. "I still miss him something fierce."

"Me, too," said Hank Phipps.

They sat for a second in silent reflection until at length Jack Pearl gave them each a curious look and said, "Well? Are we going to hit that jail wagon or not?"

"Yep, why not?" said Loot Harkens. "We'll catch

them at breakfast, before they's good and awake." All three stood up, dusted off their trousers, checked their rifles and pistols, and swung up into their saddles. Jack Pearl took the lead, heeling his horse forward into the brush.

September 16, 1871

At dawn, Marshal Tom Seals loudly raked a stick back and forth across the bars of the jail wagon. "Rise and shine! Everybody up!" Tim and Jed Strange were the first two on their feet. The other three men groaned, coughed, and cursed to themselves as they tossed their blankets aside and pulled themselves up to the bars. "Get over here and get your jewelry on, so's I take you to the bushes," Seals said to them. "Honest men would have been up two hours ago."

"Yeah, how long have you been up, Marshal?" Alley Cat Catlin asked in a sleepy voice.

"The law never sleeps, Alley Cat." Seals chuckled.

Marshals Curtis Dooley and Tom Seals reached through the bars with sets of ankle cuffs and snapped them into place on each of the prisoners. The prisoners' boots sat lined along the wall, where they had left them overnight. Anytime the men left the security of the wagon they did so barefoot, in chains. Marshal Dooley took the ring of keys from his belt, unlocked the iron door, and swung it open. The five prisoners filed down and walked to the edge of the small clearing at the bottom of a sloping hillside.

As soon as the men lined up to relieve themselves, Tim Strange caught the glint of morning sunlight streak from a rifle barrel. Tim's eyes fixed on it just in time to see the rifleman rise up from behind a rock on the hillside and level down on Marshal Dooley, who stood next to Tim, looking back toward the camp. "Look out, Marshal!" Tim shouted.

Seeing the marshal would not have time to respond, Tim shoved him hard with his left hand. As he did, Tim's right hand snatched the marshal's pistol up from his holster. He cocked it and swung it up toward the rifleman. Tim fired two rapid shots, the first hitting Loot Harkens in the shoulder, causing him to throw his arms open as he rocked back. The second shot hit Harkens squarely in the chest. On the ground, Marshal Dooley rolled up to his knees. Not seeing what Tim had just done, the sawed-off shotgun in Dooley's hand instinctively aimed at Tim and fired, just as Tim leapt out of the way.

"Dooley, don't shoot him!" shouted Marshal Christian Dane, having seen the whole thing. He and the other marshals ran forward, just as two more riflemen opened fire.

The prisoners scurried back a few feet, taking cover as best they could on the rocky ground. Tim lay flat in the grass on the edge of the clearing. Jed Strange dived over to his brother, seeing the blood on Tim's shoulder. Gunfire exploded back and forth, shattering the quiet of morning. "Tim! Are you hit bad?" Jed shouted above the melee.

"Just a couple of buckshot nicks," Tim answered, jerking Jed down to safe cover beside him as a bullet whistled past his head. Tim still held Marshal Dooley's pistol, but he didn't fire just yet. Instead, he looked around and saw Marshal Dooley taking cover behind a rock next to Marshal Dane, a few feet back near the wagon. He also saw the ring of keys on the ground where they had fallen from Marshal Dooley's belt.

Bullets from the hillside stitched up dirt all across the campsite. The other three prisoners lay pressed to the ground. Tim jerked his head toward the ring of keys on the ground behind them and said to Jed, "We've got to get out of here. Can you get to those keys?"

"I can try," Jed replied. "Keep me covered."

Jed hurried, turning and crawling on his belly, shots whizzing dangerously close to his back. He snatched the ring of keys and scurried back across the ground. Tim fired two shots from the marshal's pistol toward Jack Pearl, who rose up and fired down the hillside at Jed. Pearl ducked down as Tim's bullets sent chips of rock slicing into his forearm. "Damn! That kid can shoot," said Pearl to Hank Phipps, who lay a few feet away. Pearl grasped his forearm, then levered another round into his rifle chamber, rose up, and continued firing.

"I got them, Tim," Jed said, his breath pumping short and fast as he crawled back to his brother's side. He shot a glance back at the marshals in the clearing and saw that they were too busy firing to pay any attention to the prisoners. He drew into a ball on his side, unlocked the cuffs on his ankles, and let them fall. Quickly he rolled over and did the same for Tim.

"I've only got two shots left in this pistol, Jed," Tim said, glancing around at the prisoners, then at the marshals, then back to the hillside. "Stay close to me."

"I'm right beside you," Jed said.

They crawled faster now, rifle shots thumping the ground near their bare feet. At the edge of the clearing the brothers sprang up, running wide of the marshals' position and around the clearing until they jumped behind the wagon. At the other end of the wagon, the horses had shied around. At the horses' hooves lay Marshal Seals, his dead eyes staring up at the morning sky. "Come on, Jed! Get the horses!" Tim said, dropping down beside the dead marshal, unbuckling the gunbelt from around his waist, and slinging it over his shoulder. The gunfire continued, hard and steady. Tim grabbed the dead marshal's rifle from the ground and turned to the horses in time to catch the reins Jed threw to him.

As they mounted and turned the frightened horses, Marshal Dooley caught a glimpse of them, turned, and fired. "The prisoners are getting away!" he shouted. Marshal Dane turned and fired as well, seeing the rest of the horses scatter and race down out of sight, following the Strange twins. But the marshals' shots only hit the bars of the jail wagon and ricochetted away. On the ground a few feet to Dane and Dooley's left, Marshal Metcalf rose up and fired at the hillside, but a bullet from Jack Pearl's rifle slammed into his shoulder and spun him around in the dirt.

"Cover me!" Marshal Dane shouted, seeing Metcalf sprawled out bleeding in the dirt. He ran in a crouch, grabbed Metcalf by his boots, and dragged him back to safety from the stinging lead cutting the air all around them.

On the hillside, Jack Pearl and Hank Phipps both dropped back down behind their cover at the same time. "Did you see what I saw?" Pearl asked, levering a round into his rifle chamber.

"Yeah, I saw the look-alikes," Phipps replied, his breath heaving in his chest. "I didn't see Danny Duggin though."

"If we didn't see him, he's either dead or not there," said Pearl. "They're leading a spare horse."

"Maybe he crawled away and they're taking his horse to him?" said Phipps.

"Maybe," said Pearl. "Either way, we need to get out of here and run them down." Shots spat past overhead. "What kind of shape is Loot in?"

"I thought he was dead, but I saw him wiggle around a little," said Phipps.

"Leave him," said Pearl. "We'll be lucky to get ourselves out of here."

"We can't just leave him!" said Phipps.

"I can." Jack Pearl hissed, already lowering onto his belly and crawling away back up the hillside toward their horses. "You do what suits you."

"Damn it, Jack!" Phipps tried to raise his head enough to look over at Loot Harkens, but a rifle shot sliced past his nose. "Wait for me!" He dropped flat and hurried along behind Jack Pearl up the hillside, sticking his rifle barrel back behind himself one-handed and firing a wild shot down at the lawmen.

From his position in the clearing, Marshal Dane raised a gloved hand after the firing from the hillside had ceased. "Hold your fire, men, they're gone!" he shouted. Marshal Dane stood up and levered another round into his rifle as he scanned the hillside, saying, "Dooley, Seals, the two of you scout up there from the right. Ryan and I will take the left."

"Seals is dead, Chris," Metcalf said in a strained voice. "I saw him get shot down."

Marshal Dane glanced around, now seeing Seals's legs lying limp past the edge of the wagon. "Dooley, give me a hand!" he shouted. Helping Metcalf to his feet, Dane and Dooley propped the wounded marshal between them and walked back to the edge of the wagon where Ryan had already arrived and stooped down beside Seals's body. "Damn it, Chris," said Marshal Dooley, looking up at Christian Dane with watery eyes. "Tom didn't deserve this! He always gave a man a fair shake."

Marshal Dane helped Metcalf seat himself on the ground and lean back against the wagon wheel. "Come on, Dooley, let's get this bleeding stopped. Tom Seals was one of the best . . . but he's dead now. We'll take care of him later."

"I understand," said Marshal Dooley, wiping a hand across his face. "I'll get the prisoners back inside and go round up the horses."

"Good man," said Dane. "Ryan will help you. I'll get the medical bag and take care of Metcalf."

Dooley managed to put his grief and anger aside as he and Marshal Ryan closed the door behind the three prisoners and walked off into the distance where the horses had gathered, milling among clumps of grass. Once he and Ryan had led the horses back to the camp and hitched them to the wagon, Dooley looked down and saw that Marshal Dane had slowed the bleeding and pressed a bandage into place on Metcalf's shoulder. "As soon as we get Seals's body wrapped up and aboard, I'm heading after them look-alikes, Chris," he said in a resolved tone. "I won't stop till I've got those two facedown over their saddles. I reckon if there was any doubt before about them being outlaws, it's pretty clear now."

"Wait a minute, Dooley," said Marshal Dane, standing up and stepping back as he capped the canteen in his hand. "Don't go running off half-cocked. You didn't see how this started, did you?"

"I saw enough," said Dooley. "I heard my pistol fire four times while the fight was going on."

"Yeah, but if you'd of looked toward those twins, you'd have seen they were firing at the riflemen, same as we were."

"It's true," Metcalf said through his pain. "It looked like the riflemen were firing on them more than us."

"All's I know right now is that Tom Seals is dead, and somebody's got to face his woman and his daughter and break it to them. I want to at least be able to tell them that the buzzards who did it are dead."

Marshal Dane studied Dooley's eyes for a moment, considering everything. Then he looked at Marshal Ryan and said, "Eddie, why don't you two go see about the one we shot up there?"

He nodded toward the hillside. "When we get caught up here, we'll decide who's going after the others and who's going to get Metcalf and these prisoners back to Fort Smith."

"Come on, Dooley," said Marshal Eddie Ryan. "It'll give you time to cool down some."

Dooley seethed and cursed under his breath. But then he turned and walked off with Ryan up the hillside, the two of them with their rifles cocked and poised before them. "He'll be all right, Chris," said

Metcalf, seeing the concerned look on Marshal Dane's face as he stared after Dooley.

"I know," said Marshal Dane, "I've seen him like this before. But he'll have to settle down a whole lot before we can let him go off after those twins."

Alley Cat Catlin had been listening to the conversation, and wrapping his hands around the iron bars, he pressed his face between the bars as deep as he could and said, "Don't leave that wild-eyed fool here guarding us, Marshal Dane!"

"Shut up and sit down, Alley Cat," said Dane. "This is none of your business. I believe you were lying about those boys to begin with."

Alley Cat shrank back and slid down onto the wagon floor. "Hell, I just said what I thought you wanted to hear, Marshal. I meant no harm by it."

Dane raised up to his feet and stared at Alley Cat through the bars. "You mean they weren't with that bunch down on the other end of the Nations?"

"Marshal," said Alley Cat, "to be honest with you, I wasn't there myself."

"Then for God sakes, man!" Marshal Dane hissed. "Why didn't you say so?"

Alley Cat looked worried, casting a glance at the two other prisoners, then back at Marshal Dane. "I knew you boys always feed good—I was headed to Fort Smith anyway! Why not throw in with yas?"

Dane just stared at him.

One of the other two prisoners raised partly to his feet, saying, "Just give me the say-so, Marshal. I'll stomp his head till something squirts out both ears."

"Sit down!" Marshal Dane barked. As the prisoner dropped back to the floor, four rifle shots exploded steadily from the hillside, causing Marshal Dane to spin toward the sound with his pistol coming up cocked and ready.

Silence followed the shots until Marshal Dane took a step forward and called out, "Dooley? Ryan? Is everything all right up there?"

Ryan replied in a shaken voice, "It's all right, Chris. We're coming down."

Marshal Dane stood at the edge of the clearing as the two marshals worked their way down to him, Marshal Dooley dragging the body of Loot Harkens by the shirt collar. Ryan arrived behind Dooley with a shocked look still on his face. "There's one of 'em," said Dooley, slinging the body forward on the ground.

"What happened up there?" Dane asked in a firm voice, looking past Dooley at Ryan.

But it was Dooley who answered. "He was still alive. He made a move for his gun and I nailed him."

Marshal Dane looked down at the four exit wounds in Harkens's back. "It took four shots?" he asked.

"One shot, four shots, or a dozen," said Dooley, "what's the difference? It might have been his bullet that killed Tom Seals."

"And it might not have," said Marshal Dane.

"Yep, you're right," said Dooley, "it might not have been. That's why I want to hurry up and get after the others."

"Dooley, you ain't acting right," Marshal Dane said. "Now get a grip on yourself. We're men of the law."

"Oh? You don't believe me?" Dooley asked, jerking his head back toward Ryan, who was standing behind him. "Then ask Eddie about it."

Before Dane could say a word, Ryan cut in, saying, "I wasn't watching when the man went for his gun, but there was a gun on the ground—"

"I don't need to hear it," said Marshal Dane, cutting Ryan off to keep him from lying for Dooley. "Men, I'm as sorry as you are about losing Tom Seals. But let's not forget who we are and what we represent."

"Save it, Chris," said Dooley. "I don't know what's going on between those look-alikes and the ones who ambushed us, but they're all to blame for Seals's death."

"I'm warning you, you better calm down, Dooley," said Marshal Dane. "Acting like this ain't doing nobody any good."

Dooley had started to walk forward, past Dane toward the horses. But he stopped short and turned, facing Marshal Dane. "You're *warning* me?" he said, his voice dropping low and taking on a menacing tone.

"That's right," said Dane, "if that's what it takes. I'm the senior marshal here. If you make me pull rank on you, I will. I'm afraid there was a mistake made, us taking those boys prisoners. It was my mistake and I stand responsible for it. Let's not make another one between you and me."

Dooley studied Marshal Dane's eyes and took a deep breath. "You might have pinned a badge on a couple of months before I did, Chris, but if you think that'll stop me from going after those boys, you're badly mistaken." As he spoke, he reached up slowly with his left hand, unpinned his badge from his chest, and pitched it to the dirt at Marshal Dane's feet. "We're all square now, Chris. Don't warn me again unless you're prepared to make it stick."

"Dooley, get back here!" Ryan called out as Dooley angrily turned his back on Christian Dane and walked to the horses. "Come on now, pick this badge up and settle down! You hear me?"

"Let him go, Eddie," said Marshal Dane in a lowered tone, taking Ryan by the forearm, stopping him from running forward. "There's no talking to him right now." They watched Dooley sling a saddle up over his horse's back and ready it for the trail. When he stepped up into his saddle, Dooley took off his hat and looked at the body of Tom Seals on the ground for a brief moment. Then he put on his hat, jerked his reins, turned his horse, and booted it off in the direction the twins had taken.

"We've got to stop him somehow," said Ryan to Dane as they walked back to the wagon.

"I'll catch up to him once he's cleared his mind a little," said Marshal Dane. "You'll have to get Metcalf and the prisoners back to Fort Smith on your own. Metcalf will need some real doctoring. More than what we can give him out here."

"I'll do it, Chris," said Ryan. "Don't worry about us getting to Fort Smith."

Metcalf managed to struggle to his feet and lean back against the wagon as the two approached him. "Chris," he said, "why didn't you tell him old Alley Cat was lying on those look-alikes?"

"Because the shape his mind is in right now, he'd have likely killed Alley Cat," said Dane. "I couldn't take that chance." Dane unhitched his horse and pulled it away from the others. "I'm going to get saddled up and get after him." Dane looked off up the hillside and cursed under his breath. "Meanwhile, there goes two killers on the loose."

Metcalf said in a weak voice, "Get me up on the wagon seat. I can roll this rig into Fort Smith with a bullet hole in me. You two split up, one go after Dooley, the other after the gunmen."

"Look at you, Metcalf," said Dane, reaching down, pulling his saddle up from the ground, and tossing it atop his horse. "You're barely on your feet." Dane then turned to Ryan. "Get Seals's body wrapped up and get this wagon going." He nodded at Metcalf. "If he keeps talking foolish, crack him across the head with something. I'll take care of the rest of this mess. Those look-alikes are innocent from the looks of things."

"You be careful out there, Chris," said Marshal Ryan. "I don't know about the other one, but the one called Tim is a crack shot. I saw what he did to that rifleman."

"So, did I," said Marshal Dane. "All the more reason to catch up with Dooley. Those boys took Seals's gunbelt and rifle with them. If they are innocent now, I don't want Dooley to end up making killers out of them."

Chapter 8

Tim and Jed Strange rode hard, straight south, deeper into Indian Territory. After a full hour, they pulled their exhausted horses up alongside the shallow drop of creek bank and looked back along their horses' hoofprints. "We're awfully easy to follow, riding across country that way," said Tim. They did not take the hoof-worn trail—instead, they had cut off through the desolate brushy rock land, needing to put as much distance behind them as possible in the shortest amount of time. "You can bet they're on our tails right now."

"Yes," Jed agreed, "both the law and the outlaws, if one bunch hasn't killed the other by now. I hated leaving the lawmen there, fighting our battle for us."

"They gave us no choice, Jed. We tried explaining our situation. They didn't believe us." The two of them stepped their horses down the natural cutbank to the narrow stream of water and swung down from their saddles, loosening the cinches to let the horses drink. "If we ever live through all of this, we'll make it a point to go to Fort Smith and clear ourselves. Meanwhile, we'll do whatever we've got to do." He ran a hand across the chestnut mare's sweaty rump as she drew water.

Looking at their sister's mare painfully reminded them both of Danielle and the dangerous situation they'd left her in back in Dodge City. "What about Danielle?" Jed asked. "Is there no way we can double back and see what's become of her?"

"None that I can see right now," said Tim as he swung Seals's pistol belt down off his shoulder and strapped it on. He pitched Jed the dead marshal's rifle. Jed checked the rifle over while Tim lifted the Colt from the holster. The pistol Dooley had dropped on the ground now stuck up from Jed's waist belt. Jed had fully loaded it with cartridges from Seals's gunbelt as they'd ridden away from the battle.

"Wherever we go, we'll be bringing gunmen behind us. As long as it's been, if Danielle got back on her feet, she's gone by now. The best we can hope for is to meet up with her along the border."

"But if she didn't get back on her feet . . ." Jed offered in a air of doom. He didn't finish his words, for he couldn't bring himself to say what they knew would be the truth. By now Danielle was either on the trail, or else she was dead. Neither of them wanted to think it. They stared back toward the north for a silent moment as the horses drew the sandy water.

"I reckon going on to the border is all we can do, Jed," Tim said somberly. "If Danielle's there, she'll be going with us. If she's not there . . . well, it's what she'd have wanted us to do." They gathered the three horses, tightened the cinches, and swung up into their saddles without another word on the subject.

A half hour after the twins rode away from the narrow creek bank, Jack Pearl and Hank Phipps rode in off of the trail two miles to the west. Seeing the hoofprints of the three horses, Phipps nodded and said, "Trail or no trail, I told you they'd have to come in somewhere along this creek. It's the nearest water to the trail." He swung down from his horse's back, looking all around, wary of an ambush.

"We've got no time to waste here," said Jack Pearl, looking back at the distant line of land and sky without stepping down from his horse. "We've got law on us."

Phipps looked closely at the hoofprints on the ground. "One thing's for sure: they haven't met up with Danny Duggin. There's still no rider on that third horse."

Jack Pearl let out an exasperated breath, saying, "Damn it. It looks like we caused ourselves all that trouble for nothing."

"Maybe so," said Phipps, "but it's trouble we'll easily fix once we get into some hill country. I know for a fact that I put one marshal down back there. There's another one wounded. They can't leave the wagon sitting there alone. So that means there can't be no more than two on our trail. As soon as we get some good cover, we can take care of them when they come along."

"Then what," asked Jack Pearl, "keep on following these two look-alikes, hoping somewhere we'll run into Duggin?"

"Have you got any better ideas?" Phipps asked in a sharp tone of voice.

Jack Pearl thought about it, then grumbled. "Hell no, I reckon not. Let's get moving."

"You better water that horse," Phipps cautioned

him, whose own horse was eagerly drawing water from the creek.

"I told you, we've got no time to waste," said Jack Pearl, jerking his reins to keep the horse from bending its muzzle down into the running water. "This horse is fine until we get to the next water."

"You'll think it ain't so fine," said Phipps, "when that horse is blown and you're afoot out here. I'm not leaving here till this horse is tanked up."

"Yeah? You'll think *not leaving*, when you're laying there facedown in the water with a rifle bullet through your belly." Pearl yanked harder on his reins, kicking his tired horse forward. "I'm going on."

"What about yourself?" Phipps asked as Pearl gigged his horse up the low bank. "Ain't you going to at least fill your canteen?"

"I ain't thirsty," Jack Pearl called back to him. "Catch up to me if you ain't shot from a half mile away."

"Stupid as a mud hen," Phipps said under his breath, watching Jack Pearl ride away. Shaking his head, Phipps took his canteen down from his saddle and filled it as his horse continued drinking. When his canteen was filled, Phipps capped it and laid it by his feet. He took off his hat and held it down in the shallow creek bed, letting water run into it. Then he raised the hat and poured the water down over his head, cooling himself. Standing up, he slung his wet hair back and forth and put his hat on. He chuckled to himself. "Damn fool gets thirsty enough, I reckon I'll let him lick my shirt collar."

Within ten minutes, Hank Phipps was back in his saddle and on his way. Within another five minutes he'd caught up to Jack Pearl and sidled his horse up close to him. Seeing the way Jack Pearl's horse had slowed down almost to a walk in spite of Pearl batting his boots against the horse's sides, Phipps said, "Don't be a fool! Turn back and water that animal while there's still time, damn you! He'll be blown before we reach those low hills." He nodded toward the higher rise of purple land in the distance ahead of them.

"He's just winded is all," said Pearl, ceasing to goad the tired horse. "He'll catch his breath here in a minute." He looked at Phipps with a tight expression. "Did you fill your canteen?"

"Yes, I did, but you didn't, remember? You wasn't at all thirsty at the time." He heeled his horse ahead of Phipps by five yards and looked back. "Are you sure you don't want to go back and water that animal, you ignorant peckerwood?"

"I'll manage somehow. I ain't going back," said Pearl.

"Suit yourself, Jack." Hank Phipps chuckled.

But seeing the distance between them grow, Jack Pearl cursed under his breath and called out, "Wait up, Hank! Give me one little drink . . . just a sip!"

But Hank Phipps ignored him and rode his horse forward another fifty yards, then reined it down and waited until Jack Pearl drew nearer. "What's wrong, Jack, ain't it hot enough for you out here? That poor horse looks plumb tuckered out."

"Damn it, Hank, wait up a minute," Pearl called out in a dry, hoarse voice. "All I want is a sip! How many times have I gave you a shot of whiskey when you had none?"

"Not as many times as you should have," Phipps said, laughing and slapping his leg.

"This ain't funny, Hank! Quit fooling around!" Jack Pearl bellowed.

Phipps grinned and waited until Jack Pearl got within twenty feet of him. Then he spurred his horse, causing it to bolt forward, saying, "Ooops! This horse is just too strong to hold back!" He called out over his shoulder, "Next time you ask, you better remember to say, 'Pretty please.'"

"Son of a bitch," Jack Pearl growled to himself, running a hand across his parched lips. He gigged the horse forward, hard. But for all its effort, the hot, tired animal could barely hold a weak trot. In another five minutes, the animal had slowed to a loose walk, even with Pearl spurring and slapping his reins to its rump.

Over a low rise, Jack Pearl saw Hank Phipps sitting atop his horse, waiting for him. When Pearl got within fifty feet of him, Hank Phipps raised the canteen in his hand, took a mouthful, and spat it out in a long stream. He held the canteen out toward Phipps and said, "I've just been teasing with you, Jack. Sorry. Come on up here and get you a good long drink."

"It's about damn time," Jack Pearl said, trying to show a friendly smile on his hot dry lips. He coaxed the exhausted animal forward, the horse almost staggering beneath him. "You're lucky I've got a sense of humor, Hank."

But as Pearl got within twenty feet, Hank shook the canteen toward Pearl and said, "Sorry, you waited too long. You should have come quicker when I called you!" He spun his horse and batted it forward, calling out over his shoulder, "When you get to hell, tell the devil I said *'Howdy!'*" Laughing, he waved a hand and rode on.

This time Hank Phipps had only made it a few feet when a shot rang out behind him. He stiffened forward in his saddle, his laughter falling silent in his throat. As he rocked back in his saddle, a second shot rang out. Hank Phipps's canteen slumped onto his lap, then clattered to the ground. He managed to turn his horse around, facing Jack Pearl with a startled look on his distorted face. "I—I was only . . . fooling."

The third shot lifted Phipps from his saddle. "I wasn't fooling though," said Jack Pearl, his pistol smoking in his hand. "That'll teach you to make light of me at a time like this, you dumb bastard. I've shot more men in the back than you've got fingers and toes." He stepped down from his saddle and ran forward on foot, catching the horse's reins and drawing the animal to him. He walked the horse back to where the canteen lay in the dirt. He picked the canteen up and uncapped it on his way back to Hank Phipps's body, lying dead on the rocky ground. Raising a long drink, then lowering the canteen, Pearl said to the lifeless eyes staring up at the sky, "There now, Hank, I told you I'd manage somehow."

Up in the low hills, Tim and Jed Strange had turned at the distant sound of the first pistol shot. By the time the third shot echoed across the land to them, they had pinpointed the tiny figures of men and horses through the wavering heat. They stared as one figure stepped onto a horse and rode forward, leaving the other man stretched out on the ground.

"I don't know who it is," said Jed Strange, "but it looks like one just killed the other."

"Come on," said Tim, pushing his horse upward on the narrow path, leading the chestnut mare, "we don't need to stick around and see."

"Hold it, brother," said Jed, still looking back, "maybe we should. There's somebody farther back, one rider pushing hard."

Tim stopped his horse. Again they looked back across the land, this time seeing a single black speck at the head of a low rise of drifting dust. "I figure that one's the law, Tim," Jed said in a firm tone. "If this one in front makes it into the bottom of the hills, the next rider will be a sitting duck."

"If he's any kind of lawman he knows that already," Tim said. "Come on, let's go. Whatever they do down there just buys us more time."

"Uh-uh," Jed replied, "I don't feel right about it." He pulled the rifle from his saddle boot.

"You don't feel *right* about it?" Tim spun his horse toward him, saying, "Then you can feel *wrong* about it while we clear these hills and get out of here!"

"You don't mean that Tim." Jed levered a round into the rifle chamber and slipped down from his saddle. "It might not bother you now, but it will later if we find out one of those deputies got killed, especially if he's supposed to be hunting us."

Tim bit his lip, knowing Jed was right. "Gawl-dang it! Give me your reins," he said, reaching down and snatching the reins from Jed's hands. "I'll hide the horses out of sight." Leading the other two horses behind him, Tim guided his own horse around a shoulder-high stand of rock. When he came back on foot, Tim joined his brother a few yards off the trail, where Jed lay wiping his shirtsleeve along the rifle barrel.

"How many shots are in the rifle?" Tim asked.

"Just three," said Jed. He raised the rifle butt to his shoulder and steadied it out across the exposed half of a boulder sticking out of the ground in front of them.

"Then all we've got is a dozen rounds between us, counting what's in the pistol belt," said Tim. "If you shoot him, you best do it the first time."

"I aim to," Jed answered without looking around at Tim. "I'm not going to shoot until I have to." He clicked the long-range sight up on the rifle barrel, then adjusted it carefully with his thumb and finger. On the land below them, Jack Pearl pushed the horse up onto the slope reaching into the low hills. At the first upthrust of rock, Pearl reined the horse down, slipped out of his saddle with a rifle in his hands, and led the horse out of sight. When he returned, he carried the canteen strapped over his shoulder.

"Yep, it's an ambush sure enough," Tim said, scooting in close beside his brother.

Not answering, Jed concentrated on his target, slowing his breathing down, getting a feel for the wind across the hillside.

Jack Pearl looked out across the stretch of flatland at the distant rider and smiled to himself. The rider was coming on fast, too fast for caution, Pearl thought. He leveled the rifle out across the rock, adjusting the canteen behind his back, safely out of the way. He watched and waited.

Following the tracks of five horses ever since he'd

left the creek bank, Marshal Curtis Dooley had time to run things through his mind. Up ahead in the low hills, there were a thousand perfect spots for an ambush. But he didn't think that would happen until he was farther up along the crest of the ridges. The men had met at the creek bank, and had ridden out as one, he figured. Now that they were four guns strong, they wouldn't be so careful about watching their back trail.

As he pushed on, Dooley caught sight of the worn-out horse standing near the body on the ground. He reined down and circled wide, looking the situation over before riding in. Once he arrived at the spot where Hank Phipps's dead eyes looked skyward, Dooley stepped down and ventured closer with his rifle in his hand. "Easy, boy," he whispered to the spent horse as the tired animal sawed its weary head up and down and scraped a tired hoof on the dirt.

Dooley uncinched the saddle from the horse's wet back and let it drop to the ground. Looking all around, mostly toward the low hills ahead of him, he dropped the bit from the horse's mouth and gave the animal a shove. But the blown horse only drifted away slowly, a few feet, then stopped and stood looking back at him. Dooley had no idea why one of the men lay dead with three bullets in him. What did it matter? he asked himself. The main thing was that the men were on the run. All of the tracks leading away from the body on the ground were stretched out in the length of a run, the four sets of prints lighting out at about the same speed. These boys weren't wasting any time. Neither was he.

When a few minutes had passed, Jed saw the figure below them tense up and aim his rifle out at the closing figure in the low rise of dust. "He's getting ready," Jed said, taking aim himself. Yet, as his finger started its slow squeeze on the trigger, a flash of sunlight off the rim of the canteen below stabbed his eyes, just enough to cause Jed to hesitate for an instant. But in that short slice of time, as Jed recovered and fired, the rifle in Jack Pearl's hands bucked in a blast of fire and smoke. Then the bullet from Jed's rifle blew a hole through the canteen, nailing it to Pearl's back, causing the water to spill in a long, clear stream that soon turned bloodred.

Beside Jed, Tim Strange looked down and saw Jack Pearl slump forward against the rock, almost as if falling asleep. Then his eyes raised out across the stretch of flatland and saw the rider veer slightly in his saddle and sink to the ground. "You got your man, Jed, but not soon enough." He pointed. "Look out there!"

Jed stood up, looking out as Curtis Dooley dropped sideways off his horse and sat on his haunches in the dirt. "Dang it, Tim, we've got to go help him."

Tim grimaced, and said, "I know it. We can't leave a lawman there to die . . . besides, if he does, we'll get the blame sure enough."

They hurried back to their horses, mounted, and booted the animals down the path to the flatland. In passing the body of Jack Pearl, they only looked over long enough to assure themselves that he was dead. Then they heeled the horses up into a run.

On the ground, Marshal Curtis Dooley struggled to lift his pistol from his holster with one hand, his other hand pressed against his ribs to try and stop the steady flow of blood. He raised the pistol shoulder-high, but

the weight of it in his weak blood-slick hand kept him
from being able to cock it. "Stay back," he managed
to say in a halting voice as the twins stepped wide
of the pistol.

"Marshal, don't shoot," Tim called out. "We're here
to help you."

The pistol dropped to the lawman's lap. "Hell...
I can't do nothing... with it anyway," said Dooley.

The twins stepped down from their saddles and
ran to him, Jed carrying a canteen in his hand. "Take
it easy, Marshal."

"Why?" Dooley asked, his voice going weak and
shallow. "I'm done for."

"We didn't do this to you, Marshal," Jed said, stooping down beside him, reaching over with his hand to
take a look at the wound.

Dooley shoved his hand away. "I know you
didn't... I heard the shot. Did you get him?"

"Yep, he's dead, Marshal," said Jed.

"Good... now leave me in peace. I've got... some
things to reconcile."

"Let us help you," said Jed. He started to reach out
again, but seeing Tim shake his head slowly, Jed drew
his hand back and sat silently watching Dooley struggle to catch his breath. "Can you drink some water?"
Jed asked quietly.

"Water... would be good," said Dooley. He tried
to take the canteen, but after two attempts, Jed raised
it to his lips for him. "Much obliged," Dooley said,
water running pink from the corner of his lips.
"When... Dane catches up to you. Tell him... things
are fine... in Clay County. He'll know you didn't...
do this to me."

Tim and Jed looked at one another, then Tim said to Dooley. "We don't aim for him to catch up to us, Marshal. If he does, we won't be having time to deliver any messages."

"In my saddlebags . . . there's a pencil," said Dooley. "Take it, write down what I said. Pin it on the dead outlaw's back. Hurry on now, I want to be alone."

"We're sorry for what happened, Marshal," said Jed, standing up, capping the canteen. Behind him, Tim went through the dying marshal's saddlebags and took out a pencil stub and a scrap of paper.

"Hell . . . it weren't your fault, I reckon." Dooley looked off toward the low hills and shook his head slowly. "Damn them outlaws . . . I wish I could have shot him . . . for Tom Seals's sake."

The twins waited, standing back a ways while Marshal Dooley lay silent in the dirt. After a while when they stepped over to the marshal again Jed reached down and checked for a pulse, finding none. He stepped back and said, "I wish we had time to bury him."

"So do I," said Tim, "but we don't. There'll be somebody else along. We best get on out of here. It's a long ride across Texas."

They mounted and rode to where Jack Pearl's body lay against the rock. As Jed took off Jack Pearl's gunbelt and strapped it around his waist, Tim sat atop his horse, staring back along the trail. "If his boots will fit, you ought to take them, Jed."

"I already checked," said Jed. "Neither his nor the marshal's either one is close enough to our size."

"Looks like we'll keep riding barefoot then," said Tim. "Let's get moving."

Jed stepped in and put the note Tim had written halfway down in the dead outlaw's shirt collar. "I hope this will square us of killing the marshal." Then he backed away, swung up into his saddle, and the two of them heeled upward along the trail, leading the chestnut mare behind them.

Chapter 9

It was afternoon when Marshal Christian Dane stepped his horse down to the creek bank and watered it. Leaving the creek, he saw low-circling buzzards and, following the tracks across the stretch of flatlands, he soon came upon the body of Hank Phipps. By then the worn-out horse had wandered off, leaving a meandering path of hoofprints behind it. Marshal Dane didn't even step down from his saddle. Instead, he looked skyward in the direction of the low hills and saw the next group of circling buzzards. He nudged his horse onward until he saw the body of Marshal Curtis Dooley on the ground.

"Damn it, Curtis," he whispered to himself, stepping down, looking all around on the ground, trying to get a picture of what had gone on. Curtis's saddle lay beside his body. His horse had not wandered far. Marshal Dane walked to the horse with his rifle hanging from his hand. He brought Dooley's horse back, bridled it, and saddled it. Then he took Curtis Dooley's bedroll from behind the saddle, shook it out, and wrapped Curtis in it. "You just wouldn't listen, would you?" he said to the dead face.

With Curtis Dooley facedown over his saddle, Marshal Dane led the fallen lawman's horse, moving his own horse forward across the flatland at a steady but cautious pace. At the spot where Jack Pearl's body lay against the rock, Christian Dane stepped down again, this time with less caution. He pulled the scrap of paper loose from the dead outlaw's shirt, read the penciled words on it, then folded it in his gloved hands and put it inside his duster.

"Everything's fine in Clay County, huh?" he said under his breath. "Well, Curtis, let's see if we can get you back there." He scanned the upward-sloping hillside for a moment as evening shadows stretched long across the land. As a wind licked in from the west, he tugged his hat down on his forehead, stepped back up into his saddle, and turned his horse north, leading Dooley's horse behind him.

By nightfall, Marshal Dane had traveled along the creek bank a half mile to the east of where the twins, the outlaws, and the dead marshal had all watered their horses. He built a small fire down in between the cover of the natural cutbanks and spent the night. By mid-morning the next day, he had only traveled a few miles when he spotted the three riders rise above a crest of rolling land, spreading out abreast as they approached. Dane lifted his rifle from his lap and propped the butt of it on his thigh, his thumb across the hammer. But he relaxed as he saw the familiar face of Marshal C. F. McCord at the center of the riders. Bobbing closer at a trot atop his big dun, McCord raised a hand slightly, then checked his horse down and turned it sideways to Marshal Dane as the three riders stopped.

"Chris, what are you doing over this way?" Mc-

Cord asked, his eyes already on Marshal Curtis Dooley's horse and the blanket-wrapped corpse.

"We had a run-in a few miles east of here," said Dane, looking Danielle and Hector over as he spoke to McCord.

Danielle stepped her horse closer for a better look at the blanketed corpse. Marshal Dane stopped her in a respectful yet firm tone, saying, "That's close enough, young man. I don't believe I know you."

"This is Danny Duggin and Hector Sabio," said Mc-Cord to Marshal Dane. "Danny here is concerned it might be one of his brothers."

"One of your brothers?" Dane asked, looking Danielle in the eye. "Are they a couple of look-alikes?"

"Yes, they're twins," said Danielle. "Have you run into them out here?"

"I'm sorry to say it, but yes I have." Seeing the anxious look come upon Danielle's face, Marshal Dane added quickly, "They're all right though. I just left their trail yesterday evening."

"Who is that?" asked C. F. McCord, nodding at the body.

Christian Dane let out a regretful breath, saying, "It's Curtis Dooley. Some outlaws hit our jail wagon farther back along the breaks trail. We lost Seals . . . then Dooley went mule-head stubborn, thought those look-alikes were responsible. He got himself killed."

"Where are my brothers?" asked Danielle.

Dane jerked his head southwest. "They're headed for Texas if I guessed right. You can almost follow the bodies from here to the hills."

"My brothers aren't killers, Marshal," Danielle said

firmly. "If they had to shoot somebody it wasn't because they wanted to. I can tell you that much."

"Settle down, young man," said Marshal Dane. "I'll admit I misjudged your brothers at first. I don't know what they've got stuck in their craws or why those outlaws are after them. They've done no wrong back there as far as I can see. But they did break loose from custody." He looked at Marshal McCord. "Will you be meeting up with those two?"

McCord had stepped his horse around, raised a corner of the blanket, and looked at Dooley's face. He dropped the blanket now and said to Marshal Dane, "We're going to try our best to meet up with them between here and the border."

"Then tell them they're cleared," said Dane. "Dooley had them leave a note for me back there. There's no charges on them. We still have their gunbelts. They can pick them up in Fort Smith. I'll square things for them, as far as them breaking loose from custody." He shook his head. "I just wish our paths had never crossed. It's cost the lives of two good men, Seals and Dooley. Metcalf's wounded pretty bad. Ryan's with him. I'm going to try and catch up to them on the trail."

"I'm sorry to hear it," said McCord. He stepped his horse back around beside Danielle. Hector Sabio sat watching in silence with his wrists crossed on the fancy saddle horn.

"What are you boys up to anyway, McCord?" Dane asked, eyeing Hector Sabio as if trying to recognize him.

"It's a long story, Chris," said McCord. "But we're

headed down below the border, looking for the Delmanos."

"Hunting the Delmanos is nothing new for you, C. F.," said Marshal Dane. "You've been looking for Saul Delmano ever since I can remember."

"That's right," said McCord. "Only this time I've got a good guide who knows the country, and a man here who wants that bunch as bad as I do." He nodded toward Hector, then Danielle. "The Delmanos have a two-thousand-dollar bounty on Danny's head. Hector knows where their spread is. He's going to lead us there."

"For two cents I'd go with you," said Dane. "It's time somebody took off their badge and crossed the border. The Delmanos have had it too good for too long."

"You'd be welcome along," said McCord, "but you best get on back to Ryan and Metcalf, get to Fort Smith, and get ole Dooley here in the ground."

"I know it," said Dane. He turned his attention to Hector Sabio and said, "You look familiar."

"*Sí*, everybody tells me that," said Hector. "I have one of those faces everybody thinks they have seen." He shrugged. "But no, we have never met."

Marshal Dane studied Hector's face for a moment, then looked at McCord, saying, "The Delmanos again, huh?"

"That's right." McCord nodded. "This time for sure."

"Will you be crossing the border at El Paso?" Dane asked.

"Yep, we intend to," said McCord.

"The Delmanos have lots of men working for them.

El Paso is their stomping ground, this side of the border." Dane looked the three over as he spoke. Then focusing on Danielle, he added, "You boys watch yourselves down there. Two thousand dollars is a lot of money."

Caballo Sangriento Pasa, Mexico. September 25, 1871

Lewis Delmano stood over six feet tall, lean, but broad across his shoulders. He carried himself with the confidence and swagger of a younger man, of a man used to enforcing his will on all things within a world he'd created for himself. No sign of his age showed except for his wiry salt-and-pepper beard and hair, and the deep lines burned into his weathered face by years under the harsh Mexican sun. On the stone porch of his hacienda, Lewis Delmano struck a match to his first cigar of the morning and looked off toward the south, and the entrance to Bloody Horse Pass. Beside him, the government emissary from Mexico City, Raul Hernandez, stood quietly, his hand supporting his saucer and coffee cup. They had taken breakfast together while discussing their business. Now Hernandez waited for some sort of reply, something he could take back to his superiors.

After moments of silent consideration, Lewis Delmano said without taking his eyes off of the distant surrounding hills, "Tell them I'll pay the extra money this time. But if they keep gouging me, I'll pull up stakes and give Bloody Horse Pass back to the Apache." He turned slowly now, spreading a flat smile. "That should make for an interesting situation.

They leased me this land because they couldn't handle Victorio and his warriors. Maybe I'll tell Victorio he can have this place, house and all."

"I will tell them," said Raul, "but I will soften the words so that they sound more diplomatic, eh?"

"No, Raul, not this time," said Lewis Delmano. "This time you say it word for word the way I tell you to. I'm through fattening up every two-bit official in Mexico City."

"But we do so well here, you, me, and those who support our interests. Let us not say something hastily that we might regret later." He raised a finger for emphasis. "Don't forget, *mi amigo,* I am on your side, as always."

"You should be." Lewis Delmano stared at him. "I've made you a wealthy man since I brought my cattle operation here, not to mention that now you can travel here by buggy with no fear of getting your scalp lifted or your wallet emptied."

Raul shrugged. "All of this is true. When you and your sons came to Caballo Sangriento Pasa, it was nothing but a killing ground for the Apache and a hiding place for desperados." He swept his arm across the surrounding land. "You and your men have all of this. You are free of the gringo law here, and my government turns its eyes from what you do across the border. So why not pay these greedy *politico* officials what they want and keep them happy? You and me, we can grow old in comfort here, eh?"

"Maybe you, Raul," said Lewis Delmano, "but not me, not if the price keeps going up. Besides, I've got enough political connections back across the border that I don't have to fear the law there anymore either. I'm rich now, Raul. Money buys power and respectability on either side of the river. If the boys in Mexico City don't realize that maybe it's time I move on. They might need me more than I need them now." He shrugged a shoulder and gazed back out across the land. "I send them money all the time. What do I ever get in return?"

Raul studied Lewis Delmano's face, starting to realize that this whole conversation hadn't been about money at all. Something else was bothering Lewis Delmano. After a moment, Raul said, "What is it, *mi amigo*? Why do you stare off toward Caballo Sangriento Pasa as if you expect to see the devil?"

"Say it in English, Raul," Lewis Delmano demanded. "It's Bloody Horse Pass. As much sweat and guts as I've put into this God-forsaken furnace, I deserve to hear it said in my own damn language."

"All right," said Raul reluctantly. "Why do you stare off at Bloody Horse Pass?"

Lewis Delmano drew long on the cigar and blew the smoke in a slow, steady stream, taking his time before finally saying, "Did I tell you my oldest boy, Saul, is back?"

"No, you did not mention it," replied Raul. Hearing Saul Delmano's name prepared Raul. Whenever Saul Delmano came to Bloody Horse Pass, trouble was always close behind him.

"Yep," said Lewis Delmano, without facing him, "he's been here a little while now. He's over in the canyon, helping his brother with the branding. Maybe you'd like to go say hello to him?"

Raul Hernandez felt his chest tighten at the thought of being around Saul Delmano. He'd as soon wrestle with a rattlesnake. But he wasn't about to say so. Instead he said casually, "Not today, they are busy . . . and so am I. Soon I must return to the city and conduct our business. Please tell Saul I will see him the next time I am here perhaps?"

Lewis chuckled under his breath, saying, "He'll be disappointed I'm sure." He drew another long pull from his cigar and blew smoke out across the dusty land. "The fact is, Saul has a gunman on his tail, Raul. I'd consider it an act of respect if your pals in Mexico City would offer me their services, help me get rid of Saul's problem for him."

"Oh?" Raul looked surprised that Lewis Delmano would ask for help of this nature. "What is it that my government can do for you?"

Lewis Delmano caught the surprised tone in Raul's voice and turned to him, saying, "You've known me well enough to know that I don't back from a fight, Raul. But something tells me that this time I need to bring in somebody special who has lots of experience dealing with these kind of situations."

"*Sí*, I know my contacts in the city will be glad to help, but who has more experience in these matters than you and your men?" asked Raul. "As you have said, you have fought Apache, desperados, American lawmen."

"I know," said Lewis Delmano, "and I'll fight this gunman and whoever is riding with him, if it comes to that. But I'd like to think that I've gotten to a point in life where I can turn the dirty work over to somebody else when I feel like it. If your pals in the city did this for me, it would sure make me feel better about all the money I dish out to them every month. Do you see what I mean?"

Raul saw exactly what Lewis Delmano was asking. This was Delmano's way of seeing what power and control he might be able to wield for himself. What would be next? Raul thought. If this favor was done, how long would it be before Lewis Delmano began asking for more and more, until one day he might even have part of the military at his beck and call. Raul considered it for a second, then said, "There are men that I and my friends know who are good at this kind of work. Perhaps we can call them in for you?"

"Military men?" Lewis Delmano asked.

Raul smiled, knowing he was right. Lewis Delmano needed no help in this matter. Delmano was just seeing how far he could take this, testing the power of his American dollar. "Oh, but these men I speak of are far better than soldiers! These are the men our leaders turn to when they have things they want done that they cannot ask the *federales* to do."

Lewis Delmano thought about it. This wasn't quite what he wanted, but it might be good to see what Raul and his officials had to offer. "These are mercenaries, I take it?" Delmano asked.

"*Sí*, mercenaries who show no mercy," said Raul, grinning, wagging a finger. "Not often do we call on these men, but when we do, they act quickly and fiercely."

"Yeah?" Delmano worked the cigar back and forth in his mouth, appearing to consider it. "Well, I'd rather have army troops on my side . . ." He let his words trail, still hoping to get Raul to commit some government power to him.

But Raul held firm. "You will like these men much better, I promise."

"The thing is, Raul, I've got twenty good gunmen working right here for me. I'd just feel good knowing you and your friends think highly enough of me to put a fighting force out there between my son and his enemies."

"Oh, but that is exactly what I am doing," said Raul. "I would not trust our *federales* the way I trust these mercenaries. In political circles, these men are called *la escuadra de la muerte.*"

Hearing the name, Lewis Delmano drew on his cigar and afforded himself a slight smile. "The death squad, eh? I've heard of them. Some of them are from the U.S., some are Frenchmen and German, and some are from here. A real mean bunch as I recall."

"*Sí*, a real mean bunch of hombres. They are the *generalissimo's* personal fighting force, and they are far better at the craft of killing than our young soldiers, most of whom are simple peasants who had not fired a rifle until we take them into the army."

"And you think you can get this death squad for me?" Lewis Delmano asked. This was a good start, he thought. Delmano had all the guns he needed. But this would be interesting. The *generalissimo's* personal assassins, Lewis Delmano thought to himself, liking the idea more and more as he thought about it.

"I can have them here within a day. Just say the word, *mi amigo*, and they will set up a defense between here and the border. Nobody will get past them. You have my word."

"I don't know," said Delmano, trying to appear hesitant. "Would this death squad follow my orders? Do everything the way I tell them to do without question?"

"They obey *only* the orders of the *generalissimo*. But if I send them to you he will have told them to do what you say until the job is done. What more can you ask than that?"

Lewis Delmano's mind was already at work, seeing the great possibilities before him if he could win over the *generalissimo's* death squad. This might even be better than having some control over a column of *federale* troops. "All right, Raul," Delmano said at length, as if he had to give it a lot of careful consideration, "you've talked me into it. Send them as soon as you can." He reached inside his linen suit coat and took out a thick brown envelope. "This is for you, Raul, my friend, a little something extra that your officials needn't know about."

Raul smiled, taking the envelope and hefting it in his hand before putting it away. "As always, you are too kind, *mi amigo*," he said.

Lewis Delmano returned the smile, turning away to once again look out toward Bloody Horse Pass. "Yep, that's me all right, generous to a fault."

Chapter 10

Amid the dust and the cattle in the corral, Saul and Ramon Delmano stood up from the fire and looked toward the hacienda where their father stood talking to Raul Hernandez. Saul pitched the end of a branding iron down into the licking flames and pulled off his leather gloves. "Want to know what they're talking about, little brother?" He swabbed his brow with a damp bandanna.

"I do not care what they talk about," said the younger Ramon. "I have too many cattle to brand." There was a bitter snap to his voice.

"Yeah? Well, they're talking about me," said Saul, ignoring the tone of his brother's voice. "Pa's telling Raul about the trouble I'm causing him. He wants Raul and his politicians to make it all go away. What do you want to bet?"

Ramon looked toward the hacienda for a second longer, then shrugged and reached down and turned the branding iron in the fire, checking the color of the hot metal. "I would not bet against a sure thing." Ramon looked at the two men who stood waiting, one of them coiling his lariat and shaking it free of dust. He nodded at the two men, then turned to Saul as the men walked toward the milling cattle, unwinding a coil from their lariats. "If you resent him interfering in your trouble, why do you bring your trouble to him?"

Saul looked at his brother. "I don't resent his help, Ramon. What I don't like is his high-and-mighty attitude of late. He acts like he's better than me. I reckon he's forgotten how it was when I was just a boy. He made his living then doing the same things I do now. I robbed my first bank riding with that old man. Now that he's rich and got others doing his robbing for him, he acts like he thinks there's something wrong with the way I live."

Ramon spat and ran a hand across his dust-caked lips. "He tells me he wants a better life for me than he has had."

"Sure," said Saul, "but how much money does this better life put in your pocket? Enough to pay for all the dirt you swallow in a day's time?"

Ramon didn't answer. Instead he gave his brother a sour look as he reached down and picked up the hot branding iron. He hurried over to where the two ropers had taken down a longhorn steer. He expertly placed the tip of the iron over the older brand on the steer's rump, then stamped the iron down, cross-branding it. When he walked back to the fire and shoved the iron into the bed of glowing coals, he looked back at Saul Delmano and said, "Do you think I handle stolen cattle because I like it? This is all I get, Saul. This is all I'll ever get, hanging around here, staying under his thumb. I'm not much more than a hired hand."

"Then what's stopping you from doing something about it?" Saul asked. "You used to say it was because of your mother. Now that she's dead, what's your excuse?"

"After my mother's death," said Ramon, "I thought I should stay here until he got over his grief." He spat again, more as if to rid a bad taste from his mouth. "But I was wrong. Before my mother was in the ground two weeks, he brought the young German nurse, Greta, into his bed."

Saul chuckled, saying, "So he's gone from Irish, to Mexican, now to German. Sort of working his way around the world, woman-wise. But don't be bitter, little brother. That's the same thing that happened when my own dear Irish mother disappeared. He took right up with your ma within a week. Some say he had it all planned. Some even say it weren't the Apache who took my ma, if you know what I mean."

"And this does not bother you?" Ramon stared at him.

"Naw, I was too young to think about it at the time," said Saul, taking a bag of tobacco from his shirt pocket and rolling himself a smoke. "After I grew up some, I figured what the hell, it wasn't nothing to me. He taught me that whatever happens twixt a man and a woman is their business and nobody else's." He lifted the branding iron and lit his cigarette, then shucked the iron back into the glowing coals. "By then I was long-riding, robbing, running wild with him and his men. I didn't care for nothing . . . and I haven't since." He drew on the cigarette and let go a gray stream of smoke. "Now that I am what I am, he's acting like it ain't good enough for him." He looked off toward the hacienda. "That old son of a bitch. I'd give anything to know what he's thinking right now."

"He told you he would defend you against this gunman who is on your trail. He has placed a bounty on the man's head. What more would you have him do?"

Saul thought about it, blowing out a breath of smoke. "He's doing all that, sure enough. But don't ever think it's for me he's doing it. Our dear ole daddy ain't never done nothing for anybody unless he gets more back than he puts in. You watch. Somehow he plans on gaining something from all this."

"Yes, maybe so," said Ramon, looking over at the two ropers, then stooping down and picking up the branding iron. "Either way, no matter the outcome, I will still be doing what I do, handling stolen cattle for hired-hand wages." He stood up with the iron glowing in his gloved hand.

"Like I said, Ramon, what's your excuse now? Why don't you do something about it?"

"Like what?" Ramon asked.

"Oh, I don't know," Saul said in a cagey tone. "Me and a couple of the boys are planning to rob ourselves a little stagecoach outside of El Paso. Maybe you'd like to tag along? It ought to be worth a few hundred dollars to you."

Ramon didn't answer. He lingered for a moment, staring at his brother. Then he hurried over to the downed steer. When he came back and had raked the burnt hair from the branding iron across the sole of his boot, he stuck the iron back into the coals and said in a lowered voice, "He'll skin you alive if he finds out."

"Naw, I'm too old for a skinning anymore. He'll throw a fit, maybe try to pistol-whip me. But that ain't going to happen either. I'm thirty-three years old,

Ramon. If it came down to a serious tussle, I'd put a bullet or two in him, and he knows it." Saul grinned, then added, "But forget I said anything about it, little brother. Maybe it's best you stay here eating dust and spitting cow hair. Hell, you might get to like it after a few more years. Not everybody gets to know the ways of the world, see the big cities, and taste the finer things in life."

"Do not tease me as if I am a fool who knows nothing," said Ramon, his face glowering beneath a sheen of sweat. "While you have drifted here and there, I have spent my time fighting Apache and taking care of business. I have been to Juarez, Mexico City, and even El Paso. If you have done so well, why do you come sneaking in off the trail with men wanting to kill you?"

"Easy, little brother," said Saul Delmano, a bit of a warning in his voice. "No point in getting all riled up in the heat of the day. I'm heading out around midnight tonight with Joe Tully and Kid Jeffrey. Tomorrow, we're going to hit a stage or two, then duck back across the border. If you want to ride with us, meet us out back of the barn. If you don't, then forget I mentioned it."

"Tully and Jeffrey?" Ramon looked surprised. "I never knew they were bandits. I only knew they run cattle across the border."

Saul grinned. "There's probably lots more you don't know, little brother. Hell, Kid Jeffrey rode with the Blue Star Gang nearly a year. Joe Tully still rides with Los Pistoleros every chance he gets. If you think you can keep up with that kind of company, grab your bedroll tonight and be ready. We'll make us some quick money and get back here before Pa gets back from Sonora. He's leaving today before noon."

"I will think about it," said Ramon.

"Yeah, you do that, little brother," said Saul. "We've all got to grow up and get on our own sooner or later."

They worked until noon, neither one mentioning the proposed stage robbery. When Saul Delmano walked back to the fire from branding a downed yearling calf, he looked over past the hacienda and saw their father and two of his gunmen riding out toward the main trail. "Let's take a break," Saul said, stripping his sweat-moistened gloves from his hands and slapping them against his leather chaps. "I'm going to the cellar and crack open a bottle of wine, cool myself off a little."

"There is still much to do here," said Ramon.

"There always is," said Saul. "Let these boys do it, they're the hired hands. I told you my plans for tonight. I aim to rest up first." Saul stooped enough to untie his chaps and drop them to the ground.

"You go ahead," said Ramon, "I will take the irons and our tools to the barn." He reached down, picked up his brother's chaps, and draped them over his dusty forearm.

"Suit yourself, little brother," said Saul, walking away.

Ramon walked to the barn behind the hacienda, propped the branding irons against a tool bin, and hung both his and his brother's chaps on a wall peg. As he did so, he felt Greta's arms slip around him as she pressed herself to his back. "You must tell him, soon," she whispered in his ear, only a trace of a German accent in her voice.

Ramon turned to her, casting a cautious glance through the open barn door, then reaching out and swinging it shut. "Greta, you have to be careful doing this," he said in a hushed tone. Even as he said it, he put his arms around her and nestled his face into her soft golden hair.

"I know," she said, "but he's gone, and the others are too busy to notice anything. I came here as soon as I saw you walking over from the corrals. I can't stand it when you're not near me." She pressed her lips to Ramon's. Yet, as they kissed long and deep, Ramon opened an eye and kept watch on the barn door.

Greta felt his reluctance and ended the kiss with a sigh and laid her face against his chest. "We can't go on like this. We've got to get away from here."

Ramon gently freed himself from her embrace. "This is too risky, Greta, I'm sorry." He took a side step to the dusty window and looked out. On the rear porch of the hacienda, he watched Saul raise a water gourd dipper to his mouth, take a mouthful of water, swish it around, and spit it out. "You shouldn't have came back here," Ramon whispered over his shoulder. "My brother has the soul of a wolf. He can *sense* when something is going on."

"I—I had to see you, Ramon. If I have to hide in the shadows, that's what I'll do." He turned to her and held her. "We have to tell your father . . . we *have* to. Only last night, he told me I was to become his wife."

"No!" Ramon said, holding her closer. "He cannot

tell you what you must do! He has no right!" In his desperation, his voice trembled, and she cupped a hand to his dust-streaked cheek.

"Perhaps if we told him the truth, that you and I have been lovers since I came to take care of your mother. Maybe he would understand."

"He understands nothing." Ramon hissed. "He does not care. He knew what the outcome would be when he brought you here. He doesn't think like normal men. My father knew my mother would not live much longer. He hired you to take care of her knowing that when she died he would take you for his wife! He is a devil, my father! He would never leave us in peace! We can only flee from here and make a new life for ourselves."

"But when, Ramon?" she whispered. "I can't stand for him to touch me. When I am in his bed all I can think of is—"

"Please!" Ramon said, cutting her off. "Don't tell me about such things. I do not want to hear about you and my father. We must get away from here and never speak of, or even *think* of what has happened here."

"I have seven dollars, Ramon," Greta said. "It is money I have saved since your mother's death."

"Seven dollars won't get us very far, Greta. But don't worry. I think we'll soon have enough money to get far far away, maybe to New Orleans, or even the southern shores."

She leaned back slightly in his arms and studied his eyes, saying, "Oh? And where will you get this much money? I know your father pays you nothing until the cattle sells across the border. That will be weeks from now. Even then you'll get no more than his hired hands."

Ramon nodded through the dusty barn window toward Saul. "My brother has a way for me to make some quick money. He's going to rob a stagecoach. He told me about it while we were branding."

"But he is a thief and a killer!" Greta said, shocked at the idea. "There are men wanting to come here and kill him for the terrible things he has done. You told me so yourself!"

"It's only this one time, Greta, for us, for you and me . . . and the baby."

"No, no!" she shook her head. "Your brother will get you killed! We can take the seven dollars and run as far as it takes us! Or, if we must steal, we can take the money your father keeps in his safe!"

"Listen to me, Greta," Ramon said, holding her shoulders gently yet firmly. "I must do this. It won't be long until you cannot hide your condition. We have to get away from here while you are still able to travel. I'm leaving here tonight with Saul, and when I return, you be ready to leave with me."

"And if your father returns before you do? What then?" she asked.

"We slip away in the night and get as far away as we can before he comes after us. That's all we can do," he said.

"And if he finds us? If he forces me back to him? What will we do then?" she asked in a lowered tone.

"Then I will do what I dread even *thinking* about doing," said Ramon. "God forbid . . . I will have to kill him."

* * *

Leaving the barn through the back door half an hour later, Greta walked wide across the sand, then turned back toward the hacienda as if coming back from direction of the corrals. Saul Delmano stood up from his chair on the back porch with one of his father's cigars between his fingers and a bottle of wine hanging on his hand. "Well now," he said to Greta, stepping in front of her, blocking her way, "where have you been, out gathering jackrabbit eggs?"

She stopped, and seeing his eyes were lit and shiny from the wine, she said, "I went to the corral to tell you and Ramon that your father has left on his trip. Let me pass, Please."

"Why sure, you little yellow-haired filly you." He leered drunkenly, stepping to one side with an exaggerated sweep of his free hand. "Oops, wait a minute," he said, reaching up to her hair, running his fingers through it, "looks like you've picked up some straw here." He winked knowingly, and let a stem of straw fall from his fingertips. "Must be quite a wind out by the corrals."

She walked on into the hacienda without responding, Saul Delmano's low laughter following her through the door.

"Nothing like keeping it in the family, I reckon," Saul Delmano said to himself, sinking back down into his chair and propping his boots up on the iron porch railing. He drank wine and smoked the cigar, his hat brim pulled low on his forehead. In a few minutes, Ramon came walking from the barn, and Saul only tipped his head enough to get a glimpse of his younger brother as Ramon stepped onto the porch.

"That barn is a busy place, little brother," said Saul,

holding the bottle of wine out to Ramon without looking at him. "I'm going to have to get out there one of these times, see what the attraction is."

"What are you talking about?" Ramon took the bottle of wine and looked at it.

Saul shrugged, saying from under his lowered hat brim, "It ain't no sweat off of my neck, little brother. I'm just here for the dry air and sunshine."

"That is one of his favorite wines," said Ramon. "He's going to throw a fit when he sees you've drank it."

"His wine ain't all that's being tasted," said Saul, letting out a relaxed sigh, "but that's no sweat off my neck, either. I just hope you know what you're doing. There are things in this world even your blood kin will kill you over."

"Do you think I don't know that?" Ramon said bitterly. "There are also things in this world that men should leave alone when they see it does not belong to them."

"Well . . ." Saul Delmano let his words trail as he seemed to be considering something. Then he reached out for the bottle of wine, took a long sip from it, then said without raising his face, "Since I don't have an idea in the world what *else* you might be talking about, I'm just going to figure you're talking about taking money from stagecoaches."

"Yes, then that is what I am talking about," said Ramon.

"So, I take it you won't be riding out with me tonight?" Saul asked. "I kind of figured you wouldn't be."

"Then you have figured wrong, my brother. Yes, I

will ride with you. But only until I raise some money for myself. I will not become an outlaw."

Saul Delmano chuckled and drew on the cigar. "Now that brings up an interesting question. How many robberies does it take to make a man an outlaw?"

"Don't tease me," said Ramon, snatching the wine bottle from his brother's hand and throwing back a long drink.

Saul Delmano raised his hat brim and looked up at Ramon in surprise. "I'll be damned. You're really riding out with me tonight?" He smiled with satisfaction. "It's about time we done something together besides stick a hot iron on a steer's backside."

Ramon allowed himself a trace of a smile, handing the wine bottle back to his brother. "I think I know what stage we rob, and I think I know why."

"Oh, really now?" Saul said, cocking his head slightly in curiosity.

"Yes, the stage that runs from Pecos to El Paso, because you know there will be money on it that our father has had sent to him from his attorney there."

"That's good thinking, little brother," said Saul. "You might really have a knack for this kind of work."

"But if I have figured out that you are going to steal the very money our father has sent for to pay the bounty for whoever kills the gunman, Danny Duggin, do you not suppose our father will figure it out also? He is not a fool, and he knows how you are, my brother."

Saul raised a finger toward Ramon, saying, "See, that kind of thinking must run in our blood. We had different mothers, but damned if we both didn't get the old man's way of thinking." He grinned. "As soon as Pa hears the stage was robbed, the first thing he'll think is that I done it. But I've got that taken care of."

"How?" Ramon asked.

"Never mind how, little brother," said Saul, standing up, leveling his hat brim. "You just be racy to leave here after dark. I'll show *how* once the time comes. Until then, don't you worry about a thing."

"But what happens if someone kills this Danny Duggin and shows up here to collect the bounty, and the money is not here for them?"

"That ain't my problem," Saul grinned. "Once Duggin's dead, what do I care if Pa pays the bounty or not? Besides, Pa's got plenty more money. He didn't have to send off for more anyway. He's just strutting his stuff, wanting us to see how rich he is."

"And what about this Danny Duggin?" Ramon asked. "What if he shows up? What if we run into him while we are out there?"

"We won't," said Saul with confidence. "Hell, as many men as there are between here and Kansas after that bounty money, Duggin's probably dead already."

"You can not be sure of that," said Ramon.

"I know. But there's got to be some risk in anything we do, little brother," Saul Delmano said. "That's what makes life interesting."

Chapter 11

New Mexico Territory. September 25, 1871

Danielle, C. F. McCord, and Hector Sabio had ridden hard across Northwestern Texas. They had dropped down across the sand flats and rock country of New Mexico, stopping only long enough to take on supplies as they needed to, and to look around for any signs of her brothers at the relay stations and small desert settlements. Hector Sabio's knowledge of the land and its rocky twists and turns had proved invaluable. Once they had crossed the Pecos River and picked up the long trail toward Las Cruces, they rode southwest across the salt basin, then on toward the Hueco tanks.

"Does this Danny Duggin ever slow down?" Hector Sabio asked McCord as they rode a few yards behind Danielle in the hot afternoon sun.

"If he does, I haven't seen it," McCord answered.

"I fear he will cause us to run these horses to death," Hector said grimly. "Never have I seen a man so driven."

"Don't worry about the horses," said McCord. "I've noticed that no matter how hard he pushes himself, he never overworks the animals. He knows what he's doing," McCord added with confidence, smiling slightly as he watched Danielle from behind. "Our Danny Duggin seems to have just the right touch."

"*Our* Danny Duggin? Perhaps you admire this man, but I cannot say that I do," said Hector Sabio.

"That's because you don't understand him like I do, Hector." McCord smiled. "No, it is because he does not trust me . . . and he does not like me," said Hector.

"Well, Hector, after all you were riding with men who wanted to kill him." McCord looked at him. "You have to admit a thing like that does knock a dent in any budding friendship." McCord chuckled to himself.

"*Sí*, but still . . ." Hector started to say more, but seeing the knowing look in C. F. McCord's eyes, he shrugged, plainly puzzled. Hector scratched his head and heeled his horse forward beside McCord, both of them having to work at keeping close to Danielle.

Atop a sandy rise five hundred yards across the sand and mesquite, the gunman Cleery White lowered the telescope from his eye and scooted back a few feet before standing up and dusting himself off. "What's the doings out there?" asked one of the three other riders who had sat atop their horses while Cleery White scanned the three distant horsemen.

"You ain't going to believe this, Curly," said White. "That's Hector Sabio out there!"

Curly York stiffened in surprise at first, but then a knowing smile spread across his face. "Well, I'll be, talk about luck! He's one of the men who was riding with Tarksel, going after that bounty money. Are you sure that's him?" As he asked, Curly York reached down for the telescope, took it from Cleery White, and raised it to his eye.

"Yep, it's Hector," said White. "I'd recognize that weasel through a hailstorm. He and Tarksel and the others were going to try and hook up with Clyde Branson, if Branson would stand still for it."

"Hook up with who?" one of the other riders asked, a matchstick dropping from his mouth.

"Don't soil yourself, Duff," said Cleery White. "Branson ain't out there . . . just Sabio."

"I wasn't worried," Duff mumbled, his face reddening in embarrassment.

"Like hell you wasn't." The man beside him laughed. "You lost your matchstick just hearing Branson's name!"

"Shut up, Hale, I was through with it anyway," said Duff. He nudged his horse up beside Curly York. "Let me take a look, Curly." As Duff spoke, he fished a fresh matchstick from his shirt pocket and stuck it between his teeth.

"Just a damn minute," said Curly York, not giving up the telescope. He scanned for another few seconds, then said, "Boys, what does Delmano's pal Billy Sherman say this Danny Duggin fellow looks like?"

Donald Hale moved his horse closer, saying, "Billy said he's tall, slim, wears a brace of Colts . . . rides a chestnut mare, he said."

"Well, there's no chestnut out there, but otherwise this fellow fits the description." He hesitated, then added, "Guess who the third man is."

Donald Hale, Cleery White, and Joe Duff all looked at one another, but didn't offer a guess.

Curly York said in a wary tone, "It's none other

than U.S. Federal Marshal Charles McCord . . . in the flesh!"

"The *Fox*?" said Duff. "You don't mean it!" The fresh matchstick flew from his lips. Duff fumbled, trying to catch it, but missed.

Donald Hale gave Duff a goading grin, saying, "Guess you was through with that one too?"

"Shut up, Hale, I mean it!" said Duff. Frowning, he sidled his horse against Curly's. "Come on, Curly, let *me* see!"

Curly York shoved him away with his free elbow, still staring through the telescope. "If you want one of these things so bad, why don't you buy yourself one?" he hissed.

Duff brooded, hearing Donald Hale stifle a laugh behind him. A moment later, Curly York lowered the telescope and handed it to Duff. "There, take a look if it'll cool your fever."

Joe Duff raised the lens to his eye and searched for the three riders. Just as he found them in the tight circle of vision, Danielle, Hector, and C. F. McCord disappeared around a rocky bluff, leaving only a drift of dust in their wake. "Damn it, missed them!" Duff said, lowering the telescope and poking it back toward Curly York. Donald Hale snickered and put a hand to his mouth, hoping to keep himself from laughing out loud.

"What do you make of it, Curly?" Cleery White asked, stepping back up into his saddle.

Curly York sat in silence for a moment, feeling the men's eyes on him as he considered it. Finally he said, "Here's what I get from it." He raised a finger for emphasis and rubbed his chin as he spoke. "Hector Sabio is McCord's prisoner, which means the rest of the old Axel Eldridge Gang is either dead or in jail."

"Serves them right then," said Cleery White. "They had no business going after that bounty. They were always just thieves, and a man ought to stick to what he knows."

Curly York nodded in agreement. "The thing is, McCord had been after Saul Delmano for the longest time . . ." His words trailed as if he just stated the obvious.

"So?" said Donald Hale. "What's that got to do with the bounty money?"

"Explain it to him, White," said Curly York, sounding impatient.

"Because, you damn Georgia cracker neck!" said White. "Delmano wants this Duggin dead . . . and The Fox wants Delmano dead! Does that spark any thought at all in your mind?"

"Yeah, I get it," Hale said grudgingly, backing his horse a step away from the others. "You don't have to act that way."

Listening, Duff rolled his eyes skyward, took out a fresh matchstick, and bit down on it. "So, what do you want to do, Curly? McCord ain't no short piece of work. Neither is this Danny Duggin, from what we've heard."

Curly York turned his horse quarter-wise and looked at Duff with a flat stare, saying, "Don't blow your matchstick over this, Joe. But we're going to ride over there and kill them."

"What if that ain't Danny Duggin?" asked Hale.

"So what if it ain't?" Curly York snapped in reply,

jerking his horse around and heeling it away. "If we're wrong, all it'll cost us is a handful of bullets."

When Danielle first caught a thin distant glint of sunlight off metal, she decided not to mention it to Hector and McCord right then. Instead, she slowed her horse for a few yards, enough to let the two catch up to her. "What's wrong?" McCord asked, coming up on her right while Hector slipped his horse up on her left.

"Nothing," said Danielle, patting her gloved hand on her horse's sweaty neck. "Thought I'd walk this horse down and rest him for a couple of miles." There was something in her tone of voice that McCord picked up on right away. Danielle gave the slightest nod in the direction where she'd seen the flash of light. She let her eyes move to Hector, then back to McCord.

McCord caught on, but he saw that Hector had no idea what Danielle was doing. "It's about time you slowed down for a while, Danny," McCord said. He managed to let his gaze drift back out across the sandy stretch of mesquite and cholla. He saw nothing.

They rode on in silence for another half mile. Suddenly Hector straightened in his saddle and turned his horse sidelong to the right. "Riders are coming!" he said.

"Yep, they sure are," said McCord, giving Danielle a look. He stopped his horse short and raised his rifle from his saddle boot.

Hector looked back and forth quickly between the two of them, then said, "What? You already saw them coming? You were testing me? But that was foolish, letting them get so close!"

"This is open country, Hector. There's no place to run even if we wanted to." Danielle had also stopped her horse and stepped it sideways, putting a few feet between her and the other two. "Get ready," she said, "in case this is no social call."

"Hello, the trail," Curly York called out as the four riders came into full sight from around an upthrust of rock. As the riders drew nearer, checking their horses down to a slow walk, they spread out a few feet apart. "I thought we saw some riders over here a while ago." York forced a stiff, cordial smile. "Reckon I was right." He spoke above a hot licking wind.

"I reckon you were," said McCord. He sat facing the four men with his rifle propped up on his thigh. "What can we do for you?" Danielle sat with her right palm resting on her holstered Colt. Hector felt sweat run down the back of his neck and kept his hand near the pistol that was shoved down in his waist belt.

Curly York looked taken aback by McCord's firm tone of voice. He almost completely stopped his horse. But then, cutting a glance to White and the others, he inched the horse forward, saying, "We just saw yas, and thought we ought to come say 'Howdy.'"

"Howdy," said McCord, his tone of voice not changing. "Now stop that horse right there."

"Well, boys," Curly said to the others, "looks like we've come upon some inhospitable pilgrims today."

"Cut it short, Curly York," said McCord, letting York know that he recognized him. "It's too hot to sit here and pretend we don't know what you're after."

York feigned a surprised look, saying, "Now what

in the world are you talking about, Fox? We're just headed over toward Kansas, wanting to see what the weather's like."

Without taking his eyes off Curly York, McCord said over his shoulder, "Hector, do these boys know about the reward money?"

"*Sí*," said Hector Sabio, his gaze narrowed on Curly York. "He heard about it from Billy Sherman, the same one who told Al Tarksel and the rest of us."

"That's what I thought," said McCord, his thumb cocking the rifle hammer as he spoke. "Well, Curly, that pretty much stops the need for any further conversation, wouldn't you say?"

Curly York ignored McCord and turned his attention to Danielle, saying, "So you're Danny Duggin, huh? You don't look like much to me—not two thousand dollars, anyway. How come The Fox does all your talking for you?"

Danielle lifted her face slowly and said from beneath her lowered hat brim. "Did you come here to talk or fight, mister? So far you're doing a whole lot of one, and none of the other."

Feeling something unsettling in the calm, cold voice, Curly York called out to Hector Sabio, "What about you, Hector? What's your stake in this? Are you going to stand with them or us? We've known you a lot longer than they have."

"You see where I stand, you *hijo de una perra!*" Hector spat.

"What'd he say, White?" Curly York asked over his shoulder.

"He, uh . . . called you a son of a bitch, Curly," Cleery White said cautiously. "Maybe this ain't a good time or place," he added, seeing no sign of weakness in the eyes of the three who stood before them.

Curly York bristled and said to Hector Sabio, "It's a long trail you're on, amigo. A lot can happen between here and the border."

"Back your horses and turn them, or by the saints you will die here." Hector hissed. Hot wind whirred across the sand.

"Tomorrow's another day, Curly," Cleery White said, sounding worried.

Curly York sat staring for a second longer, then he let out a tense breath and said as he backed his horse and began turning it slowly, "I'll be seeing you farther down the trail, Mr. Danny Duggin."

As Curly York turned away, his hand suddenly snatched for his pistol. He heard the voice call out behind him, "York—!" Swinging his horse quickly, bringing his pistol up, York looked into the barrel of Danielle's cocked Colt. "You won't be seeing anything more."

The first shot lifted Curly York from his saddle before he could get his shot off. The second hit Joe Duff as the tip of his pistol cleared his holster. Beside Danielle, Hector Sabio nailed Donald Hale in the chest, Hale's drawn pistol flying from his hand as he twisted sidelong out of his saddle. Cleery White's horse reared up as he drew and cocked his big Smith & Wesson, but one shot from C. F. McCord's rifle sent both White and his horse backward in a spray of dust.

In a matter of seconds the fight was over. Dust stood high and drifted on the wind. Three of the men's horses scattered. Cleery White's horse rolled back up onto its hooves, shaking off dust, its saddle hanging down around its side. Danielle was the first to step off her horse, walking forward with her Colt pointing down from one man to the next. On the ground, Cleery White looked up at her pistol barrel, blood running down both corners of his mouth.

"Don't shoot," Cleery pleaded in a pained voice. "It . . . weren't my idea."

"Then you should have ridden away," said Danielle.

Stepping down from his horse as well, McCord hurried forward beside Danielle as she cocked her Colt toward Cleery White. "Don't do it, Danny . . . he's dead anyway!"

"Listen to the marshal!" Hector said, running up on Danielle's other side.

Danielle turned slowly toward Hector Sabio as if in a trance. It seemed to take all of her effort to lower the Colt and let the hammer down. As she stood staring at Hector with a glazed and distant look in her eyes, McCord said quietly, "There, you see, this one's dead now, too."

Danielle turned back to the blank face of Cleery White, who had slumped down on his side, his cheek pressed to the ground. It took her a moment to snap out of it. Hector and McCord looked at one another as Danielle lowered her Colt back into the holster. "See why I'm in a hurry?" she said in a hushed tone. "I want to put an end to it."

"*Sí,*" said Hector, "and you will, very soon." He stepped between Danielle and the bodies on the ground as if to shield her view of them. "Go to the horses, *por favor,* while the marshal and I bury these men."

"No," said McCord as he stepped over to White's horse, loosened its cinch, dropped its saddle and bridle, and slapped its rump, sending it out across the sand. "Let's ride on." Looking around at the four bodies sprawled in the dirt, he said, "Let the sand do all the burying."

After they had mounted and ridden away, with Danielle in front of Hector Sabio and C. F. McCord by ten yards, Hector sidled his horse close to the marshal and said, "You saw what he did . . . they were already leaving. This Danny Duggin is a cold killer, I think."

"It was too close to call, Hector," said McCord, shaking his head. "I saw Curly York go for his gun the same time as Danny called out his name. One thing's for sure though, it's all starting to take its toll. The sooner we settle with the Delmanos, the better." They rode on in the stinging wind.

No sooner than they were out of sight, Al Tarksel and Bob Dennard ventured forward around the crest of a long rise of sand. Dennard stepped his horse over to the bodies on the ground and looked down at them, holding his hat down on his head against the wind. "We lost a good chance there," he said, sounding disappointed. "I was hoping these boys would take care of things for us. We could have ambushed them afterwards." A dusty pair of binoculars hung around his neck on a long strip of rawhide.

"Damn it." Al Tarksel spat and ran a hand across his mouth. "I never seen men come on so strong, then lose their nerve so quick in my life."

Bob Dennard reined his horse away from the bodies, the blowing sand already heaping up along the dead men's sides. "Let's get out of the wind before it skins our hides off us." He nudged the horse forward, still holding his hat down on his head.

"What about them?" Al Tarksel asked, nodding toward the wind-blown trail ahead.

"Don't worry," said Dennard. "They've still got a ways to go. We ain't lost them yet."

Chapter 12

Little Hueco Pass, Texas. September 26, 1871

At a small rundown trade station west of the mountain line, Tim and Jed Strange had spent the night beneath the shelter of a canvas-covered lean-to, where three burrows grudgingly made room for them and their horses. The owner of the station, a grizzled old peddler named Martin Wheatley, had no room for the twins inside his small tent. But at the sign of distant sunlight, he came to the lean-to, carrying a hot skillet full of flat biscuits, and set it on a cleared spot on the ground. "Here you go, boys, same as last night, only fresher. I would've had us some brush-deer steak to go with them, but none came up during the night. Danged Mescaleros must be on the prowl, keeping the deer scared, I reckon."

"Are you expecting any trouble?" Tim asked, raking up a hot biscuit with his fingertips and bouncing it in his cupped hands, blowing on it to cool it.

"From the Apache? Naw sir," said Wheatley, stooping down beside the twins. "This ain't their stomping grounds no how. They're just roaming through, on the dodge, like most everybody else who comes this way lately." He eyed the gunbelts lying on a blanket, then nodded at the twins' bare feet. "I reckon wherever you boys came from, you left in a hurry? Meant to ask yas last night but I figured you was too tired to talk."

"We're not outlaws, if that's what you think," said Jed, friendly but firm.

"It wouldn't make me no difference if you are outlaws," said Wheatley. "So long as a man ain't shooting at me, I ain't shooting at him neither." He patted a weathered hand on the big saddle-style Walker Colt strapped across his belly beneath a wide wool sash. "I've shot this ole hand cannon once every Christmas for the past ten years, just to hear it bark, make sure she ain't died on me. Otherwise, it's as quiet as death here. Nobody comes this way anymore unless they ain't wanting to be seen or smelt."

"That's us," said Jed, offering a thin smile. "We're not outlaws, but we don't want to be seen or smelt."

"If you don't use your Walker," asked Tim, "how do you kill your brush-deer?"

"Bow and arrow," said the old man. "I learnt to use it years ago. A man lives in the wilds, he learns to separate himself from all mechanisms of man's device."

"What about your trade goods?" asked Jed. "How do make your living if nobody comes this way?"

"Trade goods, ha!" The old man cackled. "I ain't traded nothing since I can remember. I call this a trade station just to keep my hand into something—reminds me that I'm still alive."

"Then I guess there's no point in asking if you'd have any boots for sale, is there?" said Tim. As he asked, he looked at the old man's feet, at the worn-out boot on his right foot, and the floppy moccasin on his left.

"No, there's not," said Wheatley. "Nearest boots will be in El Paso, if you can stand all the noise there."

"How much farther are we from there?" asked Jed.

"Half a day hard ... all day easy," said Wheatley. "If you stumbled from here, you'd roll in there by nightfall."

"Much obliged for the biscuits," said Tim. "Can we pay you for breakfast?"

"I don't see why"—the old man shrugged—"I was going to eat anyway."

Jed gave the old man a level gaze and said, "We saw some fresh hoofprints coming in last evening. Has there been anybody else come through here lately who didn't want to be seen or smelt?"

The old man had to think about it as he scratched his bearded neck. "Yep, now that you mention it. Three men came past here day before yesterday. They didn't stay long though. Said they was doing some private bounty hunting." He looked away from the twins as he spoke. "Asked me had I seen any strangers passing through. I told them everybody I've seen in the past ten years has been a stranger."

"I see," said Tim. He stood up, took the last bite of his biscuit, and swung his holster belt around his waist and strapped it into place. "We'll be getting along now, thanking you for your hospitality."

"I'm still eating," Jed protested over a mouthful of hot biscuit.

"Eat on the way," said Tim, giving his brother a level stare. "I want to get into town and get me some boots."

Jed caught the look in Tim's eyes and offered no more hesitancy. He stood up, taking his gunbelt from the blanket and putting it on, still chewing his food.

"Don't know what's your hurry," Martin Wheatley said, standing up with them, brushing the ragged seat of his trousers.

"He's always in a hurry," Jed said, nodding toward Tim as he took the pistol from his holster, checked it, then put it away. "I can hardly keep up with him sometime."

Martin Wheatley watched them closely while they saddled their horses and made ready for the trail. He followed them out from beneath the lean-to, saying as they stepped up into their saddles and turned their horses, "Adios fellers. If you come back through, bring some tobacco."

"We sure will, mister," said Tim, drawing the chestnut mare up close beside him. He tugged his hat brim down onto his head, making a quick sweep with his eyes before heeling his horse forward to the narrow trail. Beside him, Jed did the same.

Neither of them spoke or looked back until they had rounded the trail past a large split boulder fifty yards away. Then Tim sidled his horse and the mare off the trail in between two tall rocks and turned to Jed, saying, "Something wasn't right was it?"

"I didn't notice until you got anxious to leave," said Jed, "but you're right, there was something wrong, sure enough. I just can't put my finger on it."

"Me neither," said Tim.

"Then what do you want to do?" Jed asked.

"I say we need to circle around, get above the place and watch him a while. I believe there's somebody back there with him. If there is, I want to know who. Danielle might be coming this way. We don't want her getting bushwhacked."

They stepped down from their saddles and led the horses up off the trail through rock and brush until they had moved to a point above the old man's run-down shack. Hitching the horses to a deadfall tangle of juniper, the twins eased out onto a rock overhang and looked down just in time to see two men step out through the door of the shack and walk toward Martin Wheatley. Beside Wheatley stood another man, this one wearing a long riding duster, carrying a rifle in his gloved hand. From sixty feet above them, Tim and Jed listened closely to make out their words.

"Hey, Carl," the man in the long riding duster called out to one of the men walking toward him, "this ole geezer wants to know if he did all right. What do you think?"

The one he spoke to was Carl Zabow, and the man walking beside Carl was his brother, Lucas. "He did all right, Ellis," said Carl Zabow. "If he hadn't he wouldn't be standing there, right, Lucas?"

Lucas Zabow only nodded. In his hands he held a short bow and a thin crooked arrow, trying to get the arrow to seat onto the bowstring. "How the hell does a man shoot one of these things?" As they neared Ellis Short and Martin Wheatley, Lucas managed to get the arrow seated and drew it back a couple of inches. When he let the arrow go, it arched slowly and stuck in the ground between Ellis's and Martin Wheatley's feet.

"Hey! Take it easy!" old man Wheatley shouted.

"That ain't no toy! I've killed deer and elk bigger than you are with it."

Lucas Zabow laughed. "I don't believe it," he said, taking another crooked arrow from the rawhide quiver under his arm. He looked the arrow over and notched it to the bowstring. "You couldn't knock wet wind out of a sick chicken with this thing."

"What do you think, Carl?" Martin Wheatley asked, "You think they're the ones you told me about, the look-alikes who travel with the man you're looking for?"

"I'd bet on it, " said Carl Zabow. "How many twins can you remember ever coming through here?"

"None that I recall," said Wheatley. "Notice how I didn't mention it to them, about them being twins?"

"Yeah, I noticed," said Carl Zabow.

On their rocky perch Jed turned to Tim and whispered, *"That's* what didn't feel right. Everywhere we go, somebody always comments on us being look-alikes."

Tim only nodded, still listening intently to the men below.

"Does this get me part of that bounty money once you kill this Duggin feller?" old man Wheatley asked. "I did it just like you asked me to."

"Sure, old man, why not," said Carl Zabow. Beside him another arrow streaked from the bow, this one a little stronger.

"Dang it, Lucas!" Wheatley said. "I told you to be careful with that thing!"

"I'm getting better," said Lucas Zabow. "Don't talk cross to me old man, I'm apt to put one of these in your chest."

Martin Wheatley looked worried. Beside him, Ellis Short only chuckled and glanced at the arrow that had pinned itself to one of the supports of the lean-to. "You ought to know better than to leave something like this laying around. You never know when some idiot is going to take it up."

"Who are you calling an idiot?" Lucas Zabow said, grinning, stringing the arrow and pointing it at Ellis Short.

Ellis Short raised a hand toward him, smiling, saying, "I take it back, don't shoot."

Lucas swung the arrow tip toward Martin Wheatley, saying, "What do you think, old man? Do you think I'm an idiot?"

Martin Wheatley ignored him and said to Carl Zabow, "What do you think about giving me a few dollars right now, Zabow? Call it an advance. You said yourself, I did a fine job lying to them boys. They never guessed anybody was here."

"No," said Carl Zabow, "no advance. When we take care of Danny Duggin, I'll remember that you're in for a couple of dollars, but that's as far as I go."

"A couple of dollars?" Martin Wheatley looked stunned. "Hell's fire, I wouldn't have wasted my time for a couple of dollars! Maybe I'll just slip atop one of the burrows and catch up to those look-alikes, see how much they'll pay me for telling them you're here."

Carl eyed him closely. "You'd do that to us?"

"I need some whiskey awfully bad," said Wheatley. "I'm apt to do what benefits me. Can you blame a man for that?"

"I reckon not," said Carl Zabow. He turned to his

brother Lucas and said, "Have you got the hang of that yet?"

"I'm getting there." Lucas pulled the arrow back from the bow and looked it up and down.

"Then shoot some arrows in this old buzzard," said Carl. "That'll teach him to keep his mouth shut."

"Now just one dang minute!" said Martin Wheatley. "I was only testing you, Carl!"

"Testing me?" Carl grinned. "Well I hope I passed."

The twang of the bowstring was followed by a deep grunt as Martin Wheatley clutched the arrow shaft sticking out of his left shoulder with both hands. "Dang!" he managed to say in a strained voice.

Another arrow hit him, this one in his thigh, causing him to buckle down onto his knee. "Boys . . . this ain't right!"

Another arrow sliced deep into his right shoulder. "Cut it out, boys, please," said Martin Wheatley, catching his breath.

"Nope, I'm just getting started," said Lucas Zabow. "Now that I got the hang of it, I could do this all day long." He grinned, stringing another arrow. "Do you hear me, old man? I said, *all . . . day . . . long.*" Lucas aimed the arrow low and let it fly, nailing Martin Wheatley's foot to the dirt. The old man bellowed and cursed.

"I got to get me one of these," said Lucas Zabow, taking another arrow and stringing it. "I bet I can put this one right smack in the middle of his forehead."

On the overhang, Tim stood up, saying to his brother, "I can't stand here and watch this."

"Neither can I." Jed jumped to his feet beside him.

Lucas Zabow took careful aim this time, drawing

the arrow back its full length. "Ten dollars says I can do it." He chuckled.

"You're on," said Ellis Short, stepping farther away from the old man.

But before Lucas Zabow could let the arrow go, a shot from Tim's pistol exploded, the bullet slicing through Lucas's hand and shattering the bow shaft. The arrow dropped down and skidded across the dirt.

"What the—?" Carl Zabow spun around, his pistol coming up out of his holster as Lucas fell to the ground, screaming, clasping his bloody hand, seeing the stub where his middle finger used to be. Ellis Short ducked back behind the lean-to pole, his pistol coming up cocked and ready.

"Up here," Tim Strange called down to them. Carl Zabow's eyes went up toward the sound of Tim's voice, his pistol following his gaze. But before he got more than a glimpse of Tim standing on the overhang above him, the second shot from Tim's pistol hit Zabow high in the chest and sent him flying backward. Jed saw Ellis Short's pistol swing around the pole and try to take aim upward. The pistol in Jed's hand exploded twice, each shot nailing Ellis Short and walking him backward into the frightened burrows. As Short fell to the ground, the burrows brayed and kicked and stomped him beneath their sharp little hooves.

"Don't shoot!" Lucas Zabow cried out from his knees, his right hand gripping his left wrist, trying to slow the flow of blood. "You shot my damned finger off!"

Ten feet away, Martin Wheatley shouted through his pain, "Shoot him again! Look what he did to me!"

"Everybody stay real still till I get there," Tim called down to them. He looked at Jed, saying, "Keep them covered while I climb down. Once I get there, you bring the horses and ride on around."

"All right, be careful," said Jed. He turned to his horse, slipped the rifle from his saddle boot, cocked it, and held it poised downward toward Wheatley and Lucas Zabow while Tim began a slow descent down the steep rocky slope.

At the bottom of the slope, Tim drew his pistol and cocked it. He kept the two wounded men covered as he walked first to the body of Carl Zabow, then to the body of Ellis Short lying broken and bloody amid the burrows' nervous hooves. Walking back from beneath the canvas lean-to, he asked Martin Wheatley, "What kind of heads do you have on those arrows?"

"They're Comanche heads," said Wheatley, giving Lucas Zabow a cold stare. "They'll have to be cut out if that's what you want to know." He tried to walk toward Zabow on his bloody knees, one hand reaching out toward him like eagle talons. "All I ask is that you kill this dirty lousy—"

"No you don't," said Tim, stepping in between the two men, stopping Martin Wheatley. "There'll be no more killing here." He looked at Zabow and nodded toward a bucket of water sitting at one end of the lean-to. "Get that water bucket and bring it over here. We're going to need some hot water and bandages."

"Like hell," said Zabow. "I can't get that bucket! Look at my hand! My finger's blown off!"

"You've got another hand," said Tim. "Now do like I tell you."

By the time Jed came down around the trail, lead-

ing Tim's horse and chestnut mare, Zabow had
dragged the water bucket over, poured water into a
battered coffeepot, and scraped together some kindling for a small fire. With a bloody bandanna
wrapped around the stub of his finger, Zabow kneeled
down and blew onto the smoldering kindling to raise
a flame.

"Have they told you anything?" Jed asked, stepping down from his horse and leading all three horses
to a hitch rail.

"Nope, not yet," said Tim. "I'm more interested in
getting those arrows out of the old man before an infection sets in."

"Hear that, you rotten jackass!" Martin Wheatley
raged at Lucas Zabow. "I'll be lucky if these things
don't kill me!"

Zabow ignored him and cursed under his breath.

"I figure there's not much to tell us anyway," said
Tim. "These gunmen were out for the bounty. Lucky
Daniel—I mean, *Danny Duggin* wasn't with us. We'd
all three've been bushwhacked."

With the flames starting to stand and grow, Zabow
raised up on his knees and fanned the fire with his
good hand, saying, "We was going to stay on your
trail. Brother Carl said it wouldn't be long till this
Duggin showed up. We heard he traveled with a couple of look-alikes. You boys ain't exactly hard to spot,
you know." His eyes went to the hand-tooled gunbelt
on Jed Strange. "Say, that's Jack Pearl's holster and
pistol. What are you doing wearing it?"

"What do you think I'm doing wearing it?" Jed
challenged.

"The man it belonged to is dead," Tim cut in.

"When the Delmanos put the word out about that reward, they must've forgot to tell all of you it would be the hardest money you ever tried to earn."

"Don't count on your friend Duggin being safe just yet." Lucas Zabow sneered. "There's plenty more guns aimed at you between here and the Delmanos."

"Yes," Tim said, offering a trace of a harsh smile, "but if they are all as smart as you all are we've nothing to worry about."

Lucas Zabow grumbled to himself, looked down at the bloody bandanna on his hand, and shook his head in contemplation. Then he raised his eyes back up to Tim and Jed as Tim walked over and put the pot of water on the fire. "Hey, can I get something done about this hand? It's bleeding pretty bad."

Tim looked at Jed, saying, "You want to take care of him while I cut these arrows out of Wheatley?"

"Yep," said Jed, "I'll do it—"

"Look out, he's got a gun!" Martin Wheatley shouted, cutting Jed off.

Even as Jed spun toward him, the derringer in Zabow's hand leveled out toward him, Zabow's thumb cocking it quickly. But he was not quick enough. Jed's pistol exploded twice on the upswing from his holster, hammering Zabow backward and down, the shot from the derringer going wild and skyward, the gun falling to the dirt. Smoke curled up from the short barrel. Jed stepped in close and kicked the derringer away, looking down at Zabow's blank, dead face. "That was the stupidest move I ever saw." Old man Wheatley gasped. "That fool was dead before he hit the ground!"

The two bullet holes in Zabow's chest lay less than

an inch apart, centered on his left shirt pocket at heart
level. Jed punched out the two spent cartridges from
his pistol and replaced them as he spoke. "We might
not get all the men out to collect that bounty, but one
thing's for sure, we're thinning them out as we go."

It was afternoon when Tim finished removing the arrows from Martin Wheatley's wounds, wrapping the
crude gashes in strips of cloth torn from a white shirt
they found in the saddlebags of one of the dead gunmen. When Tim was finished and he and Jed had
dragged the bodies of the outlaws out of sight behind
the canvas lean-to, the twins walked back and found
that Martin Wheatley had raised himself up from a
blanket on the ground, and now sat on the single
wooden step out front of the shack. He'd picked up
the blanket and wrapped it around his shoulders even
in the heat of the day. Sweat streamed down his
weathered, whiskered cheeks.

"I feel real ashamed, lying to you boys earlier," old
man Wheatley said. "I reckon the idea of big money
makes fools of all us if we let it. How can I thank yas
for what you've done for me?"

"You can keep an eye out for our pal Danny Duggin if he passes this way. If you see him, let him know
we're in El Paso waiting for him."

"I'll sure do it," Wheatley said.

"And don't go trying to collect that reward, or
telling anybody else about it, old man," Jed warned
him. "If you do you'll likely end up dead."

"Hell, don't worry, I've learnt my lesson," said
Wheatley. He nodded at his bandaged wounds.
"Every time I move a muscle it feels like a fire runs

through my bones. What made that jackass do something like this? Seems like if he wanted to kill me, he could've had the decency to put a bullet in me! Why this?"

"You'll have to figure that one out for yourself," said Jed, stepping over to the hitch rail and loosening the horses' reins.

"Are you going to be all right here alone?" Tim asked as Jed brought the horses over to him.

"Yeah, I always do better alone, it seems like." Wheatley looked off across the sky. "Ya'll go on, don't worry about me."

The twins mounted and rode away, looking back only once at the solitary figure in the afternoon shadows before rounding the turn out of sight. "He's right about something," Tim said. "We are easy to spot, looking alike the way we do. We need to do something, since the word's out that Danny Duggin travels with a pair of twins."

"What do you want to do?" Jed asked.

"I think before we ride into El Paso, I'll shave and change my appearance as much as I can." He rubbed a hand up and down on his week-old beard stubble. "You can even take your boot knife and cut my hair real short. Do you think that'll work?"

"It's worth a try," said Jed. "Another thing we need to do is put this mare somewhere out of sight for a while. There's too many people who remember it. We'll split up before we ride into El Paso. Once we're in town, we'll listen around the saloons and see what we hear. Then we'll meet up and camp somewhere outside the town limits till we hear something from Danielle."

Chapter 13

El Paso, Texas. September 27, 1871

The open-side Spanish-style coach was one of the last of its kind to provide transportation across the flats and rock lands of West Texas. It rolled around the turn in the dusty trail with its canvas covers tied down to protect its passengers from the blazing sunlight. At one time, the canvas side covers had brightly displayed hand-painted flowers and scenes of cherubs serenely above the earth. Tassels had danced on the breeze from the corners of the canvases. But now, after years of service across the harsh terrain, the sand and sun had striped away all of the garishness. Green and gold paint that had once glistened in sunlight had now faded to the color of the arid land around it.

"There she is, boys," said Saul Delmano, looking down at the coach from a sandy bluff. Beside him, Ramon rose up in his stirrups and watched the stage straighten out of the turn, its four black sweat-streaked stage horses forging ahead at a strong gallop.

"They have no one riding shotgun," Ramon said in surprise.

Saul grinned, saying, "I know . . . it's pretty foolish

of them, huh?" He raised his bandanna and adjusted it over his face.

"Why are they moving so fast?" Ramon asked. "Have they spotted us?" He pulled his own bandanna up and smoothed it down over the bridge of his nose.

Saul chuckled behind his mask. "No, little brother, they just ain't taking no chances for the next few miles. There's too many blind spots along the stretch of trail. Most times when somebody has robbed a stage along here, it's been while the stage was traveling slow. A man would just step out into the trail with a shotgun and stop it cold. But the stage company has gotten wise to that tactic. So we're going to do something a little different today, right, Tully?" he called out to his left, where Joe Tully sat atop his horse with a rifle cradled in his arm.

"That's right," replied Joe Tully, "any time you're ready."

"Come on, little brother," said Saul Delmano. "Let's get headed down there with Kid Jeffrey."

"But what are we doing?" asked Ramon.

"I'll show you." Saul grinned. "Just don't go getting nervous on me." He gigged his horse down the path toward the trail, Ramon following close behind him. Halfway down the sloping path, a shot rang out from Joe Tully's rifle. Down on the stagecoach, Ramon watched stunned as the driver melted from his seat, fell to the dirt, and rolled away, his arms flapping like the broken blades of a windmill.

"He got that sucker on the first shot!" Saul Delmano bellowed, laughing aloud, spurring his horse harder.

"Holy saints!" Ramon gasped, seeing the stage veer

off the trail, the horses spooked now and pounding into a run.

"Don't worry," Saul called out. "Kid Jeffrey's got it."

From out of nowhere, Kid Jeffrey bolted forward below them on a big silver dapple stallion. Overtaking the runaway stage horses, Kid Jeffrey reached out from his saddle, grabbed the lead horse, and began checking the stage down. From inside the canvas covers came the sound of a woman screaming. A bald head poked out through the canvas, looked all around at the riders descending on the stage, then withdrew quickly back inside.

Once the stage was halted, Kid Jeffrey backstepped his horse and called out to the passengers with his pistol drawn, "All right, everybody out!"

The canvas cover flew up enough for the bald portly man to jump out to the ground, shouting in a frenzy, "Don't shoot!" as he ran out across the sand and brush with his stubby arms raised high.

Beside Ramon came the sound of Saul Delmano's pistol, and the man spilled to the ground in a puff of dust. "Stupid bastard," Saul Delmano growled.

"You said there would be no killing!" Ramon shouted at his brother, jerking his horse into a side-long canter as they approached the stage.

"Well, that one couldn't be helped," said Saul. "Now don't lose your head over it! This is robbery most foul, little brother. Get used to it."

Joe Tully rode in hard, joining them at the stage, where a woman and an old man had stepped down from behind the canvas flaps, their hands high above their heads. "Climb on up there and get the box," Saul

Delmano said to Kid Jeffrey, keeping his smoking pistol aimed down at the two passengers. Kid Jeffrey sidled his horse to the stage and swung up out of his saddle into the driver's seat. In a second, the small iron box fell to the dirt. Saul Delmano stepped down from his saddle, staring coldly at the two terror-stricken passengers. "Bet this is your first robbery, huh?" he asked them.

The woman stood staring wild-eyed and trembling. The old man glanced away at the body on the ground, then spoke in a shaky voice. "Ye ain't going to shoot us, too, are ye?"

"That all depends, old man," said Saul Delmano, pointing his pistol down at the lock on the iron safe box. A shot exploded and the lock blew open. "Have you got any money on you?" Saul kneeled down and flipped the lid open.

"I've got about fourteen dollars . . . and a pocket watch," the old man offered, nodding at the gold watch fob on his vest.

"Well get it out and give it to us, fool!" said Saul Delmano. He reached inside the box, took a handful of letters and slung them away on the breeze while the old man drew a worn leather wallet from his coat pocket and fished out the money with quaking fingers.

"Leave the passengers alone," said Ramon Delmano. "Take what we came here for and let's go."

Ignoring Ramon, Saul Delmano lifted a cloth bag from the box, opened it, and took three stacks of bound dollar bills.

"You brother's awfully skittish," said Kid Jeffrey,

jumping down from atop the coach. "Are you sure he's cut out for this kind of work?"

Ramon shot him a harsh stare.

"Aw, don't judge him harshly," said Saul Delmano. "You know how it is, his first time and all." He stepped over and snatched the money from the old man's hand, then jerked the watch from his vest pocket, looked at it, and held it to his ear. "What are you trying to pull, old man? This watch don't work!" He slung the watch to the ground and stuck the tip of his pistol barrel beneath the man's chin.

"No, please!" the old man pleaded. "It was working earlier! I swear it was!"

"Saul, leave him alone!" Ramon shouted, jumping down from his saddle. Kid Jeffrey and Joe Tully looked at one another in surprise above their bandanna masks.

Saul Delmano turned, slowly facing Ramon. "Damn it, why'd you have to go and say my name?" He pulled his mask down and spat lint from his lips. Kid Jeffrey and Joe Tully both slumped in disgust and lowered their bandannas as well.

"Wait, no!" said Ramon. "There must be a way to—"

His words cut short beneath the sound of pistol fire. The old man and the woman crumbled to the ground like spent puppets. Ramon stood stunned, not believing his eyes.

Saul Delmano shrugged, stuffing the money inside his shirt. "It couldn't be helped, little brother. What more can I say? Things happen in this line of business."

Ramon's hand tightened on his pistol butt, yet he stood speechless.

"Easy now," said Saul Delmano. "Don't do something stupid. This is your first job . . . it'll get easier, I promise." He smiled and stooped down to the woman's body, lifting a small silk purse from her limp wrist. As he stood up, opening it, rifling his fingers inside it, he said to Kid Jeffrey and Joe Tully, "You boys cut out in different directions. Ride three or four miles, then circle around through a creek bed. Meet us tonight at the old mission. We'll split this up, and get on to something else."

"Why not split it up now?" Kid Jeffrey asked. "The way we always do?"

"Are you going to get picky on me, Kid?" Saul gave him an exasperated look, reaching back inside his shirt. "Because if you feel that way, here!" He jerked out the money and held it up to him. "You hang on to all of it! Hell, I trust you!"

Kid Jeffrey looked ashamed. "I was just asking is all."

"Then you *don't* want to hold on to it?" Saul Delmano put the money away and shook his head, saying, "Damn, Kid, as long as you've known me, you have to ask me something like that?"

"I meant no harm," Kid Jeffrey offered in a submissive voice.

"I understand," said Saul Delmano. "Now both of yas go on. We've been here too long as it is."

Ramon Delmano stood silently looking at the two bodies on the ground until he felt Saul push him toward his horse. Only when he had mounted and taken the reins in his hands did Ramon notice that Kid Jeffrey and Joe Tully had already spurred their horses out in opposite directions through the brush and rock lands. "You're going to have to get a grip on yourself, little brother," Saul Delmano said. "This job ain't over till we tie up some loose ends."

"I—I don't want any part of this," Ramon said, shaking his head.

"Well, you're a part of it now whether you want to be or not. The only question is, do you want to hang from the gallows pole for murder and robbery?" He grinned. "See? All that time you thought I was just out here having myself a grand ole hoedown . . . bet you never realized how hard this work can get." He slapped his gloved hand on Ramon's horse's rump, laughing as they both rode away.

"Where are we headed?" Ramon called out above the sound of the horse's hooves.

"Into town, just as quick as we can cut across some rock and hide our tracks," Saul replied. "We want to be seen around town like we've been there all day. Tonight we'll build ourselves an even better alibi."

"What do you mean?" Ramon asked.

"You'll see." Saul Delmano grinned.

At the edge of town, Saul and Ramon slipped in along a back trail, stepped down from their saddles, and led their horses through a narrow alley to a hitch rail out front of a crowded saloon. Then they mingled among the many passersby in the dusty street until they made their way to the next saloon a block away. Once inside the saloon, the day gamblers and drinkers looked up and some of the men who were friends of the Delmanos made room for them at the bar. A gunman called Thurman Pratt waved them forward and slapped Saul on his back as he summoned the bartender to bring them both a shot glass.

"How the hell have you boys been?" Thurman asked, snatching a bottle of rye and filling the two glasses for them. "I'm surprised to see you out and around, Saul."

"We're both fine," said Saul Delmano, answering for himself and Ramon. "We just come from Mama Rosa's up the street. Saw all the horses out front and thought we'd drop by here before heading back across the border."

"You're taking an awful big chance ain't you," said Thurman Pratt, "what with this Danny Duggin looking for you?"

Saul Delmano smiled. "You know me, Thurman, I don't scare real easy. To tell the truth I wished the ole man had never put that bounty up on Duggin. I'd kind of like to meet him myself, face-to-face." He raised his shot glass in a salute to the men along the bar and tossed back his drink.

A red-faced young man named Reggie Weil, who stood leaning on the bar next to Thurman, looked over at Saul and Ramon and said, "I hope to hell you don't meet him face-to-face. Me and Thurman are counting on making that two thousand for ourselves, so's we can chase whores all winter on it."

Saul poured himself another shot of rye and replied, "Reggie, if you're interested in that bounty, why ain't you out fanning the trails for Duggin right now?"

Before Reggie Weil could answer, Thurman Pratt cut in, saying, "Reggie talks too damn much." He cut a glance along the bar to make sure the other men weren't listening. Seeing the crowd had turned their attention to a woman dancing with her skirt raised above her waist, Thurman continued in a lowered voice beneath the sound of a twangy piano, "The only way to collect that reward, I figure, is to let this Danny Duggin come through here looking for you. Then Reggie and me will walk out into the street, pop a few shots in him, and bring you his head in a flour sack." Thurman shrugged. "It makes more sense than to be out there eating dust in the hot sun, don't it?"

"It sounds good to me," Saul answered. He threw back another shot of rye, nodded toward Ramon beside him, then asked Thurman Pratt, "You haven't seen Kid Jeffrey or Joe Tully around, have you? We've looked for them all day, in every saloon around here."

"No, we haven't seen them," said Reggie Weil, "but you don't look drunk enough to have been in every saloon in town."

Saul Delmano's expression turned dead serious. "What's that supposed to mean?"

"Nothing," said Reggie Weil, looking stuck for a response.

Thurman Pratt looked Saul and Ramon up and down. "Pipe down, Reggie," he said, "I reckon these boys know if they've been in town all day or not." He gave Saul a knowing look, adding, "Hell, Saul, you've been drinking most of the day with me and Reggie if anybody asks. Is this something important?"

"Much obliged," Saul Delmano said under his breath. "Yeah, it might be important. Seems like the law hereabouts has a pick on me. Least little thing happens, I always expect to get blamed for it."

Thurman Pratt leaned a little closer, saying between

the two of them, "You think maybe Kid Jeffrey and Tully have done something and you and your brother might catch the blame for it?"

"Yeah, something like that," Saul responded, looking a bit concerned. "Kid Jeffrey has been talking lately about hitting a stagecoach. He asked me to join him, but I'm laying low for a while."

"Don't worry," said Thurman. "I'll put the word out among these men. If anybody comes asking, you two have been in town with us since morning."

Saul nodded and threw back his shot of rye. "I knew I could count on you, Thurman." He raised his shot glass toward the bartender and called out, "Bring us all a mug of beer, something to wash down the taste of snake heads."

Ramon had been listening, puzzled, wondering what his brother had in mind. He nudged Saul, asking him in a whisper while the bartender slid beer mugs along the bar, "What are you trying to do, Saul?"

Without facing him, Saul Delmano answered in lowered voice, "I told you we was going to build ourselves an alibi. Now drink up, leave all the thinking to me."

The drinking crowd grew as the afternoon wore on. When the evening sunlight cut black slashes of shade across the dirt street, Saul Delmano nudged Ramon with his elbow and nodded at a few men who had stepped away from the bar and headed out the back door toward the outhouses. "Come on, little brother, it's time we meet Kid Jeffrey and Tully." He stepped back from the bar and said to Thurman Pratt as Thurman and Reggie stood with their arms draped around two young women. "Hey, Thurman, we're going to the jake. Keep an eye on our beers."

"Sure thing," said Thurman Pratt in a drunken voice, barely raising a drooping eye from the young woman's bare shoulder.

Once out the back door, Saul and Ramon hurried along the backs of the buildings to their horses a block up the street. Once atop their horses, they raced out on the east road to the old mission three miles out of town. It was dark by the time they slid their horses to a halt and stepped down from their saddles. Ramon saw the outline of two horses standing back at the rear edge of the old adobe church building. Kid Jeffrey called out quietly in the darkness, "Hey, Saul, we're back here."

"Hope you haven't been waiting too long," said Saul Delmano. He and Ramon led their horses back into the darkness and joined Kid Jeffrey and Joe Tully.

"No, just got here ourselves," said Joe Tully, holding an opened canteen in his hand, wiping a wet bandanna across his forehead.

"There's been nobody on your trail?" asked Saul Delmano.

"Not a soul," said Kid Jeffrey. "We've been real careful. We shook off our tracks three or four different times through creek beds and rocks. Besides, it might be sometime tomorrow before anybody finds that stagecoach."

"Let's settle up and get moving," said Joe Tully. "It's been hotter than hell out there. I'm ready to go drink myself into a blind stupor."

"Good idea," said Saul Delmano, "I'm in a hurry myself." He reached inside for what Kid Jeffrey and

Joe Tully thought would be the stacks of money. They leaned in watching him eagerly, but then stood taken aback when Saul Delmano pulled out the dead woman's small silk purse and tossed it on the ground at their feet.

"Hey," said Kid Jeffrey, "what's going on here? What are you doing with that?"

But as Kid Jeffrey spoke, Joe Tully caught on to Saul Delmano's intentions and jumped back a step, saying, "It's a setup, Kid! Kill them!" Tully's hand went for his pistol, but it was too late. Saul Delmano had already drawn his Colt and cocked it. He dropped the hammer on Joe Tully first, then quickly turned the pistol on Kid Jeffrey and put a bullet through his heart. Saul took a step back, kicked the silk purse up between the two bodies on the ground, and turned to Ramon. "Let's ride fast, little brother, our beer's getting warm."

"My God!" said Ramon Delmano, looking down at the dead men. "What kind of low monster are you? These men were your partners, your *amigos!*"

"Yeah, well, that was their mistake I reckon. We got the money, and once the law sees that purse, they'll get the blame." He grinned, taking a stack of the money from inside his shirt. "Ain't that the best kind of partners to have?" He reached out and shoved the money down into Ramon's shirt pocket. "There's a thousand dollars for a day's work, little brother. If you don't trust me, you're free to count it."

Ramon wasn't about to count the money. He didn't even want to look at it. Something told him to keep his mouth shut and go along with his brother until he found a chance to make his getaway. Saul must have read the look on his face. He turned away laughing and stepped up into his saddle. "As far as what kind of monster I am, little brother . . . I've been wondering about that my whole damn life."

Chapter 14

"What the hell took yas so long?" Thurman Pratt asked Saul Delmano when Saul and Ramon slipped in through the back door and into their places at the crowded bar. "I've already been drunk and sobered back up since you boys went to the jake! Thought I'd have to cleave the bartender's fingers off to keep him from pitching your beer out." Next to Thurman Pratt, Reggie Weil hung facedown on the bar, passed out cold, a fly walking boldly across his chin.

Saul Delmano spoke for himself and Ramon, saying, "We walked back and got our horses from out front of the cantina. Then we ran into a couple of ole boys we knew on our way here and got to talking." He sipped his beer, set the mug down, and pushed it across the bar, saying to the busy bartender, "What's it take to get a couple of beers livened up?"

Thurman Pratt eyed Ramon, then said to Saul, "What's wrong with your brother? He looks like he's seen a ghost!"

"He looks like that all the time." Saul chuckled. "I always said his ma shoulda weaned him sooner."

Ramon seethed in silence and drank his beer.

By the time Saul and Ramon Delmano had finished their beers, the young woman was back at the bar with Thurman Pratt's face buried in her sweaty bodice. Saul Delmano set his empty mug on the bar top beside Ramon's and patted Thurman on his shoulder. "I can see you're in love, ole pard. I reckon me and little brother will head back across the line. Don't forget we was with you all day."

"What's your hurry?" Thurman Pratt asked in a muffled voice without raising his face. But Saul and Ramon turned and left without answering.

Leaving the saloon, the Delmano brothers crossed the border under the cover of darkness and rode in a wandering trail across rocks and through thick brush. More than once they doubled back and followed their own tracks, just to confuse any would-be followers. Dawn churned orange and hazy in the eastern sky as they made their way along the last stretch of trail toward Bloody Horse Pass.

"You've been awfully damn quiet, little brother," Saul said, riding along with his pistol out of his holster, idly twirling it on his finger. For the past mile Ramon had been wary of the sound of his brother cocking and uncocking the big pistol.

"I have nothing to say," Ramon replied. "I only want to return home and put this thing out of my mind." He'd considered lifting his own pistol, just as a precaution, yet he realized that doing so might only progress whatever dark thoughts Saul Delmano was already harboring.

"Sorry, little brother," said Saul Delmano in a quiet tone, riding up close beside him. Ramon tensed at the sound of the pistol cocking. "But you won't be going home this morning."

Ramon jerked his eyes toward Saul, his hand

clutching around the butt of his holstered pistol. But he saw his brother uncock the pistol and twirl it, giving him a bemused look. "Take it easy now, Ramon." Saul chuckled in taunting voice. "You're strung tighter than a cheap fiddle." He slipped his pistol into his holster and let out a breath of regret. "Things went bad for us back at the stagecoach . . . you mistakenly saying my name before those people, us having to kill them. Not that I'm holding it against you. We all make mistakes. But to be on the safe side we might want to ride on through Bloody Horse Pass and take to the hideout for a few days."

"Why?" Ramon asked bluntly, not trusting anything Saul had to say. "We are already across the border . . . you set up our alibi. What are we hiding from now, this Danny Duggin who is looking to kill you? I thought you were not afraid of him."

Saul reined his horse to a halt. Ramon did the same. "Listen to me, little brother, I ain't afraid of man, beast, nor reptile. In all likelihood Kid Jeffrey and Joe Tully are going to wear that stage robbery. But don't forget there are four sets of tracks there. The sheriff is going to know there are two others involved if he pushes it—and he *will* push it, since people died, especially one of them an old codger and the other being a woman!" He shook his head. "Don't ask me why, but for some reason the law gets plumb doubled over at the death of a woman or an old person. We might have done wrong killing them. Even with Pa and the sheriff being good friends, this could get real stiff before it's over."

Ramon only stared at him for a moment, beginning to realize just how wild and bloodthirsty his brother was. "It was not we who killed them, Saul, it was *you!* Do you feel nothing at taking their lives? Does it not bother you in any way?"

"Damn it, Ramon! I just told you I might have done wrong! What do you want from me? We went to do a job, and we had to kill them. Not everything in life goes perfect, you know!" He eased down, took a deep breath to calm himself, then said, "The thing is, I've seen posses get so riled up they forget all about that border and ride right in here. So, just to be safe, we're going to lay up in the hideout for a while and cool off. There's a few others up there doing the same thing, wanted men who'll back us if something goes wrong. You never know when we might get—"

His words stopped short at the close sound of a horse nickering low in the dim morning light. His hand snapped to the pistol in his holster as his eyes cut through the darkness to the outlines of figures sitting atop their horses in a half circle around them. A deep voice said quietly, "Take your hand from the pistol, or you will both die hard." As if to state the seriousness of the man's words, six rifles levered almost as one, the metal on metal sounding harsh in the stillness of morning. "Who are you, and what are you doing in Bloody Horse Pass?" The voice had a trace of a French accent, and somehow hearing it caused Saul Delmano to sigh in relief.

"I'm Saul Delmano . . . this in my brother, Ramon. I'm guessing you men work for our pa, Lewis Delmano?"

"Stand down, men," the voice said to those surrounding the Delmano brothers, "These are his sons."

The sound of rifles uncocking brought a smile to Saul Delmano's face.

"Hear that, little brother? These boys work for us." Saul chuckled. He looked back at the ghostly looking figures in the grainy light. "Boys, you are a sight for troubled eyes," he continued. "I knew ole Daddy was getting some extra help, but I reckon he must've forgot to tell—"

The voice cut him off. "We do not work for the Delmanos. I am Henri LaBourge. We were sent here by an emissary of the *generalissimo* simply to do a small job. Then we leave. Let us be clear on that."

"Hey, that's good as gold, far as we're concerned, right, little brother?" He grinned at Ramon, who sat silent. Then he added, looking from one dark figure to the next, "We was just discussing whether or not to go hide out for a few days. Reckon there's no need in it now, eh boys?"

A silence passed, then the voice said, "Perhaps it is still best that you go there. I have more men out a half a mile or more, surrounding the place. Until I meet your father, it is best we all know who we are shooting at out here."

"You get no argument from me," said Saul Delmano. "We might stop by the house and grab something to drink. Then we'll be out of your hair until this is all over. Fair enough?"

"Fair enough," Henri LaBourge answered. "Ride quickly. If anyone stops you, tell them you have already met with me."

"You've got it all, mister," said Saul Delmano, collecting his horse beneath him and raising the ends of his reins to slap it forward. "I believe I could get used to this, having my killing done for me without me lifting a finger." He laughed aloud and batted his heels to his horse's sides. "Let's ride, little brother!"

"Two idiots," said Henri LaBourge as the Delmano brothers rode away. "This is the fool Raul Hernandez was asked to protect? It is incredible, is it not?" The men closed in together. A ripple of dark laughter rose and fell. "Come, men, back to your positions," he said.

Daylight had spread across the land by the time Ramon and Saul Delmano rode into the front yard of the hacienda. Buck Benton and Gus Latimer, two of Lewis Delmano's old outlaw partners, had heard the horses approaching at a gallop. They came running from the bunkhouse, both of them strapping their gunbelts around their waists. "Take it easy, it's only us," Saul Delmano called out to them, sounding less than respectful to the two older men as he skidded his horse down almost onto its haunches and swung down from his saddle.

"What's wrong, Saul?" asked Latimer, looking back along the trail. "Is somebody dogging you?"

Saul Delmano gave the two old men a smirk. "What would you do if there was?"

The two men caught the blunt of his sarcasm, but didn't respond.

"Leave them alone, Saul!" said Ramon, reining up his mount. He looked at the two old outlaws, saying in a friendlier manner, "There is no one dogging us. But there are men out there that our father has hired to keep watch for this Danny Duggin."

"Then we'll grab our rifles and go join them," said Buck Benton.

"No, wait," said Ramon. "These men are hired to

do the job. They asked that everyone stay back and let them do it."

Gus Latimer grumbled, "I don't see why . . . there's plenty of guns here. Nobody ever had to—"

"Because that's the way we're going to do it!" Saul Delmano shouted. "You old geezers stay the hell out of the way! Go cross-brand some stolen cattle! Leave the fighting for the ones who still know how!" He stepped close to Gus Latimer as if he were going to push the old man backward. But Ramon stepped quickly in between them.

"Let's go get what we're taking with us," Ramon said. "I will meet you back here as fast as I can."

Saul Delmano backed up a step and spread a knowing smile. "Don't bring nothing you can't tote in your saddlebags, little brother," he warned with a wink. "Those boys up at the hideout can turn randy real quick, if you get my meaning."

Ramon spun away and stomped off toward the front porch of the hacienda, where Greta stood watching through the partially open door. Gus Latimer and Buck Benton backed away from Saul Delmano, giving him a bitter look, and they both walked back to the bunkhouse. "Don't slow down on getting the branding done today, old-timers!" he called after them. "Somebody's got to tend the steers while us *men* take care of business." He stood watching them leave with a nasty look on his face. "Worthless old dogs."

"That rips it for me," Gus Latimer said to Buck Benton under his breath. "I don't care who shoots him . . . I just hope to hell somebody does."

"Something went wrong, I can tell!" Greta gasped,

seeing the look on Ramon's face as he stepped inside the hacienda, closing the door behind himself and leaning back against it. He took the first calm breath he'd drawn since leaving her the day before.

"Yes, things went very wrong. I have made a terrible mistake, thinking I could do something like this and walk away." He leaned forward from against the door and took her in his arms. "Greta, people have died! Two men and a woman. It is only a matter of time until their bodies are found."

"God, no!" Greta gasped again. "Ramon, you didn't . . . ?"

"No, I did not," he said. "But it makes no difference. I was there. I was a part of it. I am as guilty as my brother. If ever we are caught, we will both hang for it."

"What must we do now?" she asked, her eyes turning misty in fear and desperation.

Ramon held his hands on her shoulders. "I will leave the money with you, and I will ride up to the hideout with my brother. He is caught up in his own craziness right now, but I will wait until he settles down. Then I will come back for you and we will leave." He took out the stack of money and pressed it into her hands. "There are many dangerous things going on out there," he said, nodding toward the land beyond the window. "If I do not return by tomorrow night—"

"Don't talk like that, Ramon!" she said, cutting him off in a trembling voice. "If anything happens to you, I don't think I could go on living."

He shook her gently. "Listen to me. You must be strong. If I do not return, you must think of yourself and our baby. You must take this money and leave right away. Take the best horse in the stables and flee this place. My soul would find no rest, knowing that our child would grow up in this place, the same as I did."

"But where would I go?" Greta asked.

"Go far from here. Go to Fort Smith, in the territory. It is a town were there are many lawmen. My father will not follow you there."

"Fort Smith . . ." she said to herself, committing the name to memory. She looked back into his eyes. "But you will return, I know you will! I will pray for it!"

"Yes, I will return to you," said Ramon, seeing he had to give her some hope to cling to. "But you must be gone before my father comes back. If I come here and you are gone, I will meet you in Fort Smith. Do you understand?"

She collected herself and leveled her gaze. Summoning up her courage, she said, "Yes, don't worry, I will do as you say. Be careful, Ramon . . . God be with you."

El Paso, Texas. September 28, 1871

At daylight, Sheriff Lloyd Deweese and his two deputies stormed along the narrow hall above the saloon, room by room, kicking open doors and dragging blurry-eyed men out of their beds. Saloon girls screamed and cursed, grabbing whatever sheets or towels they could to throw around themselves. Once the men were downstairs, Sheriff Deweese stood in the middle of the floor with his palms resting on the pair of pistol butts sticking up from his high-riding holsters. Behind the bar, Ned Lynnly, the bartender, wiped a wet bar towel across his face and tried to wake himself up. At a table sat five men the deputies had herded in off the street. One of them was Tim Strange, who had just stepped down from his horse and hitched it to the rail out front when the deputies approached him. Tim kept quiet, watching the lawmen force the half-naked men down the stairs and line them up along the bar.

The men grumbled and staggered, looking at Sheriff Deweese as he started at one end of the line, speaking to the bartender as he went.

"All right, Ned, what about Freddie Coats?" the sheriff asked, looking the first man up and down.

"Freddie was here all day, Sheriff," the bartender replied. "Him and Norvel Yates too. You never see one without seeing the other."

Sheriff Deweese looked the next man up and down, saying, "Is that true, Norvel? You and your pard here spent the whole day drinking? Neither of yas was out on the east trail? Neither of yas was over at the old Spanish mission?"

Norvel Yates slung his stringy hair back out of his bloodshot eyes and said, "Me and Freddie at a church? Hell no, Sheriff Deweese!" He leaned forward an inch, keeping one steadying hand on the bar top. "We've been blind drunk ever since we hit town three days ago. You heard the barkeep, we was here all day, far as I remember."

"I needed to hear it from you," said Sheriff Deweese, shoving Norvel back against the bar. He stepped in front of Reggie Weil and asked, "What about you, Reggie? Have you and your pal Thurman here been out and around, stirring up trouble along the stage route?"

Before Reggie could gather himself enough to give an answer, Thurman Pratt cut in, saying, "Sheriff, you know damn well me and Reggie was here. If you can't take Ned's word, then why don't you just—"

His words were cut short in a puff of breath as Sheriff Deweese slammed a hard right into his naked stomach, lifting him up onto his toes. "Now everybody listen up!" said the sheriff, turning to the others while Thurman Pratt struggled to catch his breath, both arms thrown across his stomach. "I don't want to repeat one damn word I say here." He turned back to Thurman Pratt. "Was you and Reggie out on the east road yesterday at any time?"

"No," Thurman Pratt replied in a strained wheeze, "we wasn't, sheriff. We . . . spent the whole day here."

"That's good," said Sheriff Deweese, patting a hand on Thurman's shoulder. "Now who were the two boys I heard you was drinking with last night?"

"Sheriff, you knew who they was," Thurman rasped.

"All the same, you best tell me, Thurman Pratt," said Sheriff Deweese, "else I'll keep cracking you in the ribs till you do." He drew back a fist.

"All right, Sheriff," Thurman Pratt said, raising a hand in a show of submission, "it was the Delmano brothers, Saul and Ramon."

Hearing the name Saul Delmano, Tim Strange felt his pulse quicken. But he sat still, listening closely.

"So, you remembered the Delmano brothers being here," said the sheriff. He turned his eyes to Reggie

Weil. "I reckon you remember it too, don't you Reggie, even as blind drunk as you was?"

Reggie nodded, saying, "I do remember them being here, Sheriff, that's a fact. We drank with 'em most of the day."

Sheriff Deweese turned his gaze to Ned Lynnly behind the bar and asked, "Does that sound about right, Ned?"

"I remember them being here, Sheriff," Ned Lynnly replied.

"All day?" asked Deweese.

"I can't say, Sheriff," said the bartender. "It got awfully busy in here."

"They was here all day, for sure, Sheriff," Thurman Pratt lied, his stomach settling now. "They only left for a few minutes is all, just long enough to go to the jake and get their horses from out front of Mama Rosa's. Saul Delmano has enough trouble as it is right now ... he wasn't looking for more."

"Yeah, I know all about his trouble," said Deweese. "I heard there's a gunman dogging him. I heard all about the bounty, too." Sheriff Deweese looked around at the other men along the bar, and the ones seated at the table. "I'm going to tell every one of you. There better not be any gunplay in my town over that bounty money. I won't stand for it. If you boys want to collect some money for killing, there's plenty of *legal* bounty on Saul Delmano. Anything that ain't legal, you best leave it alone. Does everybody hear me good and plain?"

Some of the men nodded. Thurman Pratt cut in, saying, "Then why didn't you come get Saul last night, Sheriff, if you heard he was here?"

Sheriff Deweese glared at him. "Am I going have to hit you again, Thurman?"

"No, Sheriff," said Thurman, "but the fact is, we all know you and old man Delmano have something worked out between yourselves. Saul Delmano was here if you wanted him."

Sheriff Deweese let it pass. "Boys, Saul Delmano is not wanted for breaking any law in my jurisdiction, or anywhere in Texas for that matter. Leastwise not yet anyway." He looked back at Thurman Pratt. "I'm giving you boys ten minutes to get your clothes on and get out of town. I see you here after that, there'll be trouble between us."

"What's this about, Sheriff?" Thurman Pratt asked.

"What's it about?" the sheriff said, turning his level gaze to each man in turn as he spoke. "I'll tell you what this is about. Yesterday the stagecoach was hit out on the east trail. The driver and passengers were killed—one of them was a poor young woman. She was even robbed of her purse!" He had to keep his anger in check as he spoke. "I found that purse this morning on the way back. Found it beside the bodies of Kid Jeffrey and Joe Tully, two men who work for Lewis Delmano." His gaze went right back to Thurman Pratt. "But of course working for the Delmanos doesn't mean his sons were involved, does it, Thurman?" He speared a thin, knowing smile. "I mean, knowing they was both here drinking with you all day?"

Thurman Pratt winced. "A young woman was killed?"

"Yep," said the sheriff, studying the look in Thurman's red-rimmed eyes. "Are you still sure the Delmano brothers was with you all day?"

Thurman swallowed as if something was caught in his throat. He glanced at Reggie Weil, then back to the sheriff, saying, "Well, it seemed like they were."

"It seemed like?" Sheriff Deweese asked, stepping in closer with a deep piercing stare. "You just said they was *for sure*. Now, you're saying it *seemed like* they were? Do you need to talk to me in private, Thurman?"

Thurman shot a nervous glance around at the others, then shook his head, saying, "No, Sheriff, I told you all I can."

"All right then," said Sheriff Deweese to the four men along the bar, "you four men get dressed and get moving. My watch is already ticking."

Thurman Pratt, Reggie Weil, Norvel Yates, and Freddie Coats filed away from the bar and back up the stairs, the two deputies close behind them. Sheriff Deweese stepped over to the table and looked down at the first of the five men sitting there. "Stanley Bush?" he said out loud, as if surprised to see the man cowering there at the table. Deweese turned to the third deputy who stood guarding the men with a shotgun. "Hell, Wayne," he said to the deputy, "Stanley ain't got enough sense to find the east road, let along a stagecoach." He nodded toward the door, saying, "Get out of here, Stanley, before I arrest you for being stupid." Stanley Bush scurried up from the table and out the door.

The new deputy, Wayne Connick, looked embarrassed. "You said round up everybody out front, so I did."

"I understand," said Deweese, looking down at the next man, a quiet stranger with a flat-brim Stetson sitting low on his forehead. "What about you, mister?" Deweese asked, looking the stranger up and down.

"What about me?" the stranger replied, not giving an inch.

"What's your name? What are you doing here in El Paso?" Deweese asked.

"My name's Jack Smith, but you can call me *Mister* Smith. I'm here to meet a friend. I don't rob stage-coaches, I don't steal purses . . . and I don't answer a hell of a lot questions." He gave the sheriff a flat, level stare. A pistol butt shone at the edge of his black linen coat, close to his right hand. "I was on my way to breakfast when this deputy showed up. I only came in here out of courtesy. I spent yesterday and last night playing cards with two town councilmen and a Texas judge. Go ask them if you feel like it."

"Sheriff, I already asked one of the councilmen on the way in here," Wayne Connick said, cutting in. "It's true that's where he was all right."

The sheriff looked taken aback for a second. He said to the deputy, "Then what the hell is this man doing in here, Wayne?" Deweese glanced at the pistols still strapped on the remaining four men at the table. "And why are these men still armed?"

Wayne Connick squirmed in place, his face turning red in embarrassment. "I asked Smith here for his gun. He wouldn't give it to me. I reckon these others just followed suit."

Sheriff Deweese looked stunned. "Damn it, Wayne! I know you're new, but don't ever do something like this again!"

Smith stood up slowly, adjusted his hat, and said, "I'll be leaving now, Sheriff, unless you have another question."

"Get out, *Mister* Smith," Deweese snapped.

But the stranger stopped for a second and pointed down at Tim Strange. "One thing before I go, Sheriff," he said. "That man ain't one of the ones you're looking for either."

"Oh? And what makes you say that?" asked Deweese.

"Because your deputy checked his horse's shoes before we came in. They're worn thin. The deputy said the tracks you found were made by new shoes, hardly worn."

Tim Strange sat watching in silence.

"Just thought I'd mention that to you, Sheriff," said Smith, turning, walking out the door.

Sheriff Deweese turned his attention to Tim Strange, noting the Colt on his hip. "All right, young man, what's your story?"

"I've got no story, Sheriff," said Tim. "I'm here looking for my brother. He's supposed to meet me here today." Tim guarded his words, cutting a quick glance at the two remaining men at the table.

"What's you name?" Deweese asked, getting a bit testy with his job.

"Tim Coffax," said Tim, picking the first name that came to his mind. My brother's name is Jed Coffax. I got here late last night. I don't know nothing about any stagecoach robbery."

"Yeah?" Sheriff Deweese looked him up and down. "I don't suppose you know anything about a bounty on a gunman who's supposed to be coming this way either?"

"I heard about it, Sheriff," Tim admitted. "Everybody from here to Kansas has heard about it. But I'm not here for it. If I was, I wouldn't be sitting here on my rump. I'd be out there collecting it." He stared up at Deweese and said, "Can I go now?"

Sheriff Deweese didn't answer. Instead, he turned to the other two men, saying, "Dee Philpot and Early Brown. Don't even try to tell me you two ain't here looking to collect that bounty."

Dee Philpot, a young gunman with a surly smile, said, "We ain't denying it, Sheriff. Killing for bounty money is what we do. We'll keep it outside of your town. But that's all we can promise."

"That's right," said Early Brown, a heavy young man missing his right ear. "We ain't innocent lambs, Sheriff, but don't try to tell us you didn't chop off a head or two for bounty before you pinned on a badge."

"Get out, all three of you!" yelled Deweese, jerking a thumb toward the door. "Get out of my town and stay out! If you're smart you'll get out of this part of the country. From what I've heard, this Danny Duggin ain't going to be an easy day's work."

"We'll see, Sheriff," said Dee Philpot, standing up along with Tim Strange and Early Brown.

Sheriff Deweese and Deputy Wayne Connick stood in the middle of the saloon floor and watched the three men leave. Behind the bar, Ned the bartender cleared his throat and said in a sarcastic tone of voice, "Are we all through, Sheriff, or is there a few more paying customers you'd like to chase away from here?"

Sheriff Deweese spun to face him, his anger screwing up his reddening face. "Don't give me a hard time doing my job, Ned. I'll board this place up and have the town condemn it! I believe the Delmanos had something to do with that stagecoach robbery. And I believe you and Thurman Pratt are lying for them!"

"Hold it, Sheriff," said Ned Lynnly. "I told you I was too busy to pay attention to everybody's comings and goings yesterday. If you want to know more about the Delmanos, go ask their father. You and him are always on good speaking terms from what I hear."

Just outside the saloon doors, Tim Strange heard what the bartender said, but he didn't let on. He felt the eyes of Early Brown and Dee Philpot on him as he stepped down to his horse at the hitch rail. He took his time unhitching his horse. Tim knew they wanted to say something. He wanted to give them the opportunity.

"Hey, you, Coffax, hold up a minute," said Early Brown as he and Dee Philpot stepped over to the hitch rail, keeping a few feet distance between themselves and Tim Strange. "What's your hurry?"

Tim turned just enough to acknowledge them with a trace of a flat smile. "You heard the sheriff," he said. "I wouldn't want to get myself in any trouble with the law." His nervous tone of voice implied that getting in trouble with the law would be a new experience for him.

Early Brown and Dee Philpot shared a short laugh. "Right," said Dee Philpot, "that's our thoughts, too." He and Early Brown looked at one another, then

Philpot continued. "What you told the sheriff in there about not being here for the bounty? I'm betting my pard here that it wasn't quite true was it?" He spread a knowing grin.

"I hope you boys aren't calling me a liar," said Tim calmly. He looked them up and down, taking his time adjusting his saddle.

"Naw, it's nothing like that," said Dee Philpot, back-stepping the tone of his voice a little, keeping it friendly. "We're looking for this Danny Duggin . . . thought a three-way split might be worth making if a man knew something about Duggin that we don't."

Tim Strange took a deep breath and let it out, shaking his head slowly. "Fellows, why would I want to split a bounty with anybody, if I *really* was after Danny Duggin? I doubt either of you even know what he looks like, do you?"

"Well, no," said Early Brown. "Do you?"

"Yep," said Tim. "I've seen him more than a few times in Kansas."

Early Brown looked interested. "Really now? All we know is that he's young, rides a chestnut mare, and carries a brace of Colt pistols."

"So what?" Tim said. "Look at me. I'm young. I wear two pistols, *one* of them is a Colt. I don't ride a chestnut mare, but I might have changed horses along the trail. For all you know, I could be Danny Duggin."

Early Brown looked puzzled for a second, then said, "You're not, are you?"

"No. If I was, I expect you'd both be dead by now," Tim said. He turned back as if to step into his saddle. "Sorry, boys, but I don't need any partners. All I need to know is where to take this Duggin's head once I kill him."

"That's easy enough," said Dee Philpot. "We know how to get to the Delmano spread. We'd gladly show you if we was in on this together."

Tim stopped, appearing to give it some thought. Then he nodded at the doors of the saloon. "What about that Thurman Pratt and his partner? I figure if they're friends of the Delmanos they'll be after Duggin, too. There's only so many ways to split two thousand dollars before it turns into nothing more than pocket change."

Early Brown and Dee Philpot stepped in closer. Dee Philpot lowered his voice and said, "See? That's the thing about this bounty. Everybody in this part of the country is out to collect it. We figured we could catch Thurman and Reggie off to themselves and do away with part of the competition, so to speak."

"You might have something there," said Tim. "How do you know which way they'll be headed when they leave here?"

"They get on across the border," said Dee Philpot. "They'll be easy to take care of. What do you think? Have we got ourselves a deal?"

Tim looked back and forth between the two of them, knowing that whatever deal he struck with these men would be worthless. If there was a bounty to be collected, they would shoot him in the back as soon as they were through with him. "Why not," he said finally. "It would be better splitting something with you two than being cut out altogether by this Thurman Pratt and his pal." Tim stepped up into his saddle. "Come on, let's go somewhere and talk about it."

"We're right behind you," said Dee Philpot. He and Early Brown smiled at one another and reached for their horses' reins.

Chapter 15

Jed Strange had just boarded the chestnut mare at the livery barn and led his own horse out to the street when he saw the deputy round up Tim along with some other men out front of the saloon. Their intentions had been to keep a distance between themselves and work their way around town, finding out what they could about the Delmanos, and about how many men were out to collect the bounty money. But as soon as he'd seen his brother walk into the saloon under the cover of a shotgun, Jed had backed inside the livery barn and stood watching through a crack in the door.

He'd stood tense for a few minutes and breathed a sigh of relief when he'd seen the first man come out and hurry away. He'd breathed even easier when another walked out, stepped into his saddle, and rode away. Now, seeing Tim and the two other men ride their horses at a walk along the street, Jed stepped out of the door to let his brother get a look at him and hopefully give him some sign of what was going on.

As Tim and the two men came past him, Jed lowered his hat brim slightly and saw his brother nod ever so slightly toward the road leading out of town.

Jed got the message. He moved back inside the barn, waiting until the three riders were past him and on the road toward the border. Then he went back to the hitch rail, swung up into his saddle, and heeled the horse forward.

Outside of the town limits, Tim Strange, Dee Philpot, and Early Brown swung off the road, found an old path leading to the shallows of the Rio Grande, and stepped their horses down into the river. As soon as they had stepped up on the Mexico side of the river and moved away through some brush, Jed Strange nudged his horse forward, down into the river, following them. When his horse stepped out on the other side of the bank, dripping water, Jed nudged it forward, but stayed to the left of Tim and the others' hoofprints, keeping in the brush and hidden from sight. From his position, Jed could also look back on the Rio Grande, where he soon saw Thurman Pratt and Reggie Weil slip down into the shallows and come across. "Lord, Tim, what have you gotten us into now?" he asked himself in a whispered breath. Before the two men stepped their horses up onto the low banks, Jed had heeled his horse away, staying wide of the fresh hoofprints in front of him.

Two miles farther up the trail, Tim, Dee Philpot, and Early Brown had taken cover behind a low shelf of rock. Tim sipped water from his canteen and listened as Dee Philpot spoke to him. Early Brown slipped a rifle from his saddle boot and moved in a crouch to the edge of the rock. "Don't worry, pard, Early will spot them as soon as they make the bend in the trail," said Dee Philpot.

"Do I look worried?" Tim replied. "I can't say I

cotton much to ambushing, though. I always figured
a man who'll ambush another will someday ambush
me if I ain't careful."

It seemed to take a moment for his words to sink
in as Dee Philpot stood staring blank faced. But finally Dee got it and laughed, tapping a finger to his
forehead. "I see what you mean, Coffax. But you don't
have to worry about me and Early double-crossing
you."

"Like I said," Tim repeated, "do I *look* worried?"
He gazed off along the trail into Mexico and said,
"How far is it to the Delmano spread?"

"It's a day's ride, straight ahead," said Dee Philpot.

Tim smiled, saying, "If it's straight ahead why do
I need you and Early to show me?"

"Because there's more to it than just finding the
Delmano spread. Most time you have to get past the
spread and up into the rock country. The Delmanos
keep a hideout up there. You could search for days
and never find it on your own. Early and I spent the
winter up there a couple of years ago, laying low after
killing a Mexican land baron. Once you're there you
can see anybody coming at you for miles below."

"I see," said Tim. He turned his eyes back to Early
Brown as he continued speaking to Dee Philpot. Did
you ever hear why Danny Duggin is hunting Saul
Delmano?"

"Not really," said Philpot. "It had something to do
with Saul and some friends of his killing this Duggin's father is what I heard. But it doesn't matter none.
Alls I know is there is two thousand dollars in it for
us." He grinned. "Everybody's daddy dies sooner or
later I reckon."

"Yeah," said Tim, barely able to keep his anger from showing on his face, "I reckon so."

"Here they come!" Early Brown said in a lowered voice, sounding excited at the prospect of killing men from behind his cover of rock. "You best get ready, boys!"

Dee Philpot snatched his rifle from his saddle boot and hurried over in a crouch, slipping down beside Early Brown and saying over his shoulder to Tim, "Come on, Coffax. This ought to be good practice for when we get to Danny Duggin!"

"Yep," said Tim, walking over to the edge without so much as bending down as Thurman Pratt and Reggie Weil rode around the turn in the trail.

"Damn it, Coffax!" Dee Philpot hissed. "Get down here before they see you!"

But Tim only stood staring at the two riders, his hand resting on the pistol at his hip. "Thurman Pratt," he called out loudly.

"Jesus! What's he doing?" Early Brown bellowed.

"Damned if I know!" Dee Philpot tried to swing his rifle barrel up toward Tim, but seeing him make the move, Tim clamped a boot down on it, pinning it to the rock shelf. At the same time Tim drew and cocked his Colt, pointing it down at both Philpot and Brown. On the road, Thurman Pratt and Reggie Weil reined their horses to a sudden halt at the sound of Tim's voice. They looked up at him standing seven feet above them, twenty feet ahead, the cocked pistols in his hands.

"Who is it? The hell do you want?" Thurman Pratt called out, his hand going to the revolver on his hip.

"I'm Coffax," Tim called out. "I was in the saloon

when the sheriff busted you in the gut. There's a couple of boys here wanting to ambush you. I thought I'd put you all in the same circle and see which ones fall out."

"Coffax, you fool!" Dee Philpot said in a harsh growl. "We're supposed to be partners! Damn you!"

"Oh?" said Thurman Pratt. "And who might that be?" As he spoke, he and Reggie Weil stepped slowly down from their horses, dropping their reins to the ground.

"Dee Philpot and Early Brown," said Tim. "They've been waiting here to shoot you out of your saddles when you came around the turn. Are you ready to face off with them?"

"You're mighty damn right we are!" shouted Thurman Pratt. "We was friends once. Rode together! Hell, Dee still owes me seven dollars from two years ago, and I never hounded him for it! Come on out here, Dee, you sneaking son of a bitch!"

Tim stepped back, keeping his pistol pointed down at Philpot and Brown. "Come on up, *partners*," he said. "Here's you a chance to prove what kind of gunmen you are."

"You've lost your mind, Coffax." Dee Philpot hissed, standing up, unable to lift his rifle with Tim's boot standing on it. "When this is over, you better hope to God I don't come up here and—"

"Shut your mouth," Tim snapped, cutting him off. "Get on down there. Don't keep these men waiting."

"What's your interest in this, Coffax?" Thurman Pratt called out to Tim, watching Philpot and Brown pick their way down from the rock shelf to the middle of the dusty road.

"I just don't like back-shooters and bushwhackers," said Tim, keeping his pistol pointed at the two men, watching them stop twenty feet from Thurman Pratt and Reggie Weil and plant their feet a shoulder's width apart.

"Why was you boys doing this, Dee?" Thurman asked, already opening and closing his fingers to loosen them up. "I never treated either one of you any way but right."

"It's for that bounty money, Thurman," said Dee Philpot. He shot a sidelong glance up at Tim, then settled himself toward Thurman and Reggie. "We might just as well get on with it. Soon as we kill you both, me and Early is going to have to kill this jack-potting peckerwood, too."

"Don't count us dead yet!" Reggie Weil shouted, his hand going for his pistol.

"Wait, Reggie!" shouted Thurman Pratt. But it was too late. Reggie Weil's move brought the tension to a head. Dee Philpot's pistol came up from his holster, cocked and firing. Beside him, Early Brown did the same. Both of their first shots went toward Thurman, whose draw was slower than Reggie Weil's, but whose aim was known to be more deadly. Reggie Weil fired repeatedly, his shots whistling past Philpot and Brown like mad hornets, the two men flinching at the sound, yet still firing.

A shot hit Thurman Pratt in the chest, driving him back a staggering step, but not taking him off his feet. He struggled, getting a good bead on Early Brown, his shot punching through Brown's right shoulder and exiting in a long ribbon of blood. Early Brown flew backward, getting off another shot that caught Thurman Pratt in the leg, making him drop to his knees as he returned fire.

"Son of a—!" Reggie Weil screamed, his words cutting short, feeling two bullets hit him at almost the same time. His pistol exploded twice, one shot clipping Dee Philpot's hat from his head, the other shot nailing Early Brown as Brown struggled back to his feet, still firing, staggering sidelong as blood sprayed upward from his collarbone.

Dee Philpot managed to get off two more shots, both of them hitting Thurman Pratt in his chest. This time Thurman was done for. He twisted back and forth as he sank from his knees to the ground, his gun going off one last time, the shot going wild as his face hit the dirt. On his knees beside his fallen partner, Reggie Weil fired until his hammer fell on an empty chamber. He tried punching out his spent rounds to reload. Twenty feet away, Dee Philpot did the same, seeing Early Brown stagger back and forth, his pistol hanging limp in his hand.

Before Reggie Weil could snap the cylinder shut on his reloaded pistol, Dee Philpot had reloaded and cocked his Colt and stalked forward with it out at arm's length, pointing at Reggie's face.

Reggie screamed, "You rotten bastard, I never dreamed it was you who'd kill me!"

The shot from Dee Philpot's pistol kicked him backward into the dirt like a limp bundle of rags. Philpot stopped and turned, looking back at Early Brown, then up to the edge of the rock shelf, where he saw no sign of Tim. "Come on, Early! We're going to kill that peckerwood!"

Early Brown shook himself out like a horse, blood

streaming from his wounds. "Look at me, Dee! Look what he caused here!" Brown cried out. He staggered as he ran toward the path leading upward.

"Don't let him get away, Early!" Dee Philpot yelled, scrambling upward over stones and loose sand and gravel.

At the top of the rock shelf, they looked toward the horses, their pistols still cocked and ready. "It's two agin one, Early. Let's find him!"

"Over here, boys," said Tim in a quiet voice.

They spun to their right, seeing Tim with his Colt holstered, his hand poised near the handle. But before they could fire, another voice called out from their left. "No, over here!" said Jed Strange. They spun in Jed's direction, seeing the rifle in his hands.

Dee Philpot felt cold fear run through him, seeing these two men were ready and determined, and had caught them completely off guard. "Who are you people?" Dee Philpot demanded. "What's this all about?" His eyes went to Jed Strange, seeing the resemblance. "Are you Danny Duggin? Is that it? You're Duggin and you two are brothers?" His eyes flashed back and forth. Beside him, Early Brown stood frozen in place, waiting for Philpot to make the first move.

"We're neither one Danny Duggin," said Tim Strange. "But we're kin of hers."

"Kin of *hers?* What the hell are you talking about, *hers?*" Philpot shouted.

"That's right, Philpot," said Tim. "Danny Duggin is our sister."

Philpot looked baffled, but only for a second. Rage took over as he swung his pistol toward Tim Strange. "Why you crazy damn fool!" he screamed.

Three shots rang out, two from Tim's Colt, and one from Jed's rifle. In the silence that followed, Tim stepped forward and looked down at Dee Philpot's wide-open eyes beneath the bullet hole in his forehead. He cut his gaze to the bodies of Thurman Pratt and Reggie Weil lying down below them in the middle of the road. Opening his pistol and dropping out the spent cartridges, he said to Jed, "Four down . . . but how many more to go?"

"That's anybody's guess, brother," said Jed. "Come on. Let's get them bodies out of the road and get moving."

It was almost noon when Danielle walked out of the livery barn, leading the chestnut mare behind her. She walked the mare over to where C. F. McCord and Hector Sabio stood watering the horses at a trough. "They've been here," Danielle said, patting Sundown's muzzle. "The hostler said a young man named Jed paid for a week's board in advance. Said if his brother Danny showed up to let him take the mare with him."

C. F. McCord ran his sweaty bandanna across his forehead beneath his hat brim. "When was this?" he asked.

"This morning, not long after sunup," said Danielle. "He also told me there's been a stage robbery and two killings. The sheriff had questioned some men in the saloon this morning."

McCord poured himself a mouthful of water from his canteen, swished it around, and spat it out. "Saul Delmano," he said, wiping a hand across his mouth. "I'd bet on it."

Danielle reached beneath the belly of the horse she'd been riding. She loosened its saddle, taking it off as the horse drank from the water trough. She turned and laid the saddle atop Sundown and cinched it tight. Then she pulled the drinking horse's muzzle up from the trough, unfastened the bridle, and slipped the bit from its mouth. The horse slung its head and stuck its muzzle back down into the water.

"What are you doing?" McCord asked, watching her slip the bit into Sundown's mouth and string the bridle up behind the mare's ears.

"What does it look like I'm doing?" Danielle said. "I'm getting this gal ready for the road."

"But everybody who's out to collect that bounty knows that Danny Duggin rides a chestnut mare," McCord said.

"*Sí*," said Hector Sabio, "you are asking for trouble, Danny. This is not a good idea."

"Good idea or not, I'm riding her," said Danielle. "If we're in the Delmanos' stomping ground, why not let everybody know I'm here? They're out to kill me . . . I'm out to kill Saul Delmano. I've got nothing to hide."

C. F. McCord had trouble with it for a second, but then, thinking it over, he tossed Hector a quick glance and saw the worried look on his face. Then he said to Danielle, "You're right . . . why not?" He lifted his horse's muzzle from the water trough and retightened its cinch. "Let's go to the sheriff's office and see what he can tell us about the stage robbery or Saul Delmano."

"Why?" asked Danielle. "It's got nothing to do with what we're here for."

"Call it my courtesy call as a lawman," said Mc-Cord. "I still wear a badge, you know. He might also be able to tell us something about your brothers. Let's find out what we can before we move on."

"I don't know, *amigos*," said Hector Sabio. He looked greatly concerned, rubbing his chin. "I think we should go on and get into Mexico. I know this sheriff. I don't think he likes me so much."

"Is there any charge against you, Hector?" McCord asked.

"No, it is nothing like that," Hector replied.

"Then don't worry," said McCord. "You're with me now, Hector. Unless he has an outstanding charge against you, you're in good hands."

"Even so," Hector said with great reluctance, "I think it is best that I stay here and take care of the horses."

"All right then," said McCord, "you stay here and watch the horses. We won't be long." McCord turned to Danielle and together they walked along the dirt street toward the sheriff's office.

Glancing back over her shoulder, Danielle said to McCord, "I hope you're not trusting him too much, Marshal. Don't forget, he didn't exactly come into this thing with clean hands."

McCord offered a thin smile, staring straight ahead. "You have to learn to have more faith in people."

"Maybe," said Danielle, "but so far it's been my *lack* of faith in outlaws like Hector that's kept me alive."

McCord shook his head, still wearing the same thin smile. "Why, Danny, what a terrible thing to say."

Hector Sabio watched Danielle and C. F. McCord

walk away until they both stepped inside the door to the sheriff's office. "Aw, *amigos*," he whispered to himself, "you do not know how *big* two thousand dollars is to a man such as me." He rubbed his palm back and forth on the butt of the pistol shoved down in his waist belt. "But forgive me," he added under his breath, making a quick sign of the cross on his chest as his eyes darted to heaven. "I must not think such things." He leaned back against the hitch rail and let out a long breath.

Chapter 16

Riding into town, Al Tarksel was the first to spot Hector Sabio. As soon as he saw Hector, Tarksel grabbed the reins to Bob Dennard's horse and jerked them sideways, leading them out of the street and into an alley before Hector had a chance to see them. "What's going on?" Dennard said, wrestling for control of his horse. "Have you gone mad?" Dennard's hand had just dropped to his pistol butt when Al Tarksel let go of his reins and spoke in excitement.

"There's that snake, Hector!" said Tarksel. "Up by the livery barn! I saw him!"

Bob Dennard eased down, moving his hand away from his pistol. He slipped down from his horse and pitched Al Tarksel his reins. "Wait here," he said, "I'll make sure." He inched out of the alley past the edge of the boardwalk and peeped around a post toward the livery barn. Then he stepped back inside the alley, looking back and forth along the dirt street. "You're right, it's him. Danny Duggin must be close at hand."

"All right then," said Tarksel, slipping down from his saddle, "I say we gun Duggin down right here in the street, then grab his body and make a run for it." Tarksel fell silent, then added, "But damn it! What about The Fox?"

Dennard looked at him. "Settle down, Tarksel, you're getting too anxious."

"Anxious hell!" Tarksel growled. "If we wait until Duggin gets to the Delmanos', there'll be no bounty . . . they'll kill him themselves and save two thousand dollars. We've got to make our move!"

"Of course we have to," Dennard agreed. He nodded toward the livery barn. "But the Mexican is holding their horses. So wherever Duggin is, he'll have to go back there to get his horse. We're not going to start blazing away in the middle of the street! We'll wait until Duggin gets inside the livery barn, kill him nice and quiet-like, then get out of town."

"What about The Fox?" asked Al Tarksel.

"McCord will have to die, too," said Dennard.

"That might not be so easy to get away with," said Tarksel.

"Have you got any better idea?" Dennard asked, getting impatient.

Tarksel winced, trying to think of one. "Damn, I reckon not."

"Then don't argue with me." Dennard hissed. "Come on, bring the horses."

"All right, but I have some serious misgivings about killing a lawman right here in town," Tarksel grumbled. He snatched the reins to both horses and followed Dennard back to end of the alley, which led to the rear of the livery barn.

Inside the sheriff's office, C. F. McCord and Danielle poured a cup of coffee and spoke to the new deputy, Wayne Connick, who sat behind Sheriff Deweese's big desk with both hands firmly clutching the chair arms.

The deputy was plainly nervous after McCord had introduced both himself and Danny Duggin to him. "Heck, Fox—I mean, Marshal McCord, it could be all day before the sheriff gets back. He left me here because I'm the newest man he's got. I'd tell you whatever I could, except I just don't *know* much." He nodded at Danielle. "I do know that Mr. Duggin here better watch himself. All we've heard the past week is how every gunman and two-bit outlaw around is planning on collecting that bounty money."

Danielle shrugged it off. "What about this young fellow you told us about, this Tim Coffax?" she asked, already certain it was her brother.

"What about him?" Wayne Connick asked. "I took him in the saloon, Sheriff Deweese questioned him, and then he let him go. He didn't seem to be interested in the bounty money . . . but then he did leave town with a couple of back-stabbing rascals named Early Brown and Dee Philpot. Is that any help to you?"

"Yep, quite a bit," Danielle said, sipping her coffee. "Which way did they head out?"

"I heard the three of them headed for the border," said the deputy. "I hope he's not hooked up with those two. They're both killers."

"He's not. That boy is one of my brothers. You did the right thing letting him go. I've got two brothers . . . neither one of them had anything to do with a stage robbery, I can promise you that much."

Leaning against the hitch rail, Hector Sabio gave no thought to the sound of the livery barn door creaking open behind him. The street out front of the livery barn was empty except for a skinny spotted dog that stood with its nose to the hard ground. No one saw Al Tarksel slip up quietly behind Hector, throw a big arm around his neck, and drag him backward into the barn. Hector tried to let out a yell, but Tarksel's forearm cut off his air. "I'll just take that pistol, you rotten little worm!" Tarksel slammed Hector against a barn pole and snatched the gun from his waist.

Hector caught a quick breath and started to lunge forward with his bare hands toward Al Tarksel's throat. But the cold bite of Bob Dennard's pistol cocking against Hector's temple stopped him and kept him frozen in place. "Make a decision fast, Mex," Dennard growled in Hector's ear. "Either help us kill Danny Duggin or die alongside him."

Hector stalled, saying, "What are you talking about? I am not out to kill Danny Duggin for the bounty money! He has become my friend! I would not betray an *amigo!*"

"You lying weasel!" said Tarksel. "I know you, and I know how you think! You've been after that bounty money all along!" Tarksel grabbed Hector by his hair and banged his head against the pole. "Let me kill him, Dennard!" Tarksel sneered. "We don't need this little rat to lure them in here."

Dennard looked deep into Hector's eyes and said to Tarksel with a nasty grin, "Be my guest, Al. But take him back there somewhere and do it. Let's keep things quiet in here." He lowered the pistol from Hector's temple and walked to the front door, peeping out through a crack between the planks.

Al Tarksel slung the much smaller Hector Sabio toward the back of the barn. As Hector sprawled on the floor, Tarksel sprang forward beside him and kicked him in the ribs, raising Hector a foot off the dirt floor, leaving him gagging and choking for air. "We can keep it quiet all right, *Hec—tor!* But I owe you something fierce for that beating I took in Dodge. Your last minutes are going to be the worst you ever had!" He snatched Hector up from the floor and backhanded him back and forth into an empty stall.

At the front of the barn, Bob Dennard looked around and called out in a harsh whisper, "Here they come! Hurry up and finish him off."

Al Tarksel held Hector up by the front of his shirt with one hand. Hector struggled to keep his head from swaying limply. "*Sí,*" he said, managing to straighten himself and spread a battered crooked smile, "finish me off, you big tough *pig* of a man!" He spit a spray of blood into Al Tarksel's face. "Break my neck with your *cerdo* hands!"

Tarksel snatched his pistol from his holster, cocked it, and jammed it into Hector's belly, wiping blood from his face with his free shirt cuff. "Uh-uh, Hec—tor," Tarksel said in a taunting voice. "You ain't getting off that easy."

"Take that blasted gun out of his belly and kill him quietly, damn it!" Bob Dennard hissed from the front door.

"No, Bob, I'm keeping him alive till this is over. I want to take my time on this little border trash!"

"Shut up then!" Dennard hissed. "They're almost here! Get ready!"

Hector looked down at the cocked pistol jammed against his stomach and shook his bloody head. "You are such a stupid man, Al Tarksel," he whispered. "I will never allow you to kill me." Then before Al Tarksel could stop him, Hector reached down, grabbed the pistol with both hands and forced Tarksel's finger to pull the trigger. The explosion lifted Hector off the ground, then he slumped against Al Tarksel with smoke and fire rising from the open wound in the back of his shirt.

Tarksel shrieked, "This crazy son of a bitch!" jumping back from the torrent of Hector Sabio's blood as he hit the floor. Somehow, Hector was still alive and managed to start crawling toward the rear door.

"Damn you to hell!" Bob Dennard shouted at Tarksel. Seeing the element of surprise was now gone, Dennard swung the door open and sprang forward with his pistol blazing.

The warning shot that Hector Sabio had caused was all the time C. F. McCord and Danielle needed to get ready. Bob Dennard ran headlong into four shots that exploded almost as one, spinning him in place, then hammering him back inside the barn doors. As Dennard spun off a barn pole, his pistol exploded wildly in his hand. The shot hit Al Tarksel as tried to lift the latch on the rear door and make a run for it. Tarksel staggered backward and slumped down by the open stall door, where he'd left Hector Sabio lying in the dirt and straw. Outside, C. F. McCord called out, "Drop your guns and step out here with your hands raised high!"

By the time Hector Sabio had dragged his shattered body across the stall and halfway out the open gate, Al Tarksel was flat on his back, a hand pressed to the gaping exit wound in his lower stomach. He heard Hector's weak gurgling breath and turned sideways on the dirt to face him. Only inches of dirt and straw lay between them.

"This is your last chance in there!" C. F. McCord called out again.

"What . . . are you . . . grinning about?" Al Tarksel asked, his words getting hard to come by.

Hector Sabio could not answer past the thick, dark blood in his mouth, nor did he even try to. With all of his effort, he reached out and clasped both bloody hands around Tarksel's pistol lying on the dirt between them. The back of Hector's bloody shirt still smoldered in a widening circle around the gaping bullet hole.

"If you don't come out, we're coming in," C. F. McCord yelled into the barn. He and Danielle moved up closer, Danielle taking position with her back flat against the barn, her pistol raised, ready to swing around into the open door and fire.

Al Tarksel choked and said in a halting voice to Hector Sabio, "I reckon . . . you really . . . won't . . ."

Hector managed a weak nod, crawling up onto Al Tarksel's large body like a dark spirit until he lay full atop him. With the hammer cocked, Hector raised up the pistol and pointed it at Tarksel, letting all of his weight press down on it. The tip of the barrel was rooted down on Tarksel's heart as he pulled the trigger.

"Hector? Are you in there?" Danielle said into the darkness of the barn as she stepped inside with McCord. "Speak to us, Hector. We heard the shot."

McCord stepped over to Bob Dennard's body and nudged it with his boot. Danielle made out the two shapes on the floor out front of the rear stall and quickened her steps. She heard a moan as she reached down atop Al Tarksel and rolled Hector off him. Hector Sabio looked up at her with glazed eyes. She bent down, seeing the large hole blown through him, bits of straw clinging deep inside his open stomach. "Oh, God, Hector—no!" So severe was his wound, she saw no way to even cradle him on her lap without causing more torment. Biting her lip, she held her hands down close to his wound as if that was all she could do to comfort him. "You did this, didn't you, Hector? You did it to warn us!" She sobbed. She felt C. F. McCord's hand rest on her shoulder as he bent down beside her.

"*Sí . . .*" Hector somehow managed to gasp. His bloody right hand found hers and tried to squeeze it, his eyes drifting between hers and McCord's. "*Amigos,* eh . . . ?"

"*Sí, amigos,*" Danielle whispered, holding his hand to her face, McCord nodding with her as he reached a hand out and placed it on Hector's shoulder in confirmation. Hector's last breath came out softly like a child at rest, and his open eyes stared blankly into the rafters overhead.

"He's gone," McCord said gently. "Let him go."

Danielle looked up at McCord with tears streaming down her cheeks, her pistol lying loosely across her lap. Without reserve she fell forward into his outstretched arms and wept shamelessly against his chest. "I know," McCord whispered. "It's all right, let it out. It's time you got rid of it. I'm here. I'm not leaving you . . . and nobody's going to kill us. You have my word."

For the following few moments McCord held her

pressed to his chest, knowing that Danielle had seen far too many people die to let it affect her this way. Yet, there was something at work here that he knew she had to get out of her system. He, too, was remorseful about Hector Sabio's death, rightly enough. He'd brought Hector with him on a manhunt. He'd known the risk and so had Hector Sabio. But there was far deeper sorrow inside this woman than even she realized. McCord had seen it coming since the day they'd met. Nobody could remain so tough for so long without it spilling out somewhere—nobody should ever have to, he thought.

When Wayne Connick ran to the open door with a shotgun in his hand, followed by some onlookers who ventured forth to see what the shooting was about, McCord separated from Danielle and waved them all away. "Stay back, Deputy. We need a few minutes here to sort things out."

Wayne Connick turned to the gathering crowd, shouting, "All right, you heard the marshal, stay back! This is a law matter. Let us handle it!"

"Come on," McCord whispered in Danielle's ear, seeing that her tears had subsided. "Let's get up." Together they rose to their feet, Danielle's Colt falling to the dirt. McCord bent down, picked it up, and shoved it down into her holster.

"It—it needs to be reloaded," Danielle whispered. She started to reach for the pistol, but McCord's hand closed gently on hers, stopping her.

"Not this second, it doesn't. I've got you covered, Danny Duggin, for as long as you need me. Wipe your face and straighten yourself up. We'll get out here, make a camp somewhere and head out first thing come morning. We both need some rest."

They walked toward the door, Danielle leaning against McCord's side for strength. But before they reached the eyes of the onlookers, Danielle had stood straight on her own and lowered her hat brim on her forehead. "The Mexican's name is Hector Sabio, Deputy," McCord said as they walked to the hitch rail through the parting crowd. "See that he's buried proper. He's our amigo."

Danielle and McCord mounted up and rode out of town. Once across the Rio Grande, they found the fresh tracks along the Mexican side of the shallows and made a camp under the canopy of an ancient piñon, out of the afternoon heat. "It could be hard finding the Delmano's hideout without Hector along to show us," said McCord.

"My brothers are ahead somewhere," Danielle replied. "If there's any way to find the hideout, they will. But we can't let them get too far ahead of us."

"We won't," said McCord. "After we've rested, we can travel all this evening and through the night if you want to. After what happened back there, I just thought we ought to take ourselves a breather. We've pushed hard these past few days."

"I've been pushing hard this whole past year," Danielle said, spreading her blanket on the ground. She took off her hat and boots and lay down, crossing a forearm over her face. "Sometimes I have a hard time remembering what life was like before I started down the vengeance trail."

McCord came over and sat down on the corner of her blanket. "It was good," he said with a tired smile.

"How would you know my life was good?" Danielle asked.

"Anything compared to *this* kind of life had to be good." McCord reached out, pulled a long stem of wild grass and stuck it between his teeth. "I wish I'd known you then."

"You say it like you think it might have made a difference of some kind," Danielle said.

"It might have," McCord said.

She sighed. "No, it wouldn't have. I know for a fact it wouldn't."

McCord chuckled under his breath. "Funny how I can't know it *might* have . . . but you know *for a fact* that it wouldn't."

Danielle smiled with her forearm across her eyes. "You couldn't have kept me from doing what I had to do. That's the part I know for a fact."

"But knowing you, maybe I could've helped. That's the part that I think might have made a difference."

"Well, you know me now," said Danielle. A silence passed. Then Danielle added in a softer tone, "I think having you with me has made a difference. It hasn't been as lonely." She smiled playfully. "And you don't eat much . . . it's been cheaper than buying a dog."

"Thanks," said McCord. He took the stem of grass from his mouth and studied it, twirling it back and forth between his fingers. His voice turned more serious. "Once this is all over, what will you do?" he asked. "Where will you go?"

"I don't know," Danielle said. "I've tried not to ask myself that question."

"It needs asking," McCord said.

"I know." Danielle turned onto her side, facing him.

"But I haven't had the time to think about it. I haven't *allowed* myself to think about it."

"I understand," said McCord, "because it scares a person sometimes to make plans . . . knowing there's a good possibility they won't be around long enough to carry them out. I've caught myself feeling the same way."

She studied his face as he looked away, back toward the border, the river, and beyond. "You're not like most lawmen I've met," said Danielle.

"Really?" McCord smiled. "Well, you're not like any gunmen I've ever met."

"You got me there." They shared a short laugh. "I get the idea that when we're finished down here, you're not going to go back to marshaling," Danielle said, "in spite of your big reputation."

"A reputation never meant that much to me," said McCord. "I've just done my job the best I can." He shrugged. "I'd hate to think this is all there's ever going to be to life, shooting and getting shot at . . . wouldn't you?"

"Yes I would." Her voice softened as if in concern. "Maybe that's another reason I haven't thought much about what comes next. Maybe I'm afraid this *is* all there is to it."

They sat for a silent moment in the hot Mexican wind while McCord thought things over. When he did speak again, his voice was almost a whisper. "I think it's time I told you . . . Saul Delmano killed my brother. I've been looking for him far longer than you have."

Danielle let out a breath. "I figured it was something like that. There had to be some reason for you to want to come down here with me."

"No, there didn't *have* to be a reason, not after I met you, not after I got to know you. But it turns out there *is* a reason. I suppose I just should have told you sooner."

Danielle sat up on her blanket and folded her arms around her knees. "You don't have to explain yourself to me. When it's over, we'll go our own way."

"But I don't want that," said McCord. "I want us to stay together."

Danielle abruptly stood up and pushed her hair back without facing him. She then picked up her boots and hat and looked over at the horses. "They're rested enough, let's move out. I want to catch up to my brothers before they reach the Delmano spread."

With a slight sigh, McCord got to his feet and followed her over to the horses.

Chapter 17

Tim and Jed Strange had been watching three riflemen from a dark shadowed spot beneath a deep cliff overhang when they saw Sheriff Deweese ride toward them. Two of the riflemen stood no more than ten feet from the sheriff, while the other one sat in his saddle, discussing something with the Sheriff, Tim thought. Then all of a sudden the man back-stepped his horse a few inches as the rifles blasted Sheriff Deweese out of his saddle and left him lying bloody and dead on the ground. "My God," Tim whispered. They were a good quarter of a mile from the grisly scene, and he and Jed stood transfixed, watching as one of the riflemen stepped forward and viciously kicked the dead sheriff in the face.

"We ought to do something," said Jed. "It ain't right standing here doing nothing while they kill a lawman in cold blood."

"We had no idea they was going to do it till it was already done," Tim retorted. He stared at the riflemen and at the tall rocky passageway through the rock land behind them, where more rifle barrels glinted from hidden perches. "I hate to say it, but we were fortunate the sheriff rode in there before we did. He must've rode straight here when he left town—else how did he get ahead of us on the trail?"

"Beats me," said Jed, "but from the looks of that bunch of gunmen, I'd say it makes them no difference who they kill so long as they're killing somebody."

"I know," said Tim, studying the men, trying to get an idea how many were out there. "They must be some extra hired guns the Delmanos brought in. They sure don't dress like cowhands."

"What's puzzling," said Jed, "is the way Sheriff Deweese was sitting there talking to that one as if they knew one another, or as if the sheriff thought he might have been expected here or something."

"I heard talk while I was sitting in the saloon waiting for the sheriff to question me," said Tim. "It sounded like Sheriff Deweese and Lewis Delmano might have known each other pretty well. Since Deweese's badge ain't worth the tin it's made of this side of the border, he might have been coming here just to talk to Lewis Delmano."

Jed gave his twin brother a curious look. "You suppose the sheriff was on Delmano's side?"

"I won't try to guess," Tim replied, "but if he was, he sure ain't now. We're going to have to pull back out of here and wait for Danielle somewhere farther back along the trail. I know she can handle herself, but we can't let her ride into this bunch without some kind of warning."

They turned with their reins in their hands, leading the horses over to the upward path at the far end of the cliff overhang. Following the path to a stretch of flatland, both Tim and Jed were taken by complete surprise when they looked into the faces of two gunmen who had apparently been awaiting them.

One of the gunmen spoke in French, telling Tim and Jed to raise their hands. But not understanding a word the man had said, Tim and Jed only stared for a tense second, noting the way these men were dressed very much like the men who had just shot the sheriff. The man repeated the order—"*S'Elever les mains!*"—his tone of voice sounding more demanding. Tim and Jed stood frozen, watching, listening warily, until the sound of the other man cocking his pistol caused the twins to move as one, their hands snatching their pistols from their holsters with blinding speed.

The men responded quickly, but not quickly enough. Three shots erupted from Tim and Jed's pistols before the gunmen had time to take aim. The two men fell backward in a heap, a shot from one of their pistols firing wildly in the air. While Jed stood with his pistol covering the bodies on the ground, Tim swung a glance out across the land below toward the spot where the other men had shot Sheriff Deweese. "They're mounting and heading this way!" said Tim. "We better pull back fast!"

They jumped up into their saddles and batted their heels to their horses' sides, racing back along the trail they'd come in on. When they had ridden a half mile, Tim slowed his horse enough to turn and look back at the cliff where they had shot the two gunmen. There was no sign of riders on their trail, not even a rise of dust except for their own. Tim could barely make out the few men and horses standing atop the cliffs, looking toward them. "Hold up, Jed," Tim shouted, "they're not following us!"

Jed slowed his horse and turned it back to his brother in a short circle. "Why not? You know they heard the shooting. You saw them riding toward us."

"And I still see them now," said Tim, pointing a finger at the tiny figures atop the cliff overhang. "But you tell me if I'm mistaken. It looks like all they're doing is sitting there watching us ride away."

Jed looked at the distant figures, then glanced all around warily. "There's something not right about this."

"What do you think it is?" asked Tim, also looking all around.

"I don't know, but I don't trust it," said Jed. "Maybe they know there's more of them between us and the way out of here, so they're in no hurry to chase us down."

"Could be," said Tim. "But I don't think that's it. It looks to me like their job is to guard that pass, and they ain't letting nothing or nobody draw them away from it."

"Then it's going to be even harder than we thought to get through there," Jed replied. He turned his horse back along the trail leading away from Bloody Horse Pass and nudged it forward. "Come on, Tim, let's find us a good place along the trail to wait for Danielle."

They didn't have to wait very long. Danielle Strange and C. F. McCord had ridden hard throughout the night, only stopping long enough to rest their horses every few miles. When they'd heard the pistol shots moments earlier, they'd moved forward quickly yet carefully. At the sight of the twins' trail dust, Danielle and McCord had split up, the marshal making a wide half circle flanking the trail, then closing around behind Tim and Jed as the distance between them and Danielle grew shorter and shorter.

At a hundred yards, Danielle and her brothers spotted one another and raced forward the rest of the way. Danielle hugged Tim and Jed in turn without the three of them leaving their saddles. After an affectionate embrace, the three sat atop their horses in the middle of the narrow trail. "We're glad you're feeling better, Danielle," said Tim, "but I hope you ain't slipping a little, us riding up on you like that. What if it hadn't been us? A hundred yards ain't a lot of room to correct a mistake if there's rifles involved."

"Maybe you're the ones who are slipping," she said, smiling. She raised an arm and waved it back and forth, summoning C. F. McCord down from the rocky hills alongside the trail. "You've let a U.S. federal marshal get all the way around you and fan your trail." "What the—?" said Tim. The twins both looked around in surprise at C. F. McCord as the young marshal stepped his horse down toward them with his rifle propped up from his lap.

"Boys, meet Federal Marshal C. F. McCord." Danielle smiled, gesturing a hand toward McCord.

As McCord worked his way closer, Jed exclaimed, "He's the one they call The Fox! Everybody's heard of him!"

"Well," said Tim, tipping his hat to McCord as McCord's horse stopped a few feet back, "I reckon if we had to get ourselves surrounded that way, at least it was by one of the best."

"C. F., these are my brothers I've told you so much about, Tim and Jed, the family twins."

McCord looked at them and blinked, as if seeing double. Then he smiled and tipped his hat. "Your sister has said lots of good things about you two," said McCord. "I feel like I already know you both."

"Sister?" Tim and Jed gave Danielle a guarded look.

"It's all right, he knows," said Danielle.

"I thought you weren't going to tell anybody until all this was over," said Tim.

"I didn't tell him," said Danielle. "He figured it out. McCord here went all the way to St. Joseph to find out what he could about me and my family. Somewhere along the line he was able to put two and two together."

Tim and Jed passed one another a knowing glance, noting the affection in C. F. McCord's eyes as he listened to Danielle's words.

"Well, Mr. McCord, you're mighty welcome along on this trip. From the looks of things we're going to need all the help we can get," said Jed.

"We heard the gunfire earlier," said Danielle. "What's wrong?"

"The pass is guarded by a passel of riflemen," said Tim. We had a run-in with a couple of them. It looks like their sole purpose is to keep anybody and everybody out of Bloody Horse Pass. We're pretty sure Saul Delmano and his brother are in there. The sheriff from El Paso was on their trail for a stagecoach robbery, and those riflemen just shot him dead!"

McCord asked, "You mean Sheriff Deweese is dead?"

"We saw them do it," said Jed, nodding. "It looked

like he was just talking to them, then the next thing we knew he was dead on the ground."

McCord winced and shook his head. "Poor Deweese," he said. "He played both sides of the law when it came to the Delmanos. Now it looks like it all caught up to him. What do these riflemen look like?"

"The ones we ran into spoke a foreign language. It sounded like French," said Tim, "but I wouldn't swear to it."

"Yep," said McCord, "it sounds like the *generalissimo's* private bodyguards. They're a bunch of mercenaries who call themselves the death squad." McCord looked back and forth between the three of them. "We're lucky you spotted them," he said to Tim. "We'd have been in some serious trouble if we'd run into them out there all of a sudden. Once the *generalissimo* sends them out to do something, they don't stop until they get it done."

"Now that we know they're there, does anybody have any ideas how we ought to deal with them?" asked Jed. He and Tim looked to Danielle for advice.

"Let's slip in and get a look at them," Danielle said, "then we'll come up with something." She tapped her boots to Sundown's sides and moved the chestnut mare forward at a trot.

The four of them stayed back a safe distance in the cover of rocks until evening sunlight stretched long across the flatland. With the riflemen scattered out along the high walls of Bloody Horse Pass, it was next to impossible to get an accurate count of how many men were out there. "One thing's for sure," C. F. Mc-

Cord said, "as soon as some shooting starts, every man they've got between here and the Delmano spread is going to come running." He lay beside Danielle behind an upthrust of rock where they could see one of the men on horseback ride forward from the mouth of the pass, peering back and forth across the flatland. Then the man turned his horse and rode back out of sight.

A few feet away, Tim called out in a whisper, "Another thing is for sure. They're not about to let anybody through that pass unless we blast our way through."

Hearing Tim's words, Danielle asked McCord, "What if we rode around them? Is there any other way in?"

"Not that I know of," said McCord. "If there was, once a person got on the other side of the pass, they would be spotted awfully easy making their way toward the Delmanos' spread. Hector Sabio said the hideout is even harder to get to."

"Then we've got to make a rush and take our chances getting through," said Danielle.

McCord shook his head. "Even if a couple of us made it through, these men would be on our tails. The Delmanos would be tipped off. I'm afraid it would destroy any chances of getting to them."

"I've got to hand it to the Delmanos," said Danielle. "They've made themselves a safe little nest here in Mexico. No wonder they've operated so long without getting caught." She looked back and forth across the flatlands.

McCord considered things as he lay studying Danielle's face while she scanned the high walls to the pass. "We need to wait until it's good and dark. What we've got to do is create a diversion long enough for one of us to slip through the pass," he said after a few moments of thought on the matter.

"That makes sense," said Danielle, looking into his eyes, waiting to hear the rest of his plan. "I suppose you figure you'll be the one to slip through?"

McCord didn't respond to Danielle's question. Instead, he continued as if he had not heard her, "Whoever gets through is going to have to go on alone and find the Delmanos' hideout while the rest of us hold these men back here and keep them busy."

"You didn't answer me," Danielle said. "Do you plan on it being *you* who rides through and takes down Saul Delmano?"

C. F. McCord fell silent for a second, then said in a quiet, resolved tone, "It's going to be awfully dangerous for whoever goes in. But no, I've thought it out. You'll never see any peace until you've faced your father's killer yourself. If you want to be the one to slip though and get Saul Delmano . . . I won't try to stop you."

Danielle looked surprised. "But what about your brother? What about all these years you've wanted to avenge his death the same as I want to avenge my pa?"

"I've had plenty of time to think about it," said McCord, "and watching you, seeing what wanting revenge so badly has cost you, I think I've lost my thirst for it."

Danielle started to object to McCord's words, but he stopped her before she got the chance. "'Don't take it the wrong way," McCord said, "I'm not judging you. I'm just saying, so long as Saul Delmano gets what's coming to him, it doesn't have to be me who delivers the justice. I'll let go of my revenge, if it'll help you get shed of yours."

Danielle thought about it for a second, then said, "Thanks, McCord. I won't forget you doing this for me."

"It's not a favor, Danielle," McCord said. He offered a slight smile. "I just figure the sooner you get this out of your craw, the sooner you and I can talk about our future together."

Danielle looked over at her brothers a few feet away, making sure they hadn't heard what McCord had said to her. Then she lifted her pistol from her holster and checked it as she asked, "What makes you think we have a future together? For all we know neither one of us might live through this."

"I know," said McCord, "that's why I wanted to get it said now."

Danielle looked around at the harsh land in the setting sunlight, then said, "You sure picked a romantic time and place to talk about it, McCord."

"This place wouldn't have been my first choice," McCord said, "but I wanted to tell you before we split up out here. After our talk the other day, you haven't given me much of a chance to tell you how I feel about you. I'm hoping that my stepping back and letting you and Saul Delmano settle up will let you know that you're more important to me than my revenge."

Danielle nodded, slipping her pistol back into her holster. "Do you remember telling me how you'd never leave me . . . and you weren't about to get killed and be taken away from me, McCord?"

"I remember," McCord said.

"Good," said Danielle, "because I'm holding you to it." She stood up in a crouch and moved over to her brothers. McCord studied the darkening terrain as Danielle told Tim and Jed about the plan. By the time Danielle slid back in beside him, darkness had settled in for the night. "I told them," Danielle said. "They wanted to ride with me, but I told them no."

McCord nodded. "Here's the way I've got it worked out in my mind. You get about fifty yards ahead of us and lay low till we start shooting. We'll be shooting in your direction, but don't worry, we'll keep a high aim on the rocks. While we keep them attending to us, you slip though without firing a shot. We'll keep them shooting at us for an hour, giving you plenty of time to slip through the pass. Then we'll fall back a little at a time, letting them think they've turned us back. That way, you'll have none of them on your trail—provided you don't leave them a clear set of tracks to follow."

"I'll keep to the rocks," Danielle said. "They won't find any tracks."

"Then get yourself ready," said McCord. He stared at her in the darkness. Danielle could tell he wanted to say more to her. But she knew as well as he did that there was nothing more to say. Not now, she thought.

Before scooting back toward the horses, Danielle laid a hand on McCord's forearm, saying, "I know how much facing the man who killed your brother must have meant to you, C. F." She paused for a second, then added, "Thanks for stepping back."

"The only thanks I want is for you to come back to me in one piece," McCord said, almost in a whisper. He watched her slip away into the darkness without another word.

Chapter 18

Danielle slipped out across the dark flatlands, leading Sundown behind her from cover to cover until she kneeled down behind a low spreading juniper and waited for C. F. McCord and her brothers to start shooting. At the sound of the first rifle shot, Danielle felt the chestnut mare jerk against the reins, startled, yet keeping obediently quiet as if she understood the situation and what was required of her. Danielle stood up and ran a hand down Sundown's muzzle, settling her. "Easy, girl," Danielle whispered close to the mare's ear. "We'll soon be out of the firing."

Danielle waited until the return fire from the rocky walls of Bloody Horse Pass blossomed steadily in the darkness. Then she eased forward, leading the mare, knowing that she was reasonably safe, provided the riflemen in the high pass kept their sights aimed on the muzzle flashes fifty yards behind her. When she had drawn nearer to the riflemen's positions, Danielle slipped up atop the mare. Lying low in her saddle, she pressed the animal onward, searching for hard footing to keep from leaving hoofprints.

Feeling the tall, dark walls of Bloody Horse Pass close around her, Danielle rode on slowly, as quiet as a ghost beneath the constant barrage of rifle fire. A full half hour had passed by the time Danielle saw the black shadows of steep rock give way to the midnight blue of the night's sky. The firing was behind her now and she breathed a little easier. She looked back over her shoulder for a second, then heeled the mare up into a trot. "Come on, Sundown," she whispered, "they're doing their part, now let's get to doing ours." The mare carried her swiftly farther and farther away from the noise of battle.

Atop a hidden cliff in the rock work of Bloody Horse Pass, Henri LaBourge watched the muzzle flashes of rifles explode on the dark flatlands below. Beside him, a wiry German gunman known only as Vesp asked in a bemused voice, "What do these fools think they accomplish by this? Do they think they will overpower us and force their way through the pass?"

Henri LaBourge studied the darkness, tiny bursts of gunfire reflecting in his eyes. "I have stayed alive many years by never venturing a guess at what other men think."

"Yes, I know," said Vesp, "but for the sake of curiosity, do you believe that this is Danny Duggin, the one who has Lewis Delmano so upset?"

"The one Lewis Delmano would like us to kill for him?" A thin smile came to Henri LaBourge's face. "Yes, perhaps it is him." A silence passed, then Henri added, "But if this Danny Duggin *was* down there before, it is unlikely that he is down there now." His eyes scanned the darkness below, where the trail snaked though the pass like a black ribbon of silk. "If I were Danny Duggin, I would have created this little skirmish to cover me as I slipped through the pass."

Vesp looked taken aback at the thought of Danny Duggin having ridden right past them in the darkness. "Shall I send some men immediately, to make sure this has not happened?"

"No, I don't think so." Henri LaBourge chuckled under his breath. "My orders from the *generalissimo* are quite clear. I will do nothing until I have met with Lewis Delmano face-to-face."

"But meanwhile," said Vesp, "we are being attacked. Do we only sit here and hope they cannot hit us?"

"No," said Henri LaBourge, "we will not be treated like helpless fools, not even for the *generalissimo*. I have already sent some riders out to surround these riflemen. Let them shoot at these rocks all night if they wish. When morning comes, our men will move in so swiftly, these poor imbeciles will not know what hit them." He gazed out across the darkness as two shots blossomed at once on the flatland.

From his position behind an upthrust of rock, C. F. McCord looked over at Tim and Jed's black silhouettes against the purple sky. Jed whispered over to McCord, asking, "How far do you want us to pull back now?"

"Not too far," McCord replied, "fifteen or twenty yards. If we pull back too far at once, it might tip them off what we've done and send them after Danny," McCord said. "I figure by now Danny has made it through the pass, so let's cut down on our shooting, save our ammunition in case we need it later on."

"What are you expecting?" Tim asked in a lowered voice as he and his brother moved closer to McCord on their way back to a new position.

"If I was them," said McCord, "I'd be sending some men out to circle us in the dark. Come morning I'd have them sweep in for the kill."

"Do you think that's their plan?" asked Jed.

"Just my speculation," said McCord. "But to be on the safe side, by morning there'll only be one of us here on the flatland. I want you two back in those rocks behind us by then. If they circle in on me, you'll have them covered from behind."

"Uh-uh, McCord," said Tim. "That's too risky. We can't leave you down here by yourself."

"You told your sister that you'd do what I asked. Well, that's what I'm asking," McCord said firmly. "I'm going to move back and forth, firing from different positions. Now that they've seen three rifle flashes, they'll figure we're all three still here. Just be ready to throw down some long fire if they're dogging me when I light out of here in the morning."

"I don't like it," said Tim. "You're taking an awfully big chance sitting down here alone, McCord."

"Not if you boys can shoot those rifles as well as your sister thinks you can." He smiled to himself in the darkness.

"Don't worry about that, Marshal," said Jed barely above a whisper as the two of them moved back past McCord toward the black outline of scattered rock. "If you're crazy enough to stay here by yourself . . . we're crazy enough to hold the back door open once you make a run for it." Jed paused, then asked, "You do plan to make a run for it at the last minute, don't you?"

"That's exactly what I plan on doing," McCord said over his shoulder to the darkness, levering a fresh cartridge up into his rifle chamber.

Upon seeing the distant glow of light in the window of the Delmano hacienda, Danielle reined the mare toward it. She rode quickly until she knew the hacienda was within a mile, then she slowed the mare to a walk, silencing the hoofbeats and keeping down any rise of dust that might show against the night sky. At two hundred yards, Danielle stepped down from her saddle and led Sundown the rest of the way, into the dark shadows of a small adobe building facing the east side of the hacienda. Danielle stood in silence as three men stepped off the back porch, talking quietly among themselves as they walked over to a long bunkhouse. When a glow of light rose and fell as the men stepped through the door and closed it, Danielle laid the mare's reins up across the saddle. Knowing that Sundown would not move until Danielle once again took the reins in her hand, Danielle slipped forward in a crouch toward a partially open window.

Danielle reached up, eased the window open a few inches higher, then slipped inside. Taking care to look back toward the bunkhouse to make sure she hadn't been seen, Danielle eased the window back down to where it was originally. Standing for a moment in the darkness, listening to the tomblike silence of the hacienda, Danielle knew that Saul Delmano was not here. Saul Delmano would be in the hideout, up there somewhere in the rock land just like Hector had said.

Drawing her Colt, Danielle eased her way from one dimly lit room to the next until she heard the sound of soft sobbing coming through an open bedroom door. She stepped to the side of the bedroom door for a second, then took a breath and moved inside. Seeing a woman lying facedown across the bed, her face buried in a handkerchief, Danielle's first thought was to sneak closer and throw a hand across the woman's mouth to keep her quiet. Yet, before Danielle could make it all the way to the bed, a squeaking floor plank beneath her boots betrayed her, and she stopped short. "Who—who's there?" said Greta's frightened voice, turning her eyes to Danielle in the darkness.

Danielle moved quickly now, seeing Greta reach for a small pistol on the nightstand beside the bed. Her hand clamped down on Greta's wrist in time to keep her from arming herself. "Take it easy, ma'am," said Danielle, using her man's tone of voice, "I'm not here to harm you. I'm looking for Saul Delmano."

"I know who you are! You're Danny Duggin! You're here to kill Ramon!" Greta responded in a harsh whisper, bordering on desperation. She tried to wrestle her hand free of Danielle's grip, but Danielle held firmly and pulled her back away from the nightstand.

"You're wrong," Danielle said. "I came here to kill Saul Delmano, nobody else. If anyone comes at me I'll kill them in self-defense. But I have no reason to kill Ramon or Lewis Delmano unless they force me into it. I'm not a cold-blooded murderer, regardless of what they've told you about me." Danielle turned her loose.

Greta slumped on the edge of the bed, rubbing her wrist where Danielle had held her tightly. "If only I could believe that," she said.

"You're free to believe what you will," said Danielle. "But I came for Saul Delmano, and nobody's going to stop me."

"Well, he's not here, as you can see," said Greta. "None of them are here."

"I didn't really expect them to be," said Danielle. "I only stopped by here to make sure for myself. I know about the hideout up in the hills. Is that where I'll find Saul?"

Greta hesitated for a second, then answered reluctantly. "Yes, Saul is up there . . . but so is Ramon. There might be others. But listen to me, please. Ramon is trying to break away from Saul. He told me he would slip away the first chance he got and come back for me. You must promise not to kill him if you meet him along the trail!"

"I can only promise you that I won't kill Ramon, unless he tries to kill me, ma'am," said Danielle.

"But if he runs into you on the trail, he'll think you *are* out to kill him," Greta exclaimed.

"Then I suppose he and I will have to settle that between us," said Danielle.

Greta straightened up from the edge of the bed, saying in a determined voice, "I'm going with you, Mr. Duggin."

"No, ma'am," said Danielle, shaking her head, "you're not going anywhere with me."

"But I was there once, I remember the way. You

could wander around in the rock lands for days if you don't know where you're going."

"I'll follow their tracks," said Danielle.

"But don't you see," said Greta, pleading. "I must go along, to warn Ramon!"

"That's exactly what I'm *afraid* you would do, ma'am," Danielle responded.

"But you don't understand, Mr. Duggin," Greta pleaded, her eyes turning moist and full. "Ramon is a good man . . . he's not like his brother or his father."

"If he's a good man, than he'll do the right thing, ma'am," said Danielle. As she spoke, she stepped back toward the window, not knowing that outside the three men she'd seen go into the bunkhouse earlier had returned. They had caught sight of the chestnut mare standing in the shadows. Now two of the men lay in wait, while the third man slipped around into the hacienda and was headed for the bedroom with his pistol drawn and cocked.

Seeing Danielle's shadow at the bedroom window, Gus Latimer and Buck Benton braced themselves with their pistols in their hands and waited. "All right, Mr. Danny Duggin," Gus whispered to Buck Benton, "it looks like it'll be up to us to take you down."

"Hush," said Buck Benton in a nervous whisper, "he might hear you. This is no saddle tramp we're dealing with here. From what I've heard, Duggin is as tough as they come."

"Is that a fact?" Gus Latimer grinned. "Hell, I wouldn't have it no other way. I just hope Lon is in there where he's supposed to be right now."

"Lon Capps ain't never let me down," Buck Benton whispered, his hand tightening as the two of them watched the dark shadow step out through the bedroom window and onto the ground.

"All right, Mr. Danny Duggin!" Gus Latimer yelled out, his hand already coming up with his pistol. "This is as far as you get!" His shot exploded in a flash of blue-white fire, the bullet whistling past Danielle's head as her Colt streaked upward from her side. For some reason Buck Benton hadn't expected Gus Latimer to just open fire that way. But he caught on quickly and managed to get a shot off at Danielle as Gus Latimer fell backward with a bullet through his chest.

Buck Benton moved to cover as he fired, feeling Danielle's next shot only missing him by a inch. He ducked back behind an old freight wagon that sat empty in the dirt. He threw two quick shots around the corner of the wagon, then ducked farther back as three shots from Danielle's pistols tore chunks of wood from the wagon and sprayed splinters high in the air. "Damn you, Duggin!" Buck Benton shouted. "You just kilt ole Gus! Me and him was partners before you was even born!"

"It was his call," Danielle replied, coming forward a few feet from the window and down onto one knee, a Colt in either hand, fanning back and forth in the darkness lest there be more men hiding there. "Now you've got to make the same decision," she called out. "I only came here to kill Saul Delmano. If you want to die for him, that's your business."

As Danielle spoke, inside the bedroom, Lon Capps slipped across the floor with his pistol drawn and cocked. He looked over at Greta in the dim light and raised a finger to his lips, instructing her to keep quiet as he crept closer to the open window. Greta had squatted down onto the floor beside the bed. She only nodded in reply. At the window, Lon Capps ventured a glance out into the darkness, seeing Danielle's exposed back in the pale moonlight. He whispered to himself as he raised his cocked pistol and took careful aim from less then fifteen feet away. "I've got you, Danny Duggin . . . you and two thousand dollars to boot!" As he walked forward, pulling the trigger, his next step hit a creaky floorboard.

Danielle's back stiffened at the sound of the floorboard, and as a shot exploded behind her, she fell forward to the ground and spun around to return fire. But at the window all she saw was the body of Lon Capps slump forward and hang down from the window ledge, his arms swaying back and forth lifelessly. Danielle had no time to wonder what had happened. From behind the freight wagon, Buck Benton came running forward, shrieking aloud, his pistol blazing in his hand.

Danielle put two shots into his chest, lifting him and pitching him backward in the dirt. Then Danielle raised back up onto her knees, scanning the darkness for others, listening to the deathlike silence around her beneath a drift of burnt gunpowder.

At the slightest sound from the window behind her, Danielle spun toward it, both Colts aimed and cocked. "Don't shoot!" Greta said in a shaky voice. "It's only me! This one is dead. I—I shot him."

"Yes, ma'am, you surely did." Danielle stood the rest of the way up, still looking back and forth in the darkness. She lowered her left Colt into its holster, then broke open the Colt in her right hand, punched out the spent cartridges, and replaced them. "Are there more hands around here that I need to know about?"

"I don't know," said Greta. "I don't think so. These men are just the ones who handle Lewis Delmano's cattle . . . men who used to ride with him in the old days."

As Greta spoke, Danielle walked up to the window and looked at the body of Lon Capps hanging down with a bullet hole in his back. Then she looked up at Greta. "Why'd you do this, ma'am? If you had let him kill me, that would have solved all your problems, wouldn't it?"

Greta shook her head, saying, "No, it would only have put your blood on my hands. I couldn't stand by and see him shoot you in the back."

Danielle studied her face in the dim light through the open window, considering everything. Then she asked Greta, "You really believe Ramon is a good man? Not a murdering outlaw like Saul and his father?"

"I know that Ramon is a good man," said Greta. Her hand drifted instinctively to her stomach and rested there as she spoke. "I'm in love with him . . . I carry his child inside me."

Danielle lowered her right Colt into its holster, took out the left, and reloaded it as she said, "That doesn't mean he's not a gunman like his family. It just means that maybe he's pulled the wool over your eyes."

"No! Ramon and I are leaving this place!" Greta said. "We had already planned to before your name was even mentioned. He sees the kind of people his

family are. We want to get away and live our lives
and raise our baby somewhere far away from all this
murder!"

Danielle finished reloading her other Colt and said
as she shoved it down into its holster, "I hope you're
right, ma'am. Now hurry up and get yourself ready.
You're going with me."

Chapter 19

Henri LaBourge had turned his head slightly toward the distant sound of pistol fire in the darkness. But he did not say anything about it until a few moments later when he turned his head back to Vesp, who sat atop his horse beside him near the edge of a cliff.

"Did you hear anything a while ago?" LaBourge asked.

"I have heard nothing out there but the rifle fire of our own men," Vesp responded, nodding out toward the flatlands.

"Not out there," said LaBourge. "Back that way." He jerked a thumb in the direction of the Delmano hacienda.

"No, I heard nothing from that direction," said Vesp. "What was it?"

"It was pistol fire," said LaBourge, a slice of a thin smile coming to his lips as he studied the dark flatlands below them. Sporadic rifle fire blossomed in a wide circle. "If I were to guess, I would say it was coming from Danny Duggin's guns." He nodded down toward the flatland. "Whoever is down there is only acting on Duggin's behalf. Duggin is back behind us, preparing to do what he came here to do."

Vesp gave LaBourge a puzzled look. "You believe this, and yet we sit here and do nothing?"

"We do exactly what our orders tell us to do," said Henri LaBourge.

"I think I must take some men and go pursue—" Vesp's words were cut short as Henri LaBourge grabbed his horse's bridle to keep Vesp from turning away toward the narrow path.

"When the time comes for us to strike our target, we will do so quickly and without mercy," said LaBourge. "Until that time, we will do what all good soldiers do—we will wait. You were not present when I received our orders, Vesp. But you are my second-in-command, so you must pay attention and do as I tell you."

Vesp let out a tense breath and eased down in his saddle. "But of course," he said. "Forgive my exuberance."

On the floor of the flatlands, C. F. McCord stayed close to the ground even though the rifle fire was coming nowhere near him. He knew that the well-spaced shots were now only meant to harass him into returning fire and revealing his position. But now that he had given Danielle all the time she needed to get through the pass, McCord wasn't interested in keeping this gunfight going. All he wanted to do now was get back across the flatland to where Tim and Jed were waiting, without catching a stray bullet in the dark.

McCord judged the rifle fire coming from the wide half circle surrounding him, and decided there were no more than three or four men left out there now. Where had the others gone? he asked himself. While he had spent the past hour and a half firing, then hurrying to a new position to make them think there was still more than one down here, it suddenly dawned on him that these gunmen must have been doing the same thing. Had they caught on to what he was doing and gone on ahead after Danielle? He hoped not. But whatever the case, it was time for him to move out. A silver gray line was beginning to form on the eastern horizon. He wasn't about to get caught out on this flat, desolate land in broad daylight.

Moving back silently to where he'd left his horse hitched to a scrub juniper, McCord slipped atop the animal and heeled it into a quiet trot, hoping the sound of its hooves could not be heard by the riflemen. So far so good, McCord thought to himself, moving away across the flatland toward the far end of the basin where the twins would be waiting to cover his back. He'd told them to be ready to provide some long rifle fire for him if these men were close behind him. But as it now looked, McCord was going to be able to slip out of the flatlands unnoticed.

Two miles ahead, under the cover of dirty gray darkness, Tim and Jed Strange lay waiting in a low rise of rocks, seeing the distant flash of occasional rifle fire blink along the ridge lines. "Think Marshal McCord's managed to keep himself from getting shot?" asked Jed.

"I sure hope so," Tim replied. "I have a lot of respect for that lawman, not to mention the fact that Danielle thinks the world of him. I'd hate to see something happen to him."

"Me, too," said Jed with great concern. "He'd best be getting himself headed this way if he doesn't want to get caught out there in the morning light."

Out on the flatland, C. F. McCord rode with care, wanting to hurry and push the horse forward into a run, seeing the widening glow of sunlight rise up in the east. But he knew better than to press the horse too hard across this rocky land in the darkness. There were too many ways a horse could snap a leg in this rough terrain. Yet, even as McCord thought about the many things that could happen, he felt the horse veer beneath him and let out a long neigh as the sound of a rattlesnake rose up from the ground. "Easy, boy!" McCord called out in a hushed tone, sawing the reins, keeping the horse from bolting out of control.

The horse settled and sidestepped away from the sound of the rattler, but not before letting out another nervous whinny that echoed across the placid darkness. McCord knew what was coming and he booted the horse forward into a hard run just as a half-dozen rifles honed in and fired from what seemed like every direction at once.

At the sound of the horse, followed by the blasts of rifle fire, Tim straightened up from his position on the ground and hurried a few yards forward, staring out into the darkness. He whispered to his brother Jed, who ran forward beside him, "That had to be McCord's horse! He's in trouble out there!"

Another volley of rifle fire resounded, causing both Tim and Jed to wince at what dire consequences might have befallen the young marshal. "Get ready to take cover, Jed," said Tim. "I'm going to call out to him, see what we can do to help him."

"Do it," said Jed, taking a step back, getting ready to run back to their position on the ground.

"McCord," Tim shouted into the darkness. "What's wrong out there?"

Rifle fire honed in and fired on the sound of Tim's voice as he immediately ran back and joined his brother.

When the rifle fire ceased, Tim and Jed listened intently for any reply from McCord, but they heard none. All they heard was the low whimpering of a wounded horse somewhere out on the flatland.

"Do you think he's dead?" asked Jed.

"He could be," Tim replied, "or it could be that he's not going to answer and bring more fire upon himself." From the flatland came the echoing of the wounded horse's voice.

On the ground, three hundred yards out on the flatland, McCord struggled to free his leg from beneath his mortally wounded horse, who had caught a bullet high in its chest. But the weight of the horse held him pinned as another volley of rifle fire resounded. When the horse ceased its pitiful whinnying, McCord felt the animal go limp, pressing his leg even tighter to the ground. He had heard Tim Strange call out to him, but he dared not answer. Instead, he continued struggling, raising his other leg until he could reach the handle of the knife in his boot well.

McCord drew the knife and reached out with it across the dead horse's side as far as he could until he managed to slash through the cinch strap holding the saddle in place. Now that the horse had fallen silent, so had the rifles. But McCord knew he was in a bad spot. Come daylight, if he wasn't able to free himself, all the gunmen would have to do would be to walk down and shoot him to pieces. He pulled at the saddle, bracing his free knee to the dead horse's back and pushing with all his might, but to no avail. After a while he lay spent and panting in the dirt, seeing the sunrise broaden on the far horizon. "Well, Fox," he whispered aloud to himself, drawing his pistol and laying it atop the dead horse's side for easy access when the time came, "you've managed to get yourself into a real tight spot this time." He lay still long enough to catch his breath and listen to the sound of horses moving down from the rocks. "Was she worth it?" he asked himself. Then he smiled as if in reflection and answered himself in a quiet voice, "You bet she was . . ." He lay scanning the darkness surrounding him, preparing himself for whatever was to come.

Three hundred yards away, Tim said to Jed, "We've got to go get him, brother." Taking note of the sunlight creeping up over the ridgeline, he added, "I've got a feeling he'd do the same for us if it was the other way around."

"So do I," Jed agreed, standing up in a crouch and taking a step back to where they'd tied their horses. "I just hope he ain't dead already."

"Either way, at least we'll have done our best to help him," Tim said, studying the horizon as he cradled his rifle in his arms.

"I know," said Jed. "I'll go get the horses."

Tim listened to the silence of dawn as Jed moved back to the horses. After a moment when Jed didn't return, Tim turned and said in a lowered voice, "Jed? What's taking you so long?"

When Jed didn't answer, Tim felt the skin on his neck grow prickly. He drew his pistol, cocked it, and

ventured toward the horses, feeling for his steps carefully and quietly across the rocky ground. In a small
clearing amid waist-high juniper and cactus, Tim froze
at the sight of his brother Jed lying facedown on the
dirt. As soon as his senses realized what he was looking at, he instinctively fanned the pistol back and
forth, searching the gray shadows as he moved forward and bent down to his brother.

"Jed! Speak to me! Are you all right?" Tim asked,
shaking Jed by his arm. He heard Jed utter a faint
groan and would have breathed a sigh of relief had
it not been for the solid thud of a rifle butt reaching
in and slamming against the back of his head. Tim
spun half around as his legs buckled beneath him. He
tried to squeeze off a shot from his pistol into the
grinning face that swam before him as if in a fog. But
his pistol would not rise. His finger would not work
on the trigger. He felt blackness draw in close around
him as he fell.

"Get them both up and on their horses," said the
voice of the man who had just knocked Tim cold.
"We'll collect the other one on the way in."

"Why not kill them right here, Preston?" asked one
of the other riflemen who had closed into a circle surrounding Tim and Jed Strange.

"Because Henri said bring them in alive if we
could," said Preston Bendele with a slight trace of a
French accent. "I follow his orders. When Henri wants
them killed, he'll say so."

"What about the one out there on the flatland?"
asked the other rifleman. "Do you think he is dead?"

"We'll see when we get there." Preston Bendele
shrugged.

With Tim and Jed Strange lying slumped in their saddles, their pistols stripped from their holsters, the band of riflemen rode forward three hundred yards. In the thin morning light they saw the other men who had moved down from the ridgeline and now formed a wide circle around C. F. McCord, who lay with his leg still pinned beneath the dead horse. McCord raised his pistol and fanned it back and forth slowly from one man to the next. Seeing there was little he could do against such odds, he called out all the same, warning them, "Stay back, all of you! That's close enough!"

Rifles raised and cocked in unison as the men moved in, steadily closer. But before anyone fired, Henri LaBourge called out as he and Vesp rode in from the north, "You heard him, men! That's close enough! Now stand fast! I think I would like to talk to this man. I'm curious as to why a man would do something this foolish." Henri LaBourge stopped his horse and stepped down from his saddle.

"I've got nothing to say to you," Marshal C. F. Mc-Cord called out to him. "If you've got killing to do here, get it done." He aimed his pistol at Henri LaBourge, causing LaBourge to stop in his tracks and raise his hands chest-high.

"*Attente!*" Henri LaBourge chuckled under his breath at McCord's brazenness. "Wait—surely we can take a moment to talk like reasonable men before we shoot holes in one another, eh?"

"Talk then," said McCord. "I've got no plans made for this morning." Seeing Jed and Tim slumped forward on their horses, McCord asked, "Are those boys all right?"

"They have been better, I'm sure," Henri LaBourge

said with a trace of a smile. "But so much for them—where is this Danny Duggin I have heard so much about?"

"I don't know who you're talking about," said McCord, letting his pistol slump a bit, but still keeping it cocked and pointed. "Me and my friends there came all this way on our own."

"Oh, I see," said Henri LaBourge, "and for no reason at all, you decided to shoot at me and my men? Why? Just to see if we would shoot back at you?" His smile widened as he spread his arms, taking in all of the flatland. "As you see, we most certainly will."

A ripple of low laughter stirred and then settled among the gunmen. McCord struggled with his pinned leg, then said in a firm tone, "All right, I'll level with you. I'm a U.S. federal marshal who's been on the Delmanos' trail for a long time. I heard about this gunman, Danny Duggin, headed this way to clean up the Delmanos, and I couldn't stand the thought of him getting here first. So I took off my badge and crossed the border."

"I see." Henri LaBourge nodded, as if trying to believe McCord's story. "Let's you and me call a truce for a moment, eh?"

McCord didn't answer, but he did lower his pistol barrel further.

LaBourge ventured closer with his hands still chest-high, moving slowly, one step, then another, until finally he stood three feet from McCord and looked down at him, shaking his head. "It is a most tragic thing to lose a good horse."

"Yeah," said McCord, looking at the body of the

horse lying heavily on his leg. "He was one of the best I ever owned."

"And yet, you risk your life, the life of a good horse, and the life of your two friends to come all this way in order to kill Saul Delmano?" LaBourge shook his head more vigorously. "That seems too foolish," he said solemnly.

"Well, that happens to be the whole of it." McCord sighed. "Take it or leave it."

Henri LaBourge shrugged it off and said, "The Delmanos must be considered very dangerous men in America, eh?"

"No. Not for my money anyway," said McCord. "I've never thought of them as anything but two-bit thugs and killers. Why do you ask? Don't tell me you have scruples when it comes to who you do your paid killing for."

"No, of course not," said Henri LaBourge, stooping down beside McCord as he spoke. "I work only for *Generalissimo* Ortega. He gives me his orders and I follow them. It makes life simple for me." He smiled, then raised a finger for emphasis. "But still, I can't help but sometimes ask myself why I am ordered to kill a particular person."

McCord looked at him closely and said, "Don't ask me to justify what you do, mister. I came here hunting for Saul Delmano. It didn't work out the way I wanted it to . . . so that's too bad for me. I take what's coming to me with no complaints. Will you be able to do the same when your time comes?"

Henri LaBourge stared into his eyes as he seemed to work something out in his mind. Then he stood up and said, "That's an interesting question, lawman.

I don't think I can say what I will do when my time comes." He turned his back on McCord and called out to the men who sat atop their horses beside Tim and Jed, "Take them down from their horses and bring them over here."

McCord raised his pistol back toward Henri LaBourge, saying, "If you think I'll lay here and watch my friends die without trying to help them, you're badly mistaken."

Henri LaBourge seemed not to hear McCord. He gazed off toward four of his men who came riding in from the south, surrounding Lewis Delmano's open-topped buggy. "Well well, here comes the leader of the Delmano family right now," said Henri LaBourge in a detached manner.

"Do you hear me, mister?" said McCord. "Don't expect me keep our truce if you try killing my friends."

"What?" Henri LaBourge looked down at McCord as if he had forgotten he was lying there. Then he smiled and said, "Tell me, lawman, how many shots do you have in that pistol?"

"It's fully loaded," said McCord. "Six shots." He looked over to where three men had pulled Tim and Jed Strange down from their horses and were now dragging them toward him, the twins still half conscious and barely able to stand. "What are you getting ready to do?" asked McCord.

Henri LaBourge smiled. "I'm getting ready to carry out my task, of course." He gestured a hand toward the horse lying on McCord's leg. "If we removed this animal, would you be able to stand on your own?"

"I'd sure give it a try," said McCord. "I don't think my leg is broken beneath it."

Henri LaBourge motioned for two men to step in and help McCord as Lewis Delmano's buggy drew closer at a fast clip across the sand. The men struggled with the dead horse while LaBourge turned away to acknowledge Lewis Delmano. "Is that the gunman? Is that Danny Duggin?" Lewis Delmano asked in an excited voice, sliding the buggy to a halt and jumping down from it as he spoke. One of the riders had to catch the skittish buggy horse by its bridle to keep it from bolting forward.

Henri LaBourge looked Lewis Delmano up and down before answering, not liking the way Delmano had barged in without so much as a nod or a greeting. "Well," Lewis Delmano insisted, "is it him?"

Henri LaBourge shook his head, watching McCord stand up with the help of the two men beside him. "No, this is not Danny Duggin."

"What about either one of those two?" Lewis Delmano asked, cutting his glance to the twins.

"No," said Henri LaBourge. "Danny Duggin is not here. These men only ride with him. We surrounded them overnight."

"Oh, really?" Lewis Delmano's gloved hand clenched around the butt of the pistol on his hip. "Then what is this one doing wearing a gun?" He stared hard at C. F. McCord. "Why haven't all three of them been shot?"

"Because shooting these men is not the reason me and my soldiers came here," Henri LaBourge snapped in response.

"Soldiers, ha!" Lewis Delmano said in a gruff voice, turning a sarcastic expression from man to man, then back to LaBourge. "You and your men are supposed to do as you're told, nothing more, nothing less. Now whatever killing you're paid to do, I demand that you get to doing it"

"I am glad that you feel this way," said LaBourge, raising his cocked pistol. "It makes my task so much easier." Three shots fired in rapid succession from LaBourge's pistol, each shot slamming into Lewis Delmano's chest, knocking him a step backward. Delmano hit the ground with a stunned look on his dead face. "There," said Henri LaBourge, "it is done, just as the *generalissimo* ordered. Now we can all go back to Mexico City." He stood with the barrel of his smoking pistol tipped slightly toward C. F. McCord. Tim and Jed Strange stood addled and speechless, as did the rest of LaBourge's men.

McCord found his words, saying in a halting voice, "You—you mean . . . you never were out to kill Danny Duggin? It was Lewis Delmano you wanted to kill all along?" Even as McCord asked, he managed to keep his hand close to the butt of his pistol, unsure of what might come next.

"*Wanted* to kill?" LaBourge asked, lowering his pistol from McCord's direction. "I have never *wanted* to kill anyone." He nodded at Lewis Delmano's body. "But this one had become too demanding over the years. He thought he could tell the government what he wanted done and they would have to do it for him." Henri LaBourge grinned, adding, "You know how overbearing you Américains can get, left unchecked."

McCord let it sink in, then asked, "What about the sheriff, Deweese?" McCord jerked his head toward the twins. "They saw you kill him. What was his part in all this?"

"He might have been a lawman on your side of the border," said LaBourge, "but over here he was nothing more than a paid informant for Lewis Delmano. When Raul Hernandez told the *generalissimo* of how things were going out here, it was easily decided to do away with all these fools and start anew." Henri Labourge looked at Lewis Delmano's body and shook his head. "This one never had the power or the connections he thought he had. He always thought Raul Hernandez was sent here to do his bidding. In truth, Hernandez was only keeping an eye on things out here. Lewis Delmano was nothing more than a well-paid hired hand. Too bad he never realized it—he could have lived longer." LaBourge lowered the pistol into his holster and let out a breath.

"What about us now?" asked McCord, passing a glance across the twins, across the other men, then back to Henri LaBourge.

"For all the trouble you've caused I should kill all three of you," said LaBourge, his tone of voice not carrying the conviction of his words. "But I was not told to do so."

McCord asked in a cautious voice, "Then we can just leave? Nobody will try to stop us?"

"Makes you feel foolish doesn't it?" said Labourge. "Knowing that all this could have been avoided?"

"I didn't know it at the time," McCord offered. "All I knew was that I didn't want you shooting my friend Danny."

"I understand," said Henri LaBourge. "If I let all

three of you go, does it mean I will have no more trouble from any of those troublesome Delmanos?"

McCord let out a tense breath. "Just let me round myself up a horse and you have my word on it," he said.

Chapter 20

In a weathered plank shack on a narrow clearing between two craggy rock peaks, Saul Delmano reached across the small table and took a bottle of rye whiskey from an outstretched hand. In the circling glow of lantern light, he threw back a drink from the bottle and set it down on the tabletop as he wiped the back of his hand across his mouth. He stood glaring down at the outlaws seated at the table. They sat staring, waiting to hear what Saul had to say next. On a blanket on the floor beneath the front window, Ramon Delmano waited as well. He had been watching his brother drink and talk for the past hour. Ramon marveled at how the whiskey had not seemed to dull Saul's thinking or slur his speech. There appeared to be no drunkenness to Saul Delmano, only a white-hot rage that grew and swelled in intensity from somewhere inside him. With each turn of the bottle to his lips Saul Delmano became more and more a monster, less and less a man. The others saw it, too, Ramon thought, for how could they miss it? But then, how could he have missed seeing it himself all these years? His half brother Saul was a raving madman, a desperate beast who must soon be put down for good, perhaps for his own sake as well as those around him.

"There is not a stage or bank in the country that can't be robbed," Saul Delmano declared, jamming his fingertip down on the tabletop for emphasis. "Any fool can do it, provided he ain't squeamish about getting somebody's brains splattered all over his shirt." Saul tossed a glance at Ramon. "I even managed to teach my kid brother a little about the business. He spread a flat, mirthless grin that turned his face into a death mask in the lantern's glow. "For years our pa was afraid Ramon here was never going to amount to nothing. Now look at him. Out here, hiding out, just like the rest of us."

One of the outlaws, named Ruppert Terry, turned a halfhearted glance toward Ramon, saying, "Bet it makes you real proud, eh, Ramon?" Then he turned his attention back to Saul. "Bank robbing is fine, so's stage robbing. But let's get back to that reward you was talking about . . . you know, for killing this Danny Duggin?" As he spoke, his hand instinctively rubbed back and forth on the butt of his holstered Colt. "That seems like a powerful lot of money to me for just shooting one gunslinging saddle tramp."

"Forget the reward," said Saul Delmano, not wanting to talk about it. "I told you that's all over and done with. Those men Pa hired will kill him at Bloody Horse Pass—if they ain't already." Saul Delmano looked around the table at the four rough faces. "I'm ready to go on to bigger and better things. Think you four boys can keep up with me and little brother here? Wouldn't want none of you choking on our dust."

Ruppert Terry passed the question on to the others with a toss of his head. "What do you think, Wiley?

Can you and Tubbs keep up with Saul and his brother?"

Wiley Thornton sneered, giving a glance to Dick Tubbs, who sat beside him. "I expect me and Dick can hold our own." He turned his glance to the other outlaw, Hain Carnes. "What do you think, Hain? Do you see anything here that gives you pause to doubt your abilities?"

Hain Carnes spit on the dirt floor and let his eyes move up and down Saul Delmano. "Not yet I ain't." Carnes looked at Dick Tubbs and Wiley Thornton, then back at Saul Delmano, saying, "You haven't seen anything I wouldn't do, provided the money's right."

"Good!" Saul Delmano nodded, the whiskey boiling in his brain making him restless, on the verge of spinning out of control. "Come daylight, I say we saddle up, ride across the border, and commence a killing spree that'll keep the locals trembling in their boots for a long time to come." He snatched the bottle and threw back a drink.

Ramon watched for a moment in disbelief. There was no way he'd go any further with his brother. He'd hoped Saul would have passed out by now, giving him an opportunity to gather his horse and slip away in the darkness. But now that he saw that wasn't going to happen, Ramon was ready to get out of here the best way he could. He stood up and walked over to the table. "Give me a drink," he said, sweeping the bottle from Saul's hand and taking a short swig. When he lowered the bottle from his lips, he let out a whiskey hiss and headed for the door, his rifle draped over his forearm.

"Where the hell are you going?" Saul Delmano

asked, picking the bottle up from the table where Ramon had laid it. "We're getting ready to make some plans here."

Ramon gave him a flat stare, reaching for the door. "I'm going to the jake. You don't need me to make plans. It looks like you have everything worked out in your mind."

"Damn right I do," said Saul Delmano. He grinned, tapping a finger to the side of his head as he turned back to the others. Ramon slipped outside and closed the door behind himself while Saul continued speaking to the men, waving the whiskey bottle about in his hand.

Ramon moved quickly across the narrow clearing to the small corral where they had left their horses for the night. In a moment he had bridled and saddled his horse and swung atop it. He rode the animal through the corral, closing the gate behind him without leaving his saddle. Then he heeled his horse out toward the path leading east down the craggy hillside. A thin sliver of sunlight mantled the far horizon.

Inside the shack, Wiley Thornton and the other three men rose halfway from their chairs at the sound of hooves along the hard rocky path. But Saul Delmano motioned them back down with a raised hand, saying, "Don't worry boys, that's only little brother Ramon cutting out on me. I've been expecting it."

The three outlaws looked at one another curiously. "You mean you ain't going to stop him?" Ruppert Terry asked.

"Naw, there's no point in it," said Saul Delmano. "I tried to wise him up to this kind of life, see if he might have a knack for it. But it did no good at all." Saul Delmano shook his lowered head. "He just ain't got the makings."

"Do you trust him enough to think he won't bring somebody back here on us?" asked Wiley Thornton.

"If I didn't, Wiley, he'd be laying dead in the dirt right now, brother or no brother," said Saul Delmano. He shrugged. "Besides, who can he bring down on us? I told you, Danny Duggin is buzzard bait the minute he tries coming through Bloody Horse Pass." Saul walked to the door, threw it open, and gazed out through the darkness in the direction of the path his brother had taken. "Ramon won't do anything to hurt me. The fact is, he's in love with a servant gal back at the spread. I expect he'll take her and make a run for it, probably play it straight for the rest of his life." Saul spread a tired smile at the dark sky. "Hell, I wish him luck."

"Whoa, that don't sound like the Saul Delmano I know," said Ruppert Terry with a dark chuckle to his voice. "I never saw you give anybody a break, or wish anybody luck in your life."

"Well, you're seeing it now, Ruppert," said Saul, gazing away into the darkness. "Ramon leaving doesn't change a thing though. We're clearing out of here at sunup, boys, as soon as there's enough light on the trail."

"Oh, I get it now," said Ruppert Terry, standing up from the table with the bottle in his hand. "You almost had me fooled, Saul, but now I see what you're doing."

"What are you talking about, Ruppert?" asked Wiley Thornton when Saul Delmano didn't respond.

Ruppert grinned. "I'm talking about why Saul really doesn't mind that Ramon took off and left us. He knows if there's anybody on that trail, we'll hear about it sure enough. But Ramon will be the one to run headlong into them, right, Saul?"

Saul Delmano seemed to consider it for a second, then said without facing the men, "Now you're starting to get the picture, Ruppert. All my wild talking and drinking was just to rattle ole Ramon into leaving."

"Bull. I don't believe that," said Wiley Thornton. "Nobody would set their own brother up that way. You might have wanted him to leave, but just so's he'd get himself killed and we'd be warned by it? I don't believe I could ride with a man who'd do a thing like that. Tell me it ain' true, Saul."

Saul Delmano turned and looked at the four men in turn, then said to Wiley Thornton, "All right then, Wiley, it ain't true. Does that make you happy?"

Wiley Thornton nodded and looked down at the dirt floor.

"Why I done what I done ain't important," said Saul, raising his voice to the other men. "Let's get ready to move out. It'll soon be daylight." Turning to shut the door, Saul Delmano gazed off toward the path one last time, as if still listening for any lingering sound of his brother riding away.

The sound of distant gunfire resounded behind Danielle and Greta when they had left the hacienda and followed the hoofprints toward the hills. But before they had traveled a thousand yards, the guns had fallen silent, leaving Danielle to wonder if McCord and her brothers were all right. When Danielle stopped for a moment and looked back across the dark sky, Greta saw the look of concern and dread on her face.

"If we hurry on, we will be at the hideout before first light," Greta said, as if anticipating Danielle's thoughts.

"Good, " said Danielle. "The sooner I get this over with, the better." She nudged her horse, quickening the pace. "You said there might be others there . . . how many do you suppose?"

"I can't say for sure," said Greta, "but Ramon told me there are always outlaws passing through, looking for a place to lay low. Lewis Delmano still provides the hideout for them. Most of them are men he rode with in the past."

They continued steadily and quietly for the next twenty minutes as the sky in the east grew wider in silver light. At an upward turn in the trail, Danielle was the first to hear the sound of a horse's hooves descending toward them. She reached out and grabbed Greta' s horse by its bridle, stopping it. "Listen," she hissed under her breath, "there's a rider coming."

Greta whispered in reply, "Perhaps it is Ramon! He said he would return as soon as he could get away!"

"Keep quiet," Danielle whispered, pulling both horses to one side of the narrow trail and into the dark cover of a rock crevice. "If it is Ramon we'll know soon enough."

"You—you told me you would try not to shoot him!" Greta said in a shaky voice.

"I know what I said I'd do," Danielle responded, "but if this is Ramon coming, it's all up to him now."

Danielle slid down from her saddle and helped Greta step down as the sound of the hooves drew nearer. She ushered Greta back into the dark crevice and handed her both sets of reins. "Keep the horses quiet," Danielle said. "If you give up our position, it'll only make matters worse. Don't speak until we know for sure it's Ramon."

"I understand," Greta said in a grave tone of voice. "I'll be quiet . . . but if it is my Ramon, please do not kill him, Mr. Duggin, if not for his sake, then for mine . . . and the baby!"

Danielle didn't answer. Instead she stepped out into the center of the narrow trail as the hoofbeats came closer. "Ramon Delmano," she called out into the darkness, "if that's you, raise your hands and come forward slowly. This is Danny Duggin. I have Greta with me."

The sound of the horse's hooves stopped short. Danielle heard the scraping of horseshoes on rock. She saw only the faintest outline of Ramon Delmano as his voice called out, "Yes, it is me, Ramon! Where is Greta? What have you done to her?"

Before Danielle could answer, Greta called out from the rock crevice, "I'm right here, Ramon! I'm all right! Don't do anything foolish. Mr. Duggin has promised to let us go! He only wants Saul!"

"Is that right, Duggin?" Ramon called out, slipping down from his saddle as he spoke and snatching his rifle from its boot. "You only want Saul?" Ramon pushed his horse to one side and tried focusing in the darkness toward the sound of Danielle's voice. He wasn't about to venture a shot in the direction of Greta's voice, having no idea if she was behind cover or standing in the open.

"That's right, Ramon," Danielle replied, knowing that Ramon was only stalling. She prepared herself for whatever move he might make. "Point me toward Saul and you and the young lady can go your own way. I have no fight with you."

Ramon levered a round into the rifle chamber. Danielle heard the metal on metal ratchet at a distance of twenty yards. "I don't believe you, Duggin!" Ramon shouted. He fired two shots straight up in the air, levering the rifle quickly and sidestepping to his right in the darkness.

Danielle's hands acted on pure instincts. Both Colts streaked up from her holster and fired on the muzzle flash of Ramon's rifle even as she noted that Ramon's shots flew upward instead of blossoming toward her. But there was no stopping her shots now. She heard Ramon Delmano's short cry of pain as her bullets found their target. Ramon's horse also cried out, startled by the gunfire. From the rock crevice on Danielle's left, she heard Greta scream, "Ramon!" and run forward, sobbing aloud. "No, Ramon! He only wants Saul! Not you!"

Danielle watched Greta run past her in the darkness. Knowing that at least one bullet had hit Ramon, and knowing that whatever the young woman found in the trail would not be a pretty sight, Danielle hurried forward with caution. A few feet back from the body lying on the ground, Danielle caught up to Greta and grabbed her by her arm, holding her back. "Stay back, ma'am. You don't want to see—"

"No!" Greta screamed hysterically, cutting Danielle off. She slung her arm free and raced forward, sliding down beside Ramon, cradling his head in her lap and clutching his face to her bosom as she sobbed. "Why, Ramon, why?" she pleaded.

Danielle kneeled down beside Greta, noting the long bloody crease above Ramon Delmano's left ear. As Greta sobbed and rocked back and forth on the ground, Danielle looked Ramon over and saw no other wound. "I think he's alive," she said, opening Greta's arms from around Ramon's head. "Give him room to breathe!"

As Greta's arms unwrapped from his bloody head, Ramon let out a low groan and turned his face back and forth in Greta's lap. He tried to speak but the words came out broken and meaningless. Danielle reached down in the dirt, picked up Ramon's rifle, and cradled it across her forearm. Taking Ramon's pistol from his holster, Danielle stood up, saying to Greta, "Keep his head up, and keep talking to him. I'll go get some water."

Chapter 21

At the sound of the gunshots, Saul Delmano and the four other outlaws had veered slightly on the trail and came to a halt. When no other shots resounded in the gray morning darkness, Saul Delmano said in hushed tone, "Boys, there ain't a doubt in my mind that was Ramon's rifle."

"Well, as quiet as it's gotten, I'd say somebody has bit the dust," said Wiley Thornton.

Ruppert Terry stepped his horse closer to Saul Delmano and said as he slipped his rifle from its boot, "Looks like Ramon *did* warn us, whether you intended for him to or not."

"Yeah, he warned us all right," said Saul Delmano, staring ahead into the grayness, "now let's ease on down there and see what's waiting for us."

"Damn, Saul!" Ruppert said in surprise. "We've been warned. Shouldn't we swing around a different direction and get out of here?"

"Ordinarily that's exactly what I would do, Rupe," said Saul Delmano, "but not this morning." He pulled the glove from his right hand and stuffed it down into his belt. "I figure out of respect for Ramon, I'll just mosey on down there and check it out." He grinned. "I always was a nosy sort."

"But you already know it *has* to be this Danny Duggin fellow!" said Wiley Thornton. "Let's pull away from here!"

"And what," asked Saul Delmano, "have him on our trail every turn in the road?" He pulled his pistol from his holster. "No thanks, boys, that ain't my style of travel. I figured somebody would have killed Duggin by now. Since they ain't, I best do it myself." He raised the pistol and fired three shots in the air, taking his time, pausing a second between each shot. Then he lowered the pistol, replaced the spent cartridges, spun it, and put it back loosely into his holster.

"This ain't like you, Saul," Ruppert Terry murmured, shaking his head.

"I know it," said Saul. "If any of you wants to pull off to the side, I'll not hold it against yas. But I'm gonna ride down and face this Duggin fellow straight up, once and for all." He nudged his horse forward on the trail. "I've just got to see if he's as fast and tough as they all say he is."

Ruppert Terry looked at the others as Saul Delmano rode slowly into the grayness. "Well, hell, boys, I'd kinda like to see that myself." He grinned and turned his horse forward, the others following suit and forming a quiet single line down the narrow trail.

Upon hearing the three shots fired by Saul Delmano, Danielle checked her pistols and waited. Moments passed slowly until she heard the first faint click of hoof on rock. Danielle turned to Greta and Ramon. "Here they come," she said to Greta. "As soon as he's able, you get him up in a saddle and clear out of here.

If my friends run into him on the trail between here and Bloody Horse Pass, there's no telling what will happen."

Before Greta could respond, Ramon looked up at Danielle through blurry eyes. "Duggin . . . I don't know what to say."

"No need in saying anything," said Danielle. "I told this woman I was only after Saul, and I meant it. From here on the two of you get a new start in life. As far as I'm concerned, I wish you both all the luck in the world. Now do like I asked you to. I've got business to settle."

"Duggin," said Ramon, his words still a bit thick and slow coming, "I—I want you to know that I wasn't shooting at you a while ago. It was for Saul . . . I had to let him know."

"I know how it goes," said Danielle. "I have a couple of brothers of my own."

"What he does now is all up to him," Ramon went on. "I gave him all I owe him . . . didn't I?"

"Yep," said Danielle. "He can't ask for more than that. Now get on out of here." She stepped out into the trail and started walking slowly forward, a silver morning mist wafting at her shoulders. Behind her, she could hear Greta help Ramon up onto a horse. Then she heard them move away down the trail until only silence lay in their wake. She stopped and waited at a point where the trail turned upward at a steeper angle. When a few more minutes had passed, Saul Delmano called out from higher up in the gray morning swirl.

"Danny Duggin. I'm Saul Delmano. Where's my brother Ramon? Did you kill him?"

"No, I didn't kill him," Danielle called back. "Ramon left here a few minutes ago with a young woman named Greta . . . they're well on their way now. It's just you and me."

"On their way, huh?" Saul said. Then he added with a bitter snap to his voice, "Well, God love 'em, ain't that just fine and dandy. I expect the two of them will be just as happy as two coons in a corn crib . . . probably live the rest of their lives watching the sun rise and set together."

"There's worse things," said Danielle. "Are you ready to come down and finish this?"

Saul Delmano stepped down from his saddle and shooed his horse away. "Yep, as ready as you are I reckon. Is there anything we need to talk about first?"

"Not that I can think of," said Danielle. "You killed my pa, you and the others that were riding with you that day in the territory. I've killed them all but you. There's no more to say about it."

Saul stepped forward slowly, seeing the outline of Danielle's head and shoulder take form out of the morning mist. "Hell, you don't even sound mad about it, Duggin."

"I'm past mad, Delmano," she said coldly. "I'm past a lot of things since I started out looking for all of you killers. All I want now is to be done with it."

Saul Delmano chuckled under his breath, stopping forty feet away and planting his feet shoulder-width apart. Danielle saw him through the gray morning light. "Who are you trying to kid, Danny Duggin? You don't want to be done with killing. Killing ain't an easy thing to get rid of."

"I'll manage," said Danielle, reaching out slowly

with both hands and drawing both sides of her duster back behind her holsters.

"You'll manage?" Saul Delmano asked. "After killing Rufe Gaddis, Byler, Grago, Chancy Burke and all the others—no telling how many more along the way—you think you can just put it down and let it lay?"

Danielle remained silent.

Saul Delmano shook his head. "You poor fool. I reckon killing you is the best thing I can do for you then." He raised his left hand slowly and scratched his cheek, taking his time, considering things, it seemed. But Danielle had seen this kind of diversion before, and she was ready for his move when he made it. "You know something, Duggin? When I first heard you was looking for me, I told a couple of pals of mine that I was going to—" His voice stopped abruptly as his hand went for the pistol at his hip. But two rounds exploded from Danielle's Colts before Saul Delmano raised his pistol high enough to fire a shot.

"Lord God!" said Ruppert Terry in a whisper, watching with the others from ten feet back behind the cover of rock. Saul Delmano rocked backward with the impact of the first bullet, then fell to the ground as the second bullet slammed into his chest. Ruppert Terry took careful aim with his rifle as Danielle stepped forward and stopped, looking down at Saul Delmano with her right pistol pointed at his head.

Saul Delmano groaned and struggled, rising onto his elbow, his left hand clutched to his bleeding chest, the fingers of his right hand less than an inch from his pistol, where he'd dropped it in the dirt. "I reckon . . . that does it for me," Saul said in a strained voice. He managed to shake his head slowly, asking, "All this damn killing . . . just for your pa? Ain't nobody's pa . . . worth all this."

Danielle cocked her Colt, the barrel aimed steady and level at Saul Delmano's forehead. "Mine was," she said softly; and she let the hammer fall.

Before the echo of the final shot had faded off into the hill land, Danielle turned to the silver morning mist lying upward along the trail, and said, "Anybody there wants to be a part of it, come on down and face me like men . . . otherwise, lower your sights and ride out of here. I'm finished. Do you hear me? I'm through with it!" There was almost a pleading, perhaps even a trace of desperation in her voice.

"Don't shoot him, Ruppert, damn it," said Wiley Thornton in a whisper. "He ain't done no more than anybody else would if somebody kilt their pa."

"I'm not going to shoot him," Ruppert Terry whispered in reply, lowering his rifle. He looked around at the others, then called down to Danielle, "All right, Duggin . . . we're leaving here. We've got no fight with you, unless you bring it on."

"Fair enough," said Danielle, replacing her spent cartridges and closing her pistol. She stood in silence and watched the dim figures move back into the silver mist.

Farther down along the trail, riding ahead of Ramon and leading his horse behind her, Greta whispered a silent prayer under her breath and looked back at Ramon as he raised the bandanna from the side of his head and cast a glance back over his shoulder. "Don't look back, Ramon . . . we must never look back, neither of us. No matter which one died, we cannot let ourselves think about it."

Ramon started to say something, but then stopped himself and only nodded as he nudged his horse forward and rode closer to Greta's side. They rode on for another mile until the first long rays of sunlight found their way through the stands of rock and spread golden on the gannet before them. Once they reached the base of the hills, they turned onto the flatland and rode on, leaving a low rise of dust behind them.

In the distance, C. F. McCord watched the two riders through his field lens. "Who do you suppose it is?" Tim Strange asked.

"I have no idea," said McCord. "But whoever they are, they're coming off the hill trail, just below where we heard the shooting." He lowered the lens and closed it.

"Reckon Jed and I ought to catch up to them, see what's been going on up there?" asked Tim Strange.

"No, I don't think so," said McCord. "I think we best keep on your sister's tracks. Something's happened up there. We need to see what the outcome was, one way or the other. I'd hoped we might catch up to her in time to be some help once LaBourge turned us loose. Looks like we missed our chance."

Tim caught the concern in McCord's voice and said, to reassure him, "Look, Marshal, we're just as concerned about her as you are . . . you know that. But if there's one thing Jed and I have learned about our sister, it's that she's a good hand at taking care of herself."

"I know that, boys," said McCord. "There's not a doubt in my mind that she's taken care of Saul Delmano by now, if he was up there. I just want to at least be there when she comes down off the trail."

Tim and Jed Strange gave one another a knowing glance as McCord gigged his horse ahead of them on the trail. "Looks like we're apt to wind up with a lawman in the family, Jed," Tim said in a guarded tone.

"It wouldn't surprise me a bit," Jed replied, the two of them falling their horses in behind McCord, letting him lead them. They rode on for another mile and a half; and as they neared the base of the long line of hills, the sight of Danielle rounding a turn down onto the stretch of flatland caused them to stop cold in their tracks until McCord said in a breathless whisper, "Thank God! It's her! She's all right!" He heeled his horse forward and raced across the land, raising a high stir of dust. Jed started to heel his horse forward into a run as well, but Tim reached out and clasped his horse's bridle.

"Not so fast, Brother Jed . . . give the two of them a few minutes alone."

"Yeah, I reckon that's a good idea." Jed Strange settled his horse and sat watching McCord close the distance between himself and Danielle.

At thirty yards McCord began checking his horse down, the big animal turning quarterwise into a high-hoofed canter that bounced to a halt ten feet from Danielle. Then the horse sidestepped in a half circle as McCord looked Danielle up and down.

"He's dead," Danielle said bluntly.

"I figured as much," said McCord, jerking his horse to a standstill. "But what about you? Are you . . . ?" His words trailed as if he dreaded what he might hear.

"No, I'm not wounded," Danielle said, finishing his question for him. "I came out all right. That was his brother Ramon riding off over there." Danielle nodded at the rise of distant dust. "In the end it was only Saul and me, face-to-face, the way I'd hoped for it." As Danielle spoke, she swung her leg over her saddle and stepped down, taking off her hat and letting the cool morning wind blow through her hair. "How did it go for you and the twins?" she asked, glancing off to where Tim and Jed sat atop their horses.

"It was peculiar," said McCord, offering a relieved smile. "I'll tell you all about it sometime . . . but not now." He also stepped down from his saddle and swept his dusty Stetson from atop his head. "What I'd really like to know right now is your real name, Danny Duggin," he said with a sly grin.

"It's Danielle, McCord. I reckon you can call me that from now on." She reached down, unfastened her gunbelt, and swung it up over her shoulder.

McCord moved in closer, his reins in his gloved hands, the wind nipping at the bandanna around his neck. "Well, Danielle, you look no worse for the wear," he said gently, standing only a foot from her, waiting for any sign or any hint of what she might want him to do next.

Danielle tried to return his smile, but it didn't work for her. Her expression turned tired, solemn all of a sudden. "But I *am* worse for the wear, C.F. I'm worse for the wear more than I ever thought I would be." She seemed to sway slightly forward. Then she steadied herself and gazed away into the distance for a second as if trying to accept something in her mind.

"It's over, Danielle," McCord whispered.

"I know," she said, "but I can't feel it yet. It's still in me." Her eyes moved along the far horizon as if in search of something.

"Then let me help you. Tell me what you want, Danielle," McCord whispered. "I'll do whatever it takes to put this to rest. I'll go, if that's what it takes . . . or I'll stay. Just tell me what you—"

"How about if you just hold me, C.F.?" Danielle's eyes glistened wet as she turned them to McCord and stepped forward into his arms.

"Well, I can do that easy enough, I reckon," McCord said, drawing her to his chest. "The hard part might be turning you loose," he said close to her ear.

"Then don't turn me loose, C.F.," she whispered. Danielle pressed her face to his chest, feeling the warmth of his arms around her, and she stood for a moment, liking the slow steady beat of his heart through the dusty breast of his riding duster. "It's over, Pa," she said in a voice too hushed to be heard beneath the breath of the desert wind. And she closed her eyes and let the gunbelt slip from her shoulder and fall to the ground at their feet.

Rufe Gaddis

Bart Scovill

Julius Byler

Chaney Burke

Snakehead Katpana

Newt Grago

Saul Delmano

Blade Hogue

Brice Levan

Levi Jasper